"Maybe you have everyone else in Lincoln County fooled, Penny, but not me,"

the sheriff growled. "I know there's another woman inside stern, icy Judge Penelope Parker. I saw her. I made love to her."

"Why do you keep bringing that up, Ethan?" she said desperately.

Her back was to him, but the raw huskiness in her voice told Ethan she was remembering, too.

"I honestly don't know," he answered roughly. "I'm sure I'd be better off if I could forget you *and* that night."

Forget that night.

It was going to be impossible to forget now, Penelope thought wildly. A baby was already growing inside her. The *sheriff's* baby. Dear God...

How was she ever going to tell him?

Dear Reader,

Summer is a time for backyard barbecues and fun family gatherings. But with all the running around you'll be doing, don't forget to make time for yourself. And there's no better way to escape than with a Special Edition novel. Each month we offer six brand-new romances about people just like you—trying to find the perfect balance between life, career, family, romance....

To start, pick up *Hunter's Woman* by bestselling author Lindsay McKenna. Continuing her riveting MORGAN'S MERCENARIES: THE HUNTERS series, she pairs a strong-willed THAT SPECIAL WOMAN! with the ruggedly handsome soldier who loved her once—and is determined to win her back!

Every woman longs to be noticed for her true beauty—and the heroine of Joan Elliott Pickart's latest book, *The Irresistible Mr. Sinclair,* is no different; this novel features another wonderful hero in the author's exciting cross-line miniseries with Silhouette Desire, THE BACHELOR BET. And for those hankering to return to the beloved Western land that Myrna Temte takes us to in her HEARTS OF WYOMING series, don't miss *The Gal Who Took the West.*

And it's family that brings the next three couples together—a baby on the way in *Penny Parker's Pregnant!* by Stella Bagwell, the next installment in her TWINS ON THE DOORSTEP series that began in Silhouette Romance and will return there in January 2000; adorable twins in Robin Lee Hatcher's *Taking Care of the Twins;* and a millionaire's heir-to-be in talented new author Teresa Carpenter's *The Baby Due Date.*

I hope you enjoy these six emotional must-reads written *by* women like you, *for* women like you!

Sincerely,

Karen Taylor Richman
Senior Editor

Please address questions and book requests to:
Silhouette Reader Service
U.S.: 3010 Walden Ave., P.O. Box 1325, Buffalo, NY 14269
Canadian: P.O. Box 609, Fort Erie, Ont. L2A 5X3

STELLA BAGWELL

PENNY PARKER'S PREGNANT!

Published by Silhouette Books
America's Publisher of Contemporary Romance

If you purchased this book without a cover you should be aware that this book is stolen property. It was reported as "unsold and destroyed" to the publisher, and neither the author nor the publisher has received any payment for this "stripped book."

To my son, Jason. My own miracle.

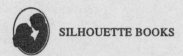

SILHOUETTE BOOKS

ISBN 0-373-24258-1

PENNY PARKER'S PREGNANT!

Copyright © 1999 by Stella Bagwell

All rights reserved. Except for use in any review, the reproduction or utilization of this work in whole or in part in any form by any electronic, mechanical or other means, now known or hereafter invented, including xerography, photocopying and recording, or in any information storage or retrieval system, is forbidden without the written permission of the editorial office, Silhouette Books, 300 East 42nd Street, New York, NY 10017 U.S.A.

All characters in this book have no existence outside the imagination of the author and have no relation whatsoever to anyone bearing the same name or names. They are not even distantly inspired by any individual known or unknown to the author, and all incidents are pure invention.

This edition published by arrangement with Harlequin Books S.A.

® and TM are trademarks of Harlequin Books S.A., used under license. Trademarks indicated with ® are registered in the United States Patent and Trademark Office, the Canadian Trade Marks Office and in other countries.

Visit us at www.romance.net

Printed in U.S.A.

STELLA BAGWELL

sold her first book to Silhouette in November 1985. Now, thirty-five novels later, she is still thrilled to see her books in print and can't imagine having any other job than that of writing about two people falling in love.

She lives in a small town in southeastern Oklahoma with her husband of twenty-six years. She has one son and daughter-in-law.

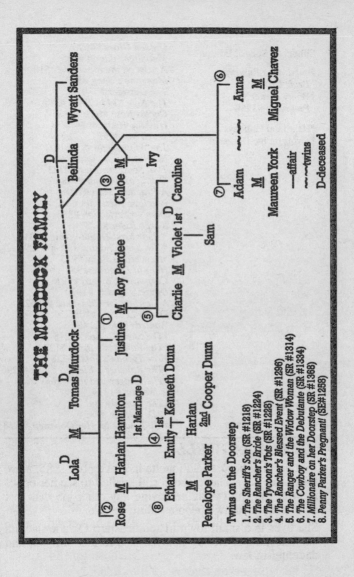

THE MURDOCK FAMILY

Lola $\overset{D}{M}$ Tomas Murdock

Rose $\overset{②}{M}$ Harlan Hamilton

Belinda $\overset{D}{M}$ Wyatt Sanders

Justine $\overset{①}{M}$ Roy Pardee ③ Chloe $\overset{M}{M}$ Ivy

Adam ～～ Anna ⑥
$\overset{⑦}{M}$ $\overset{M}{M}$
Maureen York   Miguel Chavez

1st Marriage D

Ethan ⑧   Emily ┬ Kenneth Dunn
$\overset{M}{M}$ ④ 1st
Penelope Parker   Harlan
2nd Cooper Dunn

Charlie $\overset{⑤}{M}$ Violet 1st $\overset{D}{M}$ Caroline

Sam

Twins on the Doorstep

1. *The Sheriff's Son* (SR #1218)
2. *The Rancher's Bride* (SR #1224)
3. *The Tycoon's Tots* (SR #1228)
4. *The Rancher's Blessed Event* (SR #1296)
5. *The Ranger and the Widow Woman* (SR #1314)
6. *The Cowboy and the Debutante* (SR #1334)
7. *Millionaire on her Doorstep* (SR #1368)
8. *Penny Parker's Pregnant!* (SE #1258)

——affair
～～twins
D–deceased

Chapter One

"**S**he did *what?*"

Sheriff Ethan Hamilton rounded the desk and glared down at the cowering deputy.

"You heard right, sir," the younger man answered with a helpless shrug. "Judge Parker sent me back here to you. She says she doesn't want or need protecting."

Ethan's jaw clamped down on a stream of choice words. Being the sheriff of Lincoln County, New Mexico he expected to deal with everything from a weary illegal to a crying child to the lowest snake-in-the-grass criminal. But today of all days he had more important things to do than coddle her icy highness, Judge Penelope Parker.

Slowly, he folded his arms against his broad chest and let out a long breath. "Doesn't she understand these threats were made against her personally?"

The freckle-faced deputy bobbed his head up and down. "I told her you weren't going to like this."

"And what did she say to that?"

The other man opened his mouth, paused, then let out a reluctant groan.

Ethan felt the tension in the back of his neck tighten like a chain caught in a boom. "Out with it, Lonnie! What did the woman say?"

Lonnie swallowed as though he'd rather be facing a mad Brahma bull with foot-long horns than his boss when he was riled. "She said, 'I don't particularly care if Sheriff Hamilton likes it or not. He has his job to do and I have mine.'"

Blood poured into Ethan's temples and throbbed like a bass guitar. He didn't have time for such silliness. Half his force was out combing the mountains and the desert searching for Willis Kirkland, the criminal who believed the judge was to blame for all his troubles. So far, they had yet to find a solid lead as to where he might be hiding. All Ethan did know was that the man had definite intentions to harm Penelope Parker if or when he got the chance. And Ethan couldn't let that happen.

"How the hell does she think she can do her job if some maniac murders her?!" Ethan bellowed.

Loath to say more, the deputy made a palms-up gesture.

Ethan drew in a deep breath and released it slowly. "Well, I damn well don't know, either. So get your a— your rear end back over there! I want her every move guarded."

Lonnie would normally have jumped to do the sheriff's bidding. But this time, he had the look of a man who'd just been ordered to walk through fire. "She, uh, she said for me not to come back, sir. That she was going to talk to you personally about the situation."

Ethan's brows disappeared beneath the brim of his gray

Stetson. "Is that so?" he said with finality. "Well, she's going to get her wish!"

Grabbing a leather jacket from a coat tree jammed into one corner of the cluttered room, he jerked it on as he stalked toward the door.

The deputy hurried through the door after his boss. "You goin' over to the judge's chambers?"

"Damn right I am," Ethan barked back at him. "That woman needs to be shook up."

"I don't think that's possible," Lonnie found the nerve to say.

Ethan snorted loudly as the two men pushed through the building's main entrance and stepped into the New Mexico morning. Spring was near in Lincoln County and the small town of Carrizozo. Calves and foals were beginning to drop, grass was starting to peep through the valley floors, and blossoms of wildflowers sprinkled some of the lower mesas. Normally, this was a pleasant time of the year for Ethan. He loved seeing the earth's rebirth and feeling the promise of hot weather to come. This spring, however, he'd rarely had time to look up from his desk.

"The woman is tough, sir," Lonnie felt obliged to warn him. "She'll wind up hanging you like she does everybody else."

A mocking laugh erupted from Ethan as he slid behind the wheel of a black four-wheel-drive vehicle marked with the sheriff's department emblem.

"Lonnie, no woman alive is going to tell me how to do my job. As soon as Judge Parker gets that straight, we won't be having any more problems with her."

Lonnie didn't get the opportunity to make a reply. Ethan slammed the door and gunned the vehicle out of the parking lot.

At the courthouse, he avoided passing by the county

offices where he might be caught by officials wanting to chat politics. Instead, he walked directly through the empty courtroom toward the judge's chambers.

A young secretary caught him just as he was about to enter a door marked Private. "I'm sorry, Sheriff, but Judge Parker is busy right now. Shall I tell her you need to see her?"

Ethan shook his head. "That won't be necessary. I'll tell her myself."

"But, Sheriff..." The secretary gasped as he opened the door and stepped inside unannounced.

Ethan glanced back at the distraught young woman and winked. "Don't worry, this isn't the royal chamber as she'd like for you to think," he said under his breath. "It's just the judge's chambers."

He shut the door behind him, then turned and took a quick survey of the room and its lone occupant. Compared with the bright sunlight outside, the room was dark. Blinds were shut against the windows, while only one lamp burned near a huge oak desk. Behind it, Judge Penelope Parker continued to read the legal motion in her hand.

"Julie, I told you I didn't want to be disturbed," she said quietly.

"Neither did I."

The unexpected sound of his voice brought her head up. Still, she didn't remove her reading glasses but rather peered over the rims at him as though he were a third-grader and had just walked into class fifteen minutes late.

"Sheriff Hamilton. I wasn't expecting you."

"Really? You told my deputy you were going to have a talk with me."

"That's true," she replied. "But at my own convenience."

He stepped over to the massive desk, which was polished to a high sheen. Other than a telephone, a penholder and the typed papers from which she'd been reading, there was nothing cluttering the smooth expanse of wood. A stark contrast to his own desk, which was always piled with folders, photos, scribbled notes and numbers, not to mention several days' worth of dirty coffee cups and half-eaten meals.

Ethan turned his attention to her placid expression. "And to hell with my convenience, I suppose."

She folded her small hands primly in front of her, and not for the first time Ethan wondered if there was really a female beneath her smooth face and black robes. At the moment, her pale pink lips were compressed in a tight line and that was more emotion than he'd ever seen her express.

"I realize you are a busy man, Sheriff Hamilton. But I, too, am pressed for time. And this matter of your posting a bodyguard—"

"You had no authority to dismiss him," Ethan interrupted sharply. "And I'll tell you another thing. He's coming back and you're going to leave him alone and let him do his job."

Several moments of pregnant silence passed. The only sign Ethan had that she'd digested his decree was the faint sweep of pink across her high cheekbones.

"I'm not without common sense, Sheriff. I do understand I should take precautions until you've caught this man—"

"He isn't just a man," Ethan pointed out. "Kirkland is a criminal. You sentenced him to twenty years in prison for manslaughter. He's dangerous."

Penelope's cool gray eyes followed the sheriff as he started to pace back and forth in front of her desk. She'd first met Ethan Hamilton two years ago while she'd been the practicing district attorney and he a deputy under Sheriff Roy Pardee. She'd been secretly overwhelmed by his presence then, and now after two years, she still found his looks and his bearing set her heart aflutter.

His brown hair was threaded with streaks of rust and gold and teased the back of his neck with curls most women would love to tangle around their fingers. The bones of his face were lean and angular, his eyes pale green and so limpid she felt she was looking into a tropic sea. And as though his striking coloring and features were not enough, he had the sort of body men killed themselves in the gym to acquire. Broad shoulders, long, muscled legs, a waist without an ounce of fat.

The sight of him was indecent and Penny despised herself for reacting to him in such a schoolgirl way. Especially when it was obvious he didn't see her as an attractive woman but simply as an arm of the legal system.

Jerking herself back to the point of his visit, she said flatly, "Kirkland should never have been paroled."

Her remark had Ethan pausing in midstride to glance at her. Her black hair was worn tightly pulled away from her oval face and caught in some sort of elaborate twist at the nape of her neck. Black wire-rimmed glasses were perched on her nose, and if she was wearing any makeup on her pale skin he couldn't see it. Her appearance never changed, nor did her calm countenance, making it hard for him or anyone else to believe she was only twenty-nine years old. The same age as himself.

"I agree. The parole board must have been in a generous mood that day," he retorted. "But none of that makes a damn bit of difference now. He's skipped off to God-only-knows where and you're his next target."

She shook her head. "I believe you're dramatizing the

situation, Sheriff Hamilton. The man isn't going to risk his freedom just for a chance to do me harm. I'm hardly that important."

Ethan was struck with the urge to round the spotless desk, jerk the controlled Ms. Parker from her leather chair and shake her until the carefully wound hair at the back of her head tumbled onto her shoulders.

"We've been receiving letters and calls from the man. He blames you for not allowing evidence in his trial that might have cleared him. In his mind, you're the reason he's a fugitive."

"That's nonsense," she said brusquely. "There was no evidence submitted to me that could have proven him innocent. The man was guilty."

Ethan cocked one rusty-brown brow at her. "That's the whole point, Judge. He's deranged, and as long as he's loose you're in danger. And since you're a citizen of Lincoln County, it's my duty to see that you're protected."

"I understand that. But I don't like having my privacy invaded."

Not for the first time, Ethan was amazed by this judge. Not only did he have to keep reminding himself she was a woman, he had to wonder if she was even human. Most normal people in their right minds would be shaken or distraught to hear that someone was out to kill them. But Penelope Parker showed no signs of distress. There was no quiver to her lips, no rapid rise and fall of her small bosom. No nervous twisting of her fingers or hesitation in her voice. The only thing evident to him was that she deeply resented the idea of his posting a guard on her.

"I didn't especially like getting only two or three hours of sleep for the past few nights, either," he countered. "But sometimes we have to make the best of a rotten situation."

She straightened her shoulders to an even more rigid line and planted her gray eyes on Ethan's face. "Or take control of it. I find I'd rather do the latter."

Well, lady, if you think you can find Willis Kirkland, then have at it, he thought hotly.

Outwardly, he kept his face smooth and as void of emotion as possible. The last thing he needed was to have an all-out war with the judge. To make the legal system work in this county, the two of them needed to be on amicable terms. He wouldn't jeopardize the success of his department for any amount of satisfaction he would get from telling her exactly what he thought of her. At least he wouldn't risk it at this moment.

"And how would you propose to take control, Judge?" he asked, finding it next to impossible to keep the sarcasm from his voice.

Her eyes narrowed ever so slightly on his face. "I do own a handgun. And I can use it if needed."

Damn if he didn't believe her, too, Ethan thought. She could probably pump a bullet into a man and never bat an eyelash.

"Do you think the people of this county want their judge to be put in such a situation? What sort of light do you think that would throw on my department?"

She took her time weighing the questions he'd tossed at her. Ethan waited impatiently as he felt each precious moment ticking by. He needed to be back at his office doing his job, not here trying to persuade this stubborn woman she was in danger.

Eventually, she replied, "All right, Sheriff Hamilton. Send the deputy back. I won't like his constant presence. But I'll tolerate it."

It was all Ethan could do to keep from breathing out a

loud sigh of relief. "Fine. I'll tell him to make himself as invisible as possible."

"I certainly hope you do," she said, then picked up her work and adjusted her glasses.

Ethan knew it was her way of dismissing him, but at the moment he didn't let her curtness bother him. He was just glad to be able to get the hell out of her dark chambers.

As he made his way past the secretary's desk, the young woman glanced worriedly up at him. "Was she very angry at you for butting in, Sheriff Hamilton?"

The devilish grin on his face brought a pleasurable flush to the woman's face. "Isn't she always?" he asked, then with a smug chuckle, he left the courthouse and Judge Penelope Parker behind.

The deputy was getting on her nerves. Penny couldn't help the way she felt. No one liked having their every move watched. His being around while she worked was bad enough, but to have him accompany her during every meeting and chore was ridiculous. She couldn't even go to the powder room without him standing outside the door, waiting for her to get back under his watchful eye.

Penelope understood he was only doing what his boss had ordered him to do. But enough was enough. Now he was sitting here beside her in the doctor's office while she waited to be called back to the examining room. It was humiliating and frustrating and she couldn't take much more.

If Ethan Hamilton didn't catch Kirkland soon, she was going to have another talk with him. Not that she wanted to meet with the man again. God forbid. Their last encounter two days ago had set her on such an edge she still wasn't back to normal. It was infuriating that he had such power over her. She was a judge. She wasn't supposed to be emotional over anything or anyone! But when the sheriff was around her, she turned into a different person, one that she just couldn't control.

"Penelope Parker."

The nurse's summons pulled Penelope out of her musings. As she rose to her feet, the deputy quickly glanced up at her. "I'll be waiting right here, Judge," he promised.

She sighed inwardly. "I'm sure you will," she replied, then followed the beckoning nurse down the hallway to the examining rooms.

More than an hour later, the nurse instructed Penelope to get dressed and join the doctor in his private office. Once she sat facing the fatherly man across a cluttered desk, her mind was racing with all sorts of fearful questions.

During the examination, he'd discovered something that concerned him, and now Penelope was wondering just what his findings were going to mean. Was he going to tell her she was terminally ill?

The hysterical thought that she could tell Ethan to pull off his deputy, that she was going to die anyway, zipped through her mind. But then the calm, fierce strength she'd used to get her through her parents' deaths, through years of law school to her job as a judge took over, and she faced the doctor with grim readiness.

"Penny, I'm glad you're a woman who comes in for her yearly checkup on time. Otherwise this problem might have gotten out of control before it was too late."

A lump of emotion lodged in her throat, but she refused to swallow or let the older man see she was the least bit fearful of his diagnosis. She would face whatever he had to say with quiet dignity.

"What sort of problem are you talking about, Doctor?" she asked. "You've never performed an ultrasound on me before. You must have been concerned you were going to find something."

He nodded. "When you described the monthly pain you've been experiencing, I had my suspicions." He rested his forearms on the desktop and leaned slightly toward Penelope. "From what I could tell from the test, you have endometriosis. A fairly advanced case from the pictures the ultrasound gave me."

The long word he'd used was not a familiar one. But Penelope rarely had time to read any sort of medical literature. She was constantly faced with legal briefs and motions that kept her up until the wee hours of the morning.

"What is endometriosis? Is it fatal?"

The doctor shook his head. "Only in very rare cases. For the most part, the disease is painful and insidious and after a length of time destroys the reproductive organs.'

Penelope stared at the older man as if she couldn't believe what she was hearing. "You mean I'm sterile?"

He threaded his fingers together and gave her a reassuring smile. "Without further testing, I can't be certain of that. You could be, but I'm hoping the disease hasn't reached that stage yet. However, I'm certain if things keep progressing at this rate, you'll have to conceive in the next twelve months. Otherwise, the chances of your becoming pregnant after that will probably be nonexistent."

This time, Penelope had to swallow at the painful knot that had suddenly developed in her throat again. "You mean if I don't get pregnant within a year, I might not ever conceive?"

He nodded. "That's my initial opinion right now. Of course, we need to do further testing to make sure. But as a doctor, I feel I would be remiss not to warn you that your time to reproduce is very limited.''

Very limited. The doctor went on to discuss a method of treatment he wanted to try, but it was those two words that refused to leave her as she walked dazedly out of his office. Over and over like a ceaseless mantra, his warning reverberated in her head. *She was going to be childless. Alone for the rest of her life.*

Like a robot, she walked back toward the waiting area, but halfway there, she suddenly remembered Lonnie, the deputy, would be waiting to escort her home. And once they got there, she wouldn't be able to simply drop her head in her hands and howl with pain. She'd have to pretend that nothing was wrong.

Penelope was a strong woman, but she couldn't hold up under that much strain. She had to be alone! She had to think, try to come to terms with the news the doctor had just given her.

As discreetly as possible, she turned on her heel and started back down the hallway from which she'd just come. Hopefully, she could find a back exit where she could leave the building without anyone noticing.

Ethan tossed several blocks of alfalfa into the horse's manger, and the buckskin stepped up to chomp greedily into the hay. While he patted the animal's neck, he tried to remember exactly how long it had been since he'd saddled Buckeye and ridden across the valley just for the simple enjoyment of riding.

Hell, it had been three days since he'd slept in his own bed, much less fed the livestock himself so that his hired hand could have a few hours off. And he wouldn't have come home this afternoon if it hadn't been for the necessity of taking a shower and grabbing some clean clothes.

Ethan had been born into a big ranching family and the tradition of raising cattle and horses was in his blood. As soon as he was grown and financially able, he'd purchased this spread, which was snuggled in a mountain range some fifteen miles east of Carrizozo.

During his years as a deputy, Ethan had been blessed with more time to spend on the old place. Little by little, he'd replaced the sagging fence with new barbed wire and metal posts. The roof on the main barn had been restored and the inside of the stucco house had been given a fresh face. More importantly, he'd continued to build his herd of mama cows.

Of course, Ethan's spread was only two sections of land. Small compared with his parents', Rose and Harlan's, place. But it was all he wanted and needed. Ethan's first love was the law and that would always be his main focus.

When he'd been elected sheriff a little more than a year ago, his lifelong dream had come true. And even though he'd won the election by a landslide, he was well aware he still had some way to go to earn as much love and trust from the public as his uncle, Sheriff Pardee, had enjoyed for thirty long years. But he wasn't the same man Roy was and Ethan realized he would have to do the job in his own way and at his own pace. The citizens of Lincoln County would eventually decide if he was good enough to continue wearing the sheriff's badge on his chest.

A beeping noise suddenly invaded the quiet of the feedlot. Quickly, Ethan glanced down at the pager hooked to his leather belt. The number was his office.

He gave Buckeye one last pat and headed to the house, all the while praying a good lead had turned up on Kirkland. This thing with the judge was wearing on him and the whole department.

Lonnie answered on the first ring and practically shouted in his ear. "She's gone, Sheriff! I don't know where she is!"

"Whoa, Lonnie. Just settle down and tell me who's gone."

"The judge! I can't find her."

Ethan's mind begin to whirl with all sorts of images. Many of which were too horrible to contemplate.

"What do you mean you can't find her? Damn it, Lonnie, you weren't supposed to take your eyes off the woman."

The deputy spluttered, then cleared his throat. "Sir, there's some places I just can't follow her. We were at the medical clinic. She went to see the doctor and never came back to the waiting room."

Ethan cursed under his breath. He realized he'd placed a big responsibility on the young officer's shoulders. But it was a part of the job and all the men had to learn to carry their load sooner or later. "I suppose you questioned the nurses? The doctor?"

"Yes. They don't know any more than I do."

Ethan heaved out a breath of disgust. "Have you checked all the places in town where she might be? Her home and office?"

"Me and a couple of city policemen. Her secretary said she hadn't heard from the judge since we left for the clinic. When we checked her house, the car she drives is gone."

Ethan wearily pinched the bridge of his nose as he tried to think beyond shaking the ice out of Penelope Parker's veins. "Okay, Lonnie. I'll be there in a few minutes. In the meantime, ask around about any friends or acquaintances she might have gone to see.''

"Friends? Sheriff, do you think Judge Parker has any friends?"

"Oh, hell, do as I say, Lonnie!"

Ethan drove back to town in record time. All the while, Lonnie's crass question kept running through his head. What if the woman really didn't have any friends? He didn't know her well, but the more he thought about it, the more he began to think his deputy might be right. Little as he knew, he couldn't imagine her sharing the evening with a man. He couldn't even imagine Penelope Parker having a warm, friendly visit with anyone. She was unapproachable.

By the time he arrived back in town, Ethan's office was full of harried deputies. Lonnie was pale and smoking one cigarette after the other. Ethan finally ripped the pack from the other man's shirt pocket and tossed it into the garbage pail by his desk.

"What's the matter with you anyway?" Ethan asked him. "Are you afraid I'm going to fire you? Or are you trying to kill yourself with an overdose of nicotine?"

"Are you going to fire me?" Lonnie asked meekly.

Ethan shook his head as he studied a list of possible places Judge Parker might be. Nearly all of them had been checked, but no sight of her had been reported.

"No," he barked.

"But what if something's happened to her? The judge, I mean."

"I still won't fire you. *She* was the one who ran off— like a dizzy idiot," he muttered. "Right now, I'd like to take the woman over my knee and give her a good hiding with a belt."

At that moment, another deputy walked into the office

and pushed a note in front of his boss. Ethan read it quickly and with each word his expression grew darker.

"When did you get this?"

"The call came in a few minutes ago. When the dispatcher suggested to Kirkland that he speak with you, he hung up."

Fear shot through Ethan like a bolt of lightning. "No trace on the call?"

"Not yet. But apparently he doesn't know the judge is missing. His threats are still being made in the future tense."

Ethan nodded. "Yes, I can see that."

Both telephones on his desk began to ring. Lonnie and the other deputy reached for them simultaneously and Ethan was content to let the two men deal with the callers. Right now, he had to focus all his thoughts on where the judge might have gone.

"Sheriff, it's Walter, the city councilman. He says he needs to speak with you. He says the sheriff's department is going to look like a bunch of kindergartners if we don't find the judge soon."

Several choice curse words bellowed from Ethan's lips, but since Lonnie's hand was carefully clamped over the receiver, the caller failed to hear them.

"I don't care if the whole bunch of us look like we're two years old! All I'm concerned about is a woman's safety. Not what that jackass of a councilman thinks! Tell him that!" Ethan snapped, then reached to jerk the phone from the deputy's hand. "Give me that thing. I'll tell him myself!"

Lonnie jumped back before Ethan could get ahold of the receiver. "That's okay, sir. I'll get the point across to him."

Ethan rose from his desk, tried to flex the cords of

tension binding his shoulders and neck, then scrubbed his
face with both hands. He hadn't had a decent meal in
several days, and sleep had become a luxury he only in-
dulged in when his body refused to keep going. At this
point, all he was running on was caffeine, hamburgers and
an urgent desire to face Penelope Parker once again. And
whenever he did, he wasn't going to hold back. When he
finished with the woman, she was going to know exactly
what he thought of her righteous, self-important attitude.
Not to mention her disregard for others.

In the corner of the room, Ethan discovered someone
had made a fresh pot of coffee. He poured himself a cup,
then stepped outside the back of the building for a breath
of fresh air and a few minutes away from the buzz of
telephones and voices.

The sky was darkening to blue twilight and the evening
star hung like a giant diamond over the desert. As Ethan
sipped the strong coffee, he took the opportunity to savor
the beauty of the coming night. At the moment, the small
town was quiet. Almost as tranquil as the far-off mountains where cattle, deer and coyotes slipped along shadowed trails and the pines whispered softly in the wind.

And then it suddenly hit him. Ethan knew where he
could find Judge Penelope Parker. And he was going to
take immense satisfaction in personally going after her
and dragging her back to safety.

Chapter Two

The wooden rocker creaked slowly back and forth, but Penelope was as unconscious of the movement as she was of the darkness closing in around the small cabin. Even though her gaze was locked on the windows in front of her, she wasn't seeing beyond the glass panes. All she could picture was an empty void and no way to fill it.

For the first time since her parents had been killed by a hit-and-run driver, Penny was uncertain about the course of her future. She'd been only fifteen at the time of their deaths. And because no one in the police department of the small Colorado town where they'd lived had seemed to really care about catching the person who'd run the couple down as they walked to a movie theater, Penelope had turned her entire being toward a higher law.

During all these years, her satisfaction had come from her job. Slamming the door on criminals was her sole focus in life. But now all Penelope could think of was the doctor's edict this afternoon.

She wasn't sure why the unexpected news had hit her so hard. It wasn't as if she was engaged to be married or planning on having a family any time soon. There wasn't a man in a two-hundred-mile radius who would take that sort of look at her. And up until today, she'd been fairly content to let things remain that way. She didn't want a man taking root in her heart and then being ripped away from her as her parents had been torn away and lost forever. Nothing was worth that kind of pain.

With a soul-weary sigh, she scraped her fingers through her long, loose hair and struggled to blink away the moisture forming at the back of her eyes. She never cried. She never wanted or needed to shed tears. But at this moment, they were welling up over her lashes and threatening to spill down her cheeks.

Maybe she had made the wrong choice all those years ago in college, Penelope's miserable thoughts continued. At least Hugh had offered her marriage and a family. If she'd accepted his proposal, she might have been somewhere in California with a house full of children by this time and it wouldn't matter that her reproductive organs were being scarred and ruined.

But Hugh had been possessive and old-fashioned. He'd wanted a wife. Not a wife who was also going to be a judge and in the end Penelope couldn't accept his order for her to give up her longtime dream. She'd wanted and believed she could have it all. Her job in law and a family.

But now she had to face the fact that she would never know what it was like to carry a child inside her, to give birth to it, then nourish and love it or have that child love and need her. She would never know what it was like to be called Mother or Mommy or have a pair of sticky hands reach for her. Was being a judge these past few years worth that? she asked herself.

The sound of an approaching vehicle suddenly jerked Penelope from her tortured musings. Quickly, she dashed the tears from her face and pushed her loose hair behind her shoulders. Who would know she was here? she wondered. Was Kirkland finally going to get the gratification of killing her? At this point she couldn't think of a more ironic thing happening to her.

The engine went quiet and a door slammed. Not wasting time looking out the window, Penelope raced to the kitchen where she'd left her loaded pistol on a small table. With both hands, she grabbed the ivory handle and walked grimly back to the front room.

Through the curtained window of the door leading out to the porch, Penelope made out the dim outline of a man. As he began to bang his fist against the jamb, Penelope raised the gun and shouted, "Don't come any closer or I'll shoot!"

"Penelope! It's the sheriff. It's me, Ethan."

Ethan! Her shoulders sagged with relief. "I—just a minute," she called, then with shaky hands placed the revolver on an end table and slid back the bolt on the door.

When the door finally swung open, Penelope had to fight the urge to fling herself into his arms. "Ethan, I—"

Before she could finish, he barged through the door, walked to the center of the small room and turned on his boot heel to face her.

"What the hell are you trying to do?" he demanded. "Get us both killed? Do you realize half my force had to be pulled off the search for Kirkland just so they could hunt for you?"

She opened her mouth to speak, but for once nothing

would form in her mind or on her tongue. She wanted to hate this man for his cockiness, his toughness, his sensual beauty that stirred her body and her imagination. But at this moment, she'd never been so happy to see anyone. He was the only man she knew who wasn't afraid to treat her as an equal. Who wasn't too timid to approach her as a fellow human being.

"I'm sorry," she said softly.

"And so you should be!" he bellowed. "Do you know what sort of uproar you've caused back in town?"

"I said I was sorry," she told him. "Anything else I might say at this point would be superfluous."

"*Superfluous!* By damn, lady, for two cents I'd throw your little behind in jail! At least I'd know you'd be safe there! And me and my deputies wouldn't be chasing all over the county for you! This little jaunt of yours was stupid and selfish and—"

Like the flip of a switch, the heated words spewing from Ethan's lips suddenly stopped. His green eyes narrowed, then widened. He took a step toward her and she took one back.

"What are you doing?" she whispered, fearing he really might put her in handcuffs and haul her to jail. He had Murdock blood in his veins and she knew from the long history of the family that he was not without grit. He had enough daring for ten men. "You can't legally take me to jail!" she blurted when he failed to answer.

Ethan shook his head, but still he couldn't speak. The sight of the judge had finally gotten through his anger and he was shocked. This wasn't the woman he'd confronted three days ago at the courthouse. This wasn't the person he'd seen drop her gavel on a life sentence as easily as hanging a phone back on its hook.

She was dressed in slim-fitting jeans and a blue plaid

flannel shirt. Her black hair was loose and wild on her
shoulders and red blotches of tears marred her pale,
golden skin. He'd rarely seen her in anything but her
black robe, and though he'd been aware she was petite,
he'd never once tried to imagine the shape of her body.
She was not a female who elicited sexual thoughts of any
sort. But this was a different Penelope Parker—a *Penny*
Parker—he was seeing at the moment. This was a woman
with soft, alluring curves. This was a woman who'd been
hurt and had cried and was still obviously very shaken.

"What's happened?" he asked hoarsely. "What's
wrong?"

The sight of his green eyes fastened so intently on her
face sent a shiver right down to Penelope's toes. In an
unconscious gesture of self-protection, she folded her
arms against her waist and tried to calm the rapid beating
of her heart.

"Nothing."

The one word came out so quietly Ethan could barely
hear it. He took another step closer. "I've been through
too much hell today for you to lie to me now, Penelope.
Tell me."

He used her name as though he had a right, as though
he knew her intimately. From any other man she wouldn't
have allowed such familiarity. But this was Ethan and he
was not like any other man.

"I'm—nothing is wrong. And I..." She whirled her
back to him as more tears threatened to fall. Breathe
deeply, she told herself fiercely. Pull yourself together and
bluff your way through this.

If anything could ever get to Ethan, it was a woman in
need. Before he could remember this was the ice maiden
of the courtroom, he moved up behind her and gently
placed his hand on her shoulder.

She flinched at his touch and he instinctively tightened his hold. "Penelope, I was angry a moment ago. I'm not really going to haul you to jail."

"I know," she mumbled.

His brows lifted at the simple response. And then his gaze was drawn to her hair. It was as black and shiny as a magpie's wing and hung like a curtain of silk all the way down her back. He'd never imagined she could look like this, be like this.

Unwittingly, his big hand reached out to stroke the softness of her hair, then stopped in midair as he remembered who she was. "Has Kirkland contacted you? Has the man been near you?" he demanded.

"No."

Her answer gave him a measure of relief and his voice gentled when he spoke again. "Something has upset you. If it's not these threats—"

"I said I was fine," she interrupted. "You can go back to town now." Please go back, she silently prayed. Before she made a terrible fool of herself and broke down in front of the man.

Her voice was wobbling and the sound tore at Ethan. She'd never been anything but a rock in his presence. He knew something terrible must have happened to reduce her to such an emotional state.

"I can't go back to town, Penelope. Not without you."

That brought her around and she stared up at him with wet gray eyes. As Ethan looked down at her, something twisted in his chest. Dear God, she was beautiful, he thought. How had he not seen it before?

"I'm not going back to town," she said. "Not tonight."

The quiet determination in her voice had Ethan studying her face even more closely. "Why? What happened back in town? If some of the citizens have been harassing you, I'll take care of them, Penelope. But you're going to have to tell me what's wrong first."

She knew it was his job to protect people, to reassure them and make them feel safe. But there was something in his voice, or maybe it was just something in her troubled heart, that made it sound as though he'd lay down his life for her. Not as a sheriff, but as a man.

"I can't...I mean, no one has been harassing me. I simply came out here to...get some peace and quiet."

She was avoiding the truth, but Ethan decided not to push her for the present. He'd give her a few minutes to calm down before he tried to reason with her again.

"All right, Penelope. I'm going outside to radio my office and let them know you're safe, then I'm coming back and making a pot of coffee. Is there anything to eat in this place?"

The sudden switch in subject jarred her and for a moment she could only stare at him blankly. Ethan couldn't recall one other time Judge Parker had missed a word. But he was obviously dealing with an entirely different woman now.

"Food," he stated patiently. "Did you come out here without anything to eat?"

Penelope had been so desperate to escape the deputy and her tortured thoughts, she'd simply jumped in her car and driven the ten miles to the cabin as quickly as she could. Fortunately, she'd been out last week and stocked the place with canned goods and staples.

"There's coffee and a few things to eat," she told him.

He nodded. "I'll be back in a minute."

He left the cabin and Penelope used the time to scurry to the bathroom and dash cold water on her face. As she hurriedly pushed back her hair with a black headband, she couldn't help noticing her eyes were red and her lips puffy. From her experience with him in the courtroom, she knew Ethan was a man who noticed every minute detail. It would be foolish to try to pretend she was in her normal state of mind.

Still, there was no way Penelope could tell him the real reason for her flight out to the cabin. He was a man who, as far as she knew, had never even come close to having a wife or children. He wouldn't understand her feelings. And even if he could, it would be too embarrassing to share such an intimate problem with him.

Hearing the front door open and close, she drew in a fortifying breath and walked out to meet him.

Ethan was relieved to see she'd been attempting to compose herself. Next to having a missing woman on his hands, a hysterical one would be almost as bad.

"The kitchen's through here," she said, then motioned behind her with one hand.

Ethan nodded and followed her through a short, darkened hallway into another room equipped with a small, antiquated cookstove, an equally outdated refrigerator and a small pine table with two matching straight-backed chairs. Rather than cabinets, open shelves lined one wall. Canned goods of all sizes shared the storage space with an odd assortment of dishes, cups and glasses.

"If you'll tell me where everything is, I'll make the coffee. You sit down," he told her.

She shook her head. "No. I'm fine, really. I can make the coffee."

Ethan started to argue but quickly decided the small task might help take her mind off her problem. Whatever it might be.

"How did you find me?" she asked after a few minutes.

Since she had her back to him, Ethan watched her openly as she poured coffee grounds and struck a match to the gas burner. Her voice was much more steady now, but her hands were not. The deepest part of him longed to go to her and take her hands between his two, to hold on to her little fingers until the quaking inside her stopped. He wasn't sure why he wanted to comfort her. He only knew he didn't like seeing her suffering.

"I remembered I'd come out here one weekend to ask you to sign a search warrant. Since you were nowhere to be found around town, I figured you had to be here."

She released a sigh so small he almost missed it.

"Lonnie said he lost you at the clinic," he went on. "Does your visit to the doctor have anything to do with your reason for being here?"

Penelope carefully kept her back to him. "No. I just…couldn't take being followed around anymore."

Ethan didn't believe her entirely, but she was still too shaky to push the matter. "I think Lonnie is taking this whole thing personally. He thinks you skipped out because you don't like him."

Surprised by his statement, Penelope glanced over her shoulder at him. "I seriously doubt whether your deputy cares if I like him or not."

He frowned at her. "He was worried about you. Along with the rest of us," he added.

She turned to face him and her heart begin to thump as she took in the sight of his hat and revolver hanging on the back of the chair. He'd made himself at home as though he had a right to be in her kitchen, a right to be sitting there expecting her to serve him as if he were her husband and she a woman who lived just to please him.

The idea sent a flame licking at her cheeks and she desperately hoped the lighting in the little room was too dim for him to notice she was blushing. "I realize I shouldn't have...left town like I did, but I knew if I told you...well, you wouldn't have let me come out here alone."

"Damn right," he said. "What would you have done if it had been Kirkland at the door instead of me?"

"Shot you."

For a long moment, his gaze dwelled on her face. Behind her, the coffee began to perk and the first scent of the brew filled the air.

"You're a strange woman, Penelope."

It was not so much his words as the soft inflection in his voice that caused her gaze to drop from his and settle on the bare wood floor.

"I've always known people considered me odd," she said quietly. "It doesn't surprise me to hear you say it."

He sighed. "You must admit, you're not exactly the typical woman. At least, not the kind I've known."

Lifting her gaze back to him, she said, "There's nothing strange or complex about me. I simply do my job to the best of my ability and the rest doesn't concern anyone."

It was the rest that Ethan would have liked to know about. He'd met her more than two years ago and since then had seen her frequently in and around the courthouse. Yet he knew little about her personal life. And up until now he'd honestly never wondered about what she might be like outside the courtroom. To him, she'd been a judge, not a woman.

"You're not from here originally," he said.

Her brows lifted ever so slightly. "How do you know that?"

"You don't exactly act like a native. Besides, I know everyone who grew up in Lincoln County."

She grimaced. "I grew up in Colorado, then went to college in California."

"That's a long ways from Carrizozo," he remarked.

"That's the whole point."

He waited for her to say more. When she didn't, he wondered if she was deliberately being closemouthed about her past. Or maybe she had the notion he wouldn't be interested in hearing her talk about herself.

Penelope moved over to one of the shelves on the wall and took down two brown mugs. "Would you like cream or sugar?"

"Black is fine."

She poured the coffee and joined him at the small table. "Do you want to eat now?"

"No. I've changed my mind about the food. We need to be going soon."

She felt her insides began to quiver again and she silently berated herself for being so weak. It shouldn't upset her to think about going back to her house. Back to reality. But it did. "I told you I'm staying here tonight."

She plopped the coffee down on the table. Some of it sloshed over the rim of the mug and made a puddle on the table. With a little cry of dismay, she snatched up a tea towel and quickly sopped up the spill.

Ethan calmly reached out and covered her hand with his. The moment his fingers touched hers, her gaze shot up to his face. And suddenly, she couldn't breathe or still the rapid thud of her heart.

"Penelope, it's obvious you're upset about something. But this isn't the time to—"

"Don't you realize I don't care if I'm in danger?" she whispered hoarsely. "Just let me be responsible for myself."

"I can't do that." Gently, he tugged her onto the chair next to him. "Sit down and drink," he ordered.

Penelope didn't argue. Sometime during the past few minutes, her legs had become useless. She'd never forgive herself if she allowed Ethan to see her wilt like a flower in the noonday sun.

Cupping her hands around the warm coffee mug, she dared her eyes to meet his. "You can't force me to go back," she said with as much bravado as she could muster. Then, in not much more than a whisper, she added, "Please, Ethan, don't make me."

In his wildest imaginings, he never would have pictured Penelope pleading with him for any reason. And at one time, he might have enjoyed hearing the humbleness in her voice. But none of it pleased him now. To know that she was hurting cut at him more than he wanted to admit.

"If you'd only tell me what it is you don't want to face back in town, I'd deal with it for you."

A hysterical laugh climbed up her throat and struggled to burst past her lips. This brave, handsome sheriff could fix many things for many people. But he couldn't change the course Penelope's life was taking. Even she couldn't change it.

"There's nothing for you to deal with, Ethan." She lifted the mug to her lips and carefully sipped. When she lowered the drink back to the table, he was still studying her with a thoughtful expression. "Okay. Send Lonnie out here," she told him. "I won't like having the man here. But I'll endure his company."

"It's Kirkland, isn't it?" Ethan asked after a pause. "Knowing we haven't caught him yet is becoming too much for you."

Penelope figured it would be much easier to let Ethan think her odd behavior was due to the fugitive's dark threats. But that was so far from the truth, so against her normally strong nature, she couldn't bear for him to believe such a thing.

Closing her eyes, she passed her fingers across her furrowed brow. "Why are you pumping me for information?" she asked wearily. "I've given in. I've told you to send Lonnie here to guard me. Can't you be satisfied with that?"

Ethan probably should be content to radio for Lonnie, drink his coffee and be on his way. He'd chewed on Penelope Parker and she'd admitted she'd been wrong. She'd even apologized. He should let it drop. Yet, for some reason he didn't understand, he was loathe to leave her in the hands of a deputy. He was loathe to leave her. Period.

Rising from the chair, he walked over to the single sink wedged between the cook stove and the refrigerator. Above it a small window looked out on the land behind the cabin. Even though darkness hid the encroaching mountains, he knew the view would be a pretty sight with the piñon pine and blue sage growing right up to the back door.

"I'm not sending for Lonnie. If you're so all fired on staying I guess I'll be staying, too."

Her eyes flew open as though a bolt of electricity had just shot through her. "You!" she cried, her gaze stabbing the middle of his back. "You can't stay here!"

"Why?"

She didn't answer.

He turned back around and as she spotted the look of calm determination on his face, Penelope had never felt so helpless or out of control in her life.

"Because you—you're the sheriff," she finally managed to say. "You have more important things to do than guard me."

"You're the judge in this county. Your safety is important to all of us."

"I'm no different from any other citizen," she argued.

He returned to his chair and picked up the mug of cooling coffee. "I think we could argue that point. But I'm not going to. I'm too tired. And anyway, you'd lose."

Penelope gripped her own drink and stared down at the brown liquid. How had things gotten to this point? she wondered wildly. Normally, her life never altered. Her days consisted of work and home. Nothing more or less. She wasn't accustomed to fugitives threatening her life, lawmen tracking her down or doctors telling her she could very well be sterile. It was all too much for her to bear.

"Does this mean I have nothing else to say in the matter?" she asked.

"That's exactly what it means."

Penelope couldn't believe she was sitting here, quietly allowing him to have his way. This was somebody else crumbling beneath the sheriff's orders. Not her.

"You won't be comfortable."

He grimaced and flexed his shoulders. The movement drew her gaze from his face to the wide expanse of his chest. He was wearing a tan khaki shirt styled with western yokes and pearl snaps. A small oval badge was pinned on the left pocket.

From hearsay, she knew he was a rancher and had come from a long line of ranchers before him. She could picture him in the role of cowboy as easily as she could sheriff. His big hands were lean and tough skinned, his face burned brown from the fierce New Mexico sun. Without having to ask, she knew he was a man who loved the outdoors and was totally attuned to nature.

"Since you probably only have one bed in this place, I should take it and make you sleep on the couch," he told her. "After all, you're the one who got us in this situation. But my mother tried to raise me as a gentleman and I wouldn't take a woman's bed—unless she offered it to me."

And Penelope figured he'd had many offers. Ethan Hamilton was one of the most sought-after bachelors in several counties. She didn't know why he hadn't gotten married yet. It certainly wasn't for lack of willing women. She could only guess that he was, in his own way, like her. He'd committed his life to the law.

"I'll offer you the couch," she said while desperately trying to keep a blush off her face. "I have an extra pillow and blankets, so you should be all right. Maybe a little cramped."

"Lady, it's been so long since I've had a full night's sleep, the thought of a couch and a few quiet hours sounds like heaven."

She was still wondering about his motive for staying when he suddenly rose to his feet and reached for his hat and gun belt.

"What are you doing?" she asked as he strapped the weapon back on his hips.

"I'm going out to my vehicle to use the radio. Unless you have a telephone in here somewhere."

She had a cellular telephone and normally brought it with her in case of emergencies. But this afternoon, she'd not even taken time to gather extra clothes.

"No. There's no phone."

He jammed his Stetson back on his head. "I'll be back in a few minutes. While I'm gone, do you think you could rustle up something in those cans for us to eat?"

Penelope was certain her knotted stomach couldn't hold

a bite, but she'd do her best to prepare him some sort of meal. "I'll try."

He left the room and Penelope pushed herself to her feet. As she searched through the cans of food, the hysterical thought that she was going to cook for Sheriff Ethan Hamilton kept popping into her head. She, the sterile old maid of the courthouse, was going to spend the night with the sexiest man in southern New Mexico. She couldn't think of anything more hilarious nor could she stop the laughter from erupting from her throat.

Though she tried to stifle the foreign sound, it went on and on until tears flowed from her eyes like twin rivers of pain. Eventually, she managed to compose herself and once again went to the bathroom and soaked her face in cold water. This time when she looked into the mirror, she was completely disgusted with herself.

So what if she was never going to bear a child? So what if she was going to be alone for the rest of her life? She was still a worthwhile woman. She could still serve society. And wasn't that all she'd ever set out to do anyway?

Setting her jaw with grim resolution, Penelope went back out to the kitchen and began to prepare supper.

Outside, Ethan reached for the two-way mike hanging on the dashboard of the vehicle, then swiftly changed his mind and picked up the cellular phone attached to the floorboard. Even though cellular calls could be picked up by scanners, it would still be far more private than the two-way radio. And he didn't necessarily want this conversation to be public news.

Lonnie answered the phone on the first ring and Ethan quickly explained he'd be staying at the judge's cabin for the night.

The brash young deputy began to splutter and Ethan

wearily closed his eyes as Lonnie's voice came back in his ear. "But, sir, the judge is my responsibility. I won't mess up again. Besides, if people find out you two stayed together under the same roof, all sorts of gossip will start."

Any other time, Ethan would have counted to ten and tried to be patient, but tonight he didn't have the time or the will to deal with Lonnie's nonsense. "Who the hell is going to tell anybody anything?"

"Well, uh, not me, sir. But—"

"Good! See that it stays that way. In the meantime, if anything changes in the Kirkland case, page me immediately."

"When are you coming back to the office?"

"I don't know. It depends on Penelope."

The telephone went silent for a long moment. Ethan was about to push the end button when the deputy's voice finally came back at him.

"Sheriff, are you sick or something?"

"I'm dog tired," he snapped. "Other than that, I don't think I need medical attention."

"Well, sounds like you do. You never let the judge call the shots before. Not when you two are outside the courtroom."

"Lonnie, one of these days you're going to learn that issuing a woman orders isn't the best way to handle her."

"But, sir, the judge—well, she's not a woman. I mean, not like a real, regular woman. I'm warning you, she'll hang you if you give her the chance."

Ethan glanced at the log cabin. People around town called her the hanging judge. And in a sense the term fitted. But if Penelope had a noose waiting to wrap around his neck, she was hiding it well.

"I think I'll manage to survive one night in the woman's company."

"But, sir, she's not a woman—"

"Good night, Lonnie." Ethan quickly ended the connection and headed back to the cabin.

He found Penelope in the kitchen at the little cookstove. The moment his footsteps reached her ears, she cast a glance back over her shoulder at him.

And as Ethan looked into her soulful gray eyes, it dawned on him that his deputy's warning had been all wrong. Penelope didn't have a noose waiting for him. She had something far more dangerous.

Chapter Three

The odd notions going through Ethan's head must have shown on his face because Penelope was staring uneasily at him.

"Is something wrong?" she asked.

He mentally shook himself and stepped forward. "No," he said quickly. "Everything is settled and if I'm needed back in town my deputies will contact me."

She nodded with a measure of relief, then turned back to the cookstove and switched off the burners. "This is ready to eat," she announced. "There's a bathroom off to the left of the hallway where you can wash."

"Thanks. I'll be right back," he told her.

When Ethan returned, the pine table was set with two plates and three dishes of food. Their coffee mugs were steaming with fresh brew and Penelope was waiting beside the chair she'd sat in earlier.

"I'm sorry I don't have any fresh bread or tortillas. I didn't take time to stop by a store before I drove out."

"This will be fine." He motioned for her to take a seat, then quickly eased down in his own.

There were tamales, corn and brown beans. She took a small portion of each before passing the bowls on to him.

"How did you come by this place anyway?" he asked as he shook hot sauce over the mounds of food on his plate.

His presence filled the room and it wasn't simply because he was a big man or that he was sitting only inches from her. There was something commanding about him, something that said he was not of ordinary stock.

Penelope had always been a confident woman. When she'd lost her parents, she'd been forced to be strong and stand on her own two feet. When she'd told Hugh their relationship was over, she'd done it with calm certainty and had refused to give in to sadness or regret.

But Ethan Hamilton was like no one she'd ever encountered. He was the only person who could shake her reserve. And he was the only man who reminded her she was a woman and that somewhere in the deepest part of her she had a woman's needs.

Releasing a pent-up breath, Penelope tried to concentrate on her plate as she answered him. "When I first became district attorney, I approached a real-estate agent for a place where I could get away from the pressures of my job. At the time, he said all he had was an old hunting cabin and he figured I wouldn't be interested. But I came out and took a look anyway."

"And you liked it," he stated the obvious.

She nodded. "It's rustic. But I've never been a frilly person."

"Maybe that's why you wound up living in New Mexico,'' he suggested. ''It's stark in a lot of places, but oh, so enchanting.''

As was he. Penelope wondered if he knew how much. ''My parents used to own a summer home in Ruidoso. When I was small, we'd spend several weeks there. That's how I came to love the state. By the time I finished law school, I had my mind set on returning.''

''Do your parents still own the place?''

Her gaze dropped to her plate. ''My parents are no longer living,'' she said flatly.

''Oh. I'm sorry. Do you have other relatives in Colorado where you grew up?''

She shook her head. ''A few distant relatives in California. But I'm not close to them.''

Ethan wasn't surprised by her admission. He figured she wasn't close to anyone and wondered if she deliberately wanted to live that way. The only thing he could figure was that she didn't like people. Or she simply didn't know how to make friends or keep a lover.

''That's too bad,'' he said between bites of tamale. ''I have a whole herd of relatives in Lincoln County and I'm close to all of them.''

''Our former sheriff was your uncle.''

''That's right,'' he said with a nod of his head. ''Roy had a big influence on me. He's the reason I first became interested in being a lawman.''

''When was that?''

''When I was seven years old and I understood he had the power to put bad people in jail. You see, there was a bully at school who was always hitting the other kids and stealing their lunch money. I swore when I grew up I'd be like my uncle Roy and put Freddie in jail.''

''What did you do in the meantime? With Freddie, I mean.''

He chuckled. "My father taught me some wrestling holds and I worked the kid over on the playground. After that, he changed his ways."

The corners of her lips tilted into a faint smile. Ethan told himself he always enjoyed making a woman smile, but seeing the look of amusement on Penelope's face gave him such a surge of pure pleasure he felt downright foolish.

"I'm sure a hammerlock would have that effect," she said, then with a glance at him asked, "What did your parents think about your becoming a lawman?"

"At first, they weren't too keen on the idea," Ethan admitted. "But once they both realized I was serious, they stood behind my decision."

Penelope had no way of knowing what her parents would have thought of her becoming a judge. She'd always been a good student and they'd proudly encouraged her to be all that she could be. Their guidance had been important to her. But she'd lost them. And now she'd never have a child of her own to guide, support or love.

Tears suddenly burned her throat, but she determinedly swallowed them down and reached for her coffee. "I'm sure your mother must worry about you," she told Ethan.

"Why do you say that?"

The question put a mocking twist to her lips. "You do have a dangerous job," she pointed out. "In fact, not too long ago, I was going through the local newspaper archives and ran across a piece about how you were shot in the line of duty."

He continued to eat as though she'd been remarking about the weather rather than a life-threatening event. "That was a long time ago when I was a deputy. It was nothing. Just a little fracas with an armed robber."

"The article said you were seriously wounded."

He shook his head dismissively. "You know how news stories are. Three-quarters of them are overdramatized. Actually, the only thing my mother worries about is whether I'm going to be a bachelor for the rest of my life."

Her dark brows lifted with surprise. "I'd think the danger of your being shot is far greater than your remaining single."

He chuckled and her gaze lingered on his lips. No doubt he'd kissed many women in his time and it was an art he enjoyed. As for herself, Penelope's experience with kissing was very limited.

"Why do you say that?" he asked.

She looked down at her food. "There's always gossip to be heard in the courthouse. You've been linked with a number of women."

He made a sound of disgust. "Well, I can assure you that's all it is, gossip. I'm not *linked* to anyone."

"Why is that?" she asked, then immediately wished she'd bitten her tongue instead. This wasn't like her to ask personal questions. So why was she? He was going to think she'd slipped a cog, or even worse, that *she* was interested in him.

"Because I haven't found anyone I want to be married to. What's your reason?"

Her heart gave an odd little jump. "Reason?"

"Yes. Why you're not married."

To her horror, she laughed. The unfamiliar sound had Ethan laying down his fork and leaning back in his chair to stare at her. "I didn't realize the question was amusing," he said.

There was nothing funny about love or marriage. In fact, the subjects were both so painful to Penelope she rarely allowed them to enter her mind.

"I'm sorry. I really didn't mean to laugh. Something is—I'm just not myself tonight."

She rose to her feet and carried her plate over to the sink, her meal half-eaten. From his seat at the table, Ethan watched her and wondered.

"Well, there's gossip about you, too, you know," he said.

Without turning to look at him, she gripped the edges of the porcelain sink. "What sort of gossip?"

"About your love life. Or should I say the lack of one?"

Her lips pressed together as an odd little pain coursed through her chest. "Why do people have to talk about you or me? Or things that are none of their business?"

"Because it's human nature," he replied. "Because their own lives are so boring they don't know what else to do."

"Well, the reason I'm not married is because…I don't want to be." She turned to face him. Her chin unconsciously lifted as she added, "I know everyone thinks I'm too—well, that I can't attract a man, but the truth is I've chosen to live my life alone and they should respect that decision."

And so should Ethan. But tonight, as he looked at her pale, beautiful face, her silky curtain of hair and the alluring curves hidden beneath her plain clothes, he could only think how wasteful and sad that she'd chosen to be without a mate.

Rising to his feet, he gathered his empty plate and carried it the few steps over to where she still stood. "And why have you decided to live alone? Do you hate men?"

This time, there was nothing to do to stop the blaze of heat scorching her face. "Of course I don't hate men. But I serve the public. I don't have time to serve a man, too."

One corner of his mouth crooked upward. "You think to love a man means to serve him?"

Dear heaven, what was making her say these things and how was she ever going to face this man in her courtroom? "I think this conversation is absurd. And I'm tired. I'm going to bed."

Other than the pretty blush on her face, this was more like the judge he knew. Stern and distant. Obviously, whatever had been wearing on her mind had left for the moment and she was gathering herself together. A part of him was ridiculously disappointed.

"What about dessert? One thing you might not know, Penelope, is that men always want dessert."

A big part of her job was being able to read people. But she was suddenly finding it next to impossible to believe what she was seeing on Ethan's face. He wasn't joking or even being impertinent. He was being downright suggestive. With her! Prim Penelope Parker!

Quivering at the mere thought, she quickly stepped around him and walked over to the shelves of food. After a moment's search, she set a tin of butter cookies and a can of peaches on the table.

"Here's your dessert," she told him. "I'll put your blankets and pillow on the couch. Good night."

She walked out of the room before Ethan could say a word. With a regretful shrug of his shoulders, he found a can opener and went over to the table to finish the last of his meal.

As Penelope had predicted, the couch was too short for him. By morning, he was sure to be feeling cramped. But just the plain relief of being in a recumbent position after spending the past twenty hours awake was enough for Ethan.

Penelope had provided him with two blankets. Since the April nights were still very cool, especially here in the mountains, he'd folded both of them double. He didn't need the cold to add to his misery.

On the floor below his shoulder lay his colt .45, pager and cellular phone. The first item he didn't expect to need. But with Kirkland on the loose, he wasn't going to take any risk with Penelope's safety. The least little sound would alert him to be ready for the man.

With a weary sigh, he shifted on the lumpy cushions and tugged the blankets higher onto his shoulders. As he did, his fingers came in contact with scar tissue, a result of a bullet tearing through his flesh.

Even though he'd played it down to Penelope, the wound had been serious, missing his heart only by inches. After the incident, his mother had begged him to quit his job as deputy, but he'd not allowed his tender feelings for her to sway his resolve. He'd argued that most lawmen work until retirement without getting involved in any sort of shoot-out. The odds of having it happen to Ethan twice would be as high as winning a state lottery.

That had been nearly eight years ago and he still wasn't sure his mother was convinced. And as for getting married, he couldn't stay interested in a woman when once they got serious, the first thing that came out of her mouth was, "How soon can you find another job?"

His lips twisted wryly. It seemed as ironic as hell that the very thing that drew women to him in the first place was eventually the thing that drove them away. Being a figure of authority attracted women, but it didn't necessarily keep them hanging around for the long haul. Trisha had definitely taught him that hard lesson. At first, she'd thought his being a deputy sheriff was well and dandy until she'd met someone higher on the totem pole. In the end, it hadn't mattered to her that Ethan had planned on running for sheriff with a great chance of winning. His being just a sheriff hadn't been good enough for Trisha. She'd wanted someone in the state capitol who wrote the laws. Not just a peon who enforced them.

The memory of her dejection still burned with anger and humiliation. Yet he hadn't let her betrayal sway him from his plans. Serving Lincoln County as its sheriff was the essence of who and what Ethan was as a person. He couldn't make himself into something else just to please a woman so she might eventually agree to marry him. And even if there was a woman out there who considered his position prominent enough to suit her, he still might be wrong to expect her to take the risk of becoming a young widow, he argued with himself.

During the past few years, he'd watched his sister and cousins get married and start having children of their own. Ethan was happy for all of them. Although, at times whenever he was in their company, he couldn't help but feel very much alone. Even his cousin Charlie, who was a Texas Ranger, had managed to find a woman who adored him and supported his career in law.

Ethan grimaced in the darkness. Maybe he just wasn't as lucky as Charlie, he thought. Besides, after what Trisha had put him through, he figured a little loneliness was a small price to pay compared with what another woman might cost him.

Hell, he mentally cursed as he shifted once again on the too short couch. He didn't know why he'd been digging at Penelope to explain why she was still single. She was like him, but only in a different way. They were both meant to be loners and nothing could change that fact.

Penelope couldn't believe her parents were really back with her. She could see them clearly in the afternoon sun as they smiled and waved to her from across the city street. As she eagerly lifted her hand and waved back to them, the loneliness, the burden of grief she carried inside her, vanished and joy spread through her like the warmth of the desert sunshine.

She waved again and began to run toward them. Her arms were outstretched, her heart bursting with joy. Then, out of nowhere, an engine raced, tires squealed loudly on pavement, and Penelope screamed in terror.

Her cry pierced the walls of the little cabin. Ethan was instantly awake. Without bothering to pull his jeans over his boxer shorts, he snatched up the colt and moved soundlessly through the little cabin.

Ethan was always ready for the unexpected. But not this time. When he stepped into her room, he was immobilized by the sight of Penelope sitting straight up in bed. Her hair was a mass of wild tangles on her bare shoulders. Her face was gripped with an expression of sheer horror.

"Penelope?"

Her only response was a vacant stare. Ethan squashed the urge to rush to her. Instead, he put his training in gear and searched the windows and shadowed corners of the room for intruders. After a few moments, he concluded nothing appeared to be amiss. Except for Penelope. She was yet to acknowledge his presence.

"Penelope, it's me, Ethan," he said softly as he approached the bed.

She continued to stare blankly at him and Ethan knew she was somewhere other than the dark bedroom. Reaching out, he touched her bare shoulders with the tips of his fingers. She flinched and blinked her eyes.

Bending his head closer, he spoke again. "Penelope, are you awake?"

The moonlight filtering through the bare windowpanes was enough to illuminate her face. He could see her searching his face, his eyes, his lips.

"I…they're gone," she said simply.

Ethan frowned as he tried to decipher her meaning. "They? Who's gone?"

"I thought—" She broke off abruptly, then swallowed as a look of utter desolation washed over her face.

"You thought what? What is it, Penelope? You screamed out a moment ago. Were you dreaming?"

Dreaming. It was a nightmare, she thought sickly. Her parents hadn't been alive. The joy, the contentment that had poured all too briefly through her heart had been merely a cruel illusion of her troubled mind.

When she failed to answer, Ethan began to worry she was still disoriented. Grasping both her shoulders, he forced her to look up at him. "Do you know where you are?"

The realization of where she was and why came rushing back to her, and as it did, her body began to shake. "Yes, I know I'm at the cabin. I'm sorry, Ethan. I…"

To her humiliation, tears suddenly choked off the rest of her words. Instinctively, Ethan's hands slid against her back and drew her gently against his chest.

"There's nothing to be sorry about, honey," he murmured. "You had a bad dream. But you're going to be all right now."

She wasn't going to be all right and the reality of the fact was almost more than she could bear.

"I wish that were true," she mumbled, and then it dawned on her that she was in Ethan's arms. Her face was pressed against his warm, bare chest. Her lips were almost touching his skin.

"Nothing is going to hurt you, Penelope. I'm not going to let that happen," he told her, and then he could not stop his hand from tangling itself in her long hair and stroking down the silky strands lying against her back.

The hypnotic touch of his hand coupled with the luscious warmth of his hard body was like a drink of water after a trek across the desert. Without thinking, her hands latched onto his shoulders and she buried herself closer.

If Ethan was surprised by her needy response, he didn't give himself time to question it. She felt so warm and small and vulnerable in his arms. He wanted to hold her, soothe her, show her that she was not alone.

Eventually, her silent sobs lessened, and beneath the quilt separating their bodies, he could feel the rapid rise and fall of her breasts. The soft caress of her breath skimmed across his shoulder and the touch of her fingers began to burn his skin.

He tried to remember she was not his for the taking. She was the stern, cold judge who could stare down the meanest snake. But this soft, warm woman in his arms was not that person.

Penelope suddenly tilted her face up to his and Ethan's mental argument came to a grinding halt. His head bent and his lips touched hers. Instantly, she flinched away from him, and her wide, shocked eyes scanned his face.

"Ethan."

She breathed his name as though he were a precious wonder to her, as though she had waited all her life for this very moment. And then before he could understand what any of it meant, she was groaning low in her throat and sliding her arms around his neck.

That was all the invitation Ethan needed to fasten his

lips roughly over hers. The quilt between them slipped
and the sudden shock of her bare breasts pressing against
his chest rivaled the overwhelming taste of her kiss.

When the need for breath finally forced him to break
the contact of their lips, he buried his face in the side of
her hair. Like her skin, it smelled of wildflowers and sunshine. He breathed deeply, filling himself with the heady
scent.

"Penelope, do you know what you're doing?" he whispered hoarsely.

Her small hands lifted and cupped his whisker-rough
jaw. He leaned his head back to look at her and it was all
he could do to keep from crushing her in the circle of his
arms, kissing her until neither of them could breathe or
speak.

"Yes."

That one word was enough for him. It had to be. He'd
never had a woman in his arms who tasted like honey and
felt like velvet. She was like nothing he'd ever imagined
and he wanted more. Much more.

With a growl of desperation, he found her lips again
and this time he didn't hold back. This time the need in
him roughened his touch. His tongue delved boldly between her teeth while his hands slid to her breasts.

Their softness filled his palms, and once his thumbs had
rubbed their centers to hard, rosy buds, he pulled his
mouth from hers to hungrily taste the sweetness.

By the time he lifted his head, Penelope's breaths were
coming rapid-fire, her head swirling like the dancing shadows on the wall. Then, without giving her senses a chance
to cool, he eased her down on the mattress and pushed
away the quilt tangled over the lower part of her body.

To his utter surprise, she'd been sleeping in the nude,

and now all he had to do was look down to feast his eyes on her small, perfectly shaped body.

She blushed beneath the slow inspection of his gaze, but when he slid beside her and gathered her into his arms, she could only think how right it felt, how precious to have him touching her, wanting her as though there were no tomorrow.

Starting with her chin and ending with her eyelids, he worshiped her face with kisses, then moved his attention to the pulse beating near the hollow of her throat. Her skin was like warm cream against his tongue. The throbbing beneath his lips matched the wild beat of his own heart and he wondered if she was feeling the same terrifying pleasure that was rushing through him.

Lifting his head, he looked at her for a long, breathless moment. "Are you frightened of me, Penelope?"

"No!" she answered hoarsely, then her head twisted back and forth against the pillow. "I want you, Ethan."

With shaking fingers, he pushed back the hair at her temple. "You're the most beautiful woman I've ever known."

Tears sprang to her eyes. "You don't have to tell me that. You don't have to tell me anything."

Somehow Ethan knew she didn't expect words from him. She only wanted what he was able to give her. And that in itself turned his heart inside out.

"Are you protected?" he asked, his voice thick with desire.

Penelope hesitated only a second before she nodded her head. It was the answer Ethan wanted to hear. He snatched her tight against him and devoured her lips with his. She greedily accepted the thrust of his tongue and her body arched against his. He rolled her onto her back and her arms clamped around his waist.

The need to absorb her, to be connected to her in the most primal way, was more than he could bear. Quickly, his knee nudged her thighs apart and he entered her warm, soft body.

And Ethan's last conscious thought before the blinding pleasure overtook him was that she was a virgin.

Chapter Four

The aromas of freshly brewed coffee and frying bacon slowly tugged Penelope from a deep sleep. Blinking her eyes, she groggily tried to figure where the delicious smells were coming from. She was still in bed. She wasn't cooking breakfast.

Slowly, the last cobwebs of sleep drifted from her mind and reality came flowing in like a wave of icy water.

Ethan!

Totally awake now, her head twisted to the right and she stared in wild disbelief at the pillow next to hers. Dear God, the indentation of his head was still there where he'd slept beside her! What had she done? What must he think of her?

She swallowed convulsively as her thoughts raced from the wild ecstasy she'd experienced in his arms to the idea of facing him in the cold light of morning. At this very moment, he was probably in the kitchen wondering how he'd let himself fall into bed with a woman like her. He'd already described her as strange. No doubt he was cursing himself a thousand times over for letting things get so out of hand between them.

Clutching the patchwork quilt to her naked breasts, she swung her legs over the side of the bed and immediately groaned as her body reacted in outrage. Every muscle, and some she didn't even know she possessed, was sore. And she was suddenly overwhelmed with flashes of memory from the night before as Ethan had slowly and surely turned her into a woman. His woman.

No! She couldn't let herself start thinking along those lines. She wasn't Ethan's woman. Nor would she ever be. She was a judge in Lincoln County and that's all she'd ever be. Ethan hadn't really been making love to her. He'd only been trying to comfort her. What had happened afterward had been her own weak doing. And being a man, he'd simply responded to her need. She had to remember that.

After a quick wash in the bathroom, she dressed in jeans and another flannel shirt, then tied back her hair with a string of leather. As she walked into the kitchen, Ethan was placing crisp pieces of bacon onto a platter.

Even though Penelope was barefoot, he somehow heard her as she entered the room. Glancing over his shoulder, he greeted her with a faint smile. "Good morning."

Heat instantly stung her cheeks, but she refused to look away from his green eyes. Not for anything did she want him to think she was embarrassed at giving herself to him. Because she wasn't. For two long years, she had quietly fantasized about him. Yet her fantasies had not come close to the tender passion he'd shown her. And no matter what happened in the days ahead, she would always cherish the fact that he was the man who had gently led her into womanhood.

"Good morning," she replied as normally as she could.

"Are you hungry? I found bacon and eggs in the refrigerator. The bacon wasn't moldy and the eggs seemed to be fresh."

She nodded. "I brought those things out here last week."

He gestured to the percolator on the cookstove. "The coffee is ready if you'd like a cup."

Thankful for anything to do besides stand in the middle of the floor and gawk at him, Penelope went over to the cabinets and took down a mug.

While she poured it full of strong coffee, he stepped up beside her and began to break eggs into the bacon grease. "How do you like your eggs?" he asked.

Penelope had never had a man cook for her before. But then, she'd never had a man make love to her for half the night, either, and all of a sudden she knew that she, or the world around her, would never be the same.

"I'm not sure I could eat," she admitted.

"Of course you can eat," he said with a frown. "You barely picked at your supper last night."

She couldn't believe he'd noticed. People never did. Or if they did, they kept their observations to themselves. No one wanted to risk irking a judge.

"Has anyone from the department notified you?" she asked.

"No."

"Is that a good sign?"

"It's a sign nothing bad has happened. But it also tells me there's no news about Kirkland."

Kirkland. The fugitive's name was a sudden reminder of why Ethan was here at the cabin in the first place. Last night, it had been his duty to find her, to make sure she was safe. Making love to her had not been a part of the job. And even though he had a reputation for attracting the ladies, Penelope somehow knew he was not a man who took sex casually. Still, she wasn't a foolish, naive teenager. Ethan didn't love her. He'd simply wanted her.

"These eggs are ready if you are."

His words jarred her solemn thoughts and she joined him at the table. It was already set with plates and cutlery and a platter of bacon, eggs and toast. Obviously, Ethan was a man used to taking care of himself.

"Where did you find the bread? I didn't think there was any here," she commented.

"In the freezer."

"I should have looked there last night," she murmured.

There were a lot of things she should have done last night, Ethan thought as he slid into the chair across from her. Especially when he'd come to her bedroom. But none of that could be changed now. He couldn't give her back her virginity. Nor could he forget how her body had felt beneath his.

As she filled her plate with one of the fried eggs and a meager ration of bacon, Ethan allowed his gaze to slip over her face. In spite of all that had happened, she looked far better than she had when he'd first arrived at the cabin last night. There was a bit of pink color to her cheeks and the tears that had wet her eyes were now long gone. He still didn't know what had driven her out to the cabin. And since their sleeping together he supposed the problem seemed mundane to her now.

"Penelope," he said as he began to fill his own plate, "I want you to know…"

He stopped and Penelope's heart throbbed with pain and dread. It was obvious he was going to say something about last night, and from the grave look on his face, it was clear there was a mountain of regret inside him.

"If you're going to start apologizing for what happened, please don't," she said quickly. "I think—" she glanced down at the food on her plate as a knot of emotion lodged in her throat "—if anyone should apologize, it should be me."

Ethan's brows lifted as he tried to study what he could see of her downcast face. "Why should you think that? You didn't hold that gun of yours to my head."

Scarlet heat filled her cheeks and Ethan tried to recall the pale, emotionless judge he oftentimes faced in the courtroom back in Carrizozo. It seemed impossible that the woman sitting across from him was the same person. And even more incredible that it was that same stern judge who had loved him so passionately last night.

"No. I didn't force you to do anything. But I was behaving like an emotional, needy female and—"

"Is that so wrong? You are a woman," he pointed out.

"I'm a judge first and foremost. An officer of the court. Just like you are the sheriff before anything else."

Ethan had to admit being the sheriff was his first priority. But he realized he was also human and it was that part of him that had reached out to Penelope last night. And he'd thought that was the part of her that had clung to him.

"You believe judges aren't supposed to make love?" he asked with wry disbelief.

Not to the sheriff! "We, uh, you and I didn't make love," she said quietly, then with all the strength inside her, she forced her gaze to lift to his.

Ethan's coffee cup stopped midway to his lips. "The hell you say."

More hot color poured into her face, but she was determined to play the whole thing down. She had to. Because she knew once they left this cabin, it would all be over. She would have to go on with her life and forget the exquisite pleasure this man had given her.

"Look, Ethan, just because I was a virgin doesn't mean I was also a fool. What transpired between us was just sex. Nothing more."

Her frankness knocked the air clean out of him. Though he didn't necessarily know why. What she was saying was essentially true. But damn it, the things he'd felt with her were like nothing he'd ever experienced before. To label what had happened between them as "just sex" seemed so wrong to him.

With a small sigh, Ethan forced himself to sip his coffee, then shove a bite of food to his mouth. When he'd first sat down at the table, he'd been ravenous. Now instead of buttered toast, he felt as though he were chewing a wad of cotton.

"I guess there's nothing like calling a spade a spade."

She winced inwardly as images of his strong hands cupping her breasts, stroking her thighs and tangling in her long hair shot through her mind like white-hot lightning. He'd transported her to paradise, yet now in the cold light of day, she could not let him know just how much of her heart she'd given him last night. As she'd learned to do long ago, she would push her tender feelings aside and face reality.

She picked up her fork and began to eat. Inside her chest, her heart felt like a lead weight. "I just don't want you to feel guilty or regretful," she went on after a moment.

Ethan couldn't feel guilty or regretful. To do so would mean he wished that night had never happened. And that would be a hell of a lie. Especially when it was just about all he could do to keep from jerking her up from the table and carrying her back to the bedroom. "I don't. Do you?"

"No," she said quickly. "So please, let's not talk of it anymore. You've cooked this nice breakfast. We should enjoy it before we head back to town."

Her comment took him by surprise. "You're willing to go back to town now?"

She couldn't stay here with him. Not after last night. Maybe he'd be willing to send Lonnie out to guard her, but even with Ethan out of the cabin, his memory would linger behind to haunt and taunt her.

No, she thought grimly, she might as well go home. Trying to run from her problems had gotten her into deeper water. Now she'd have to return to Carrizozo and try to come to terms with all that had happened.

"We both have work waiting on us," she answered bluntly.

His brows arched with speculation. "Last night you were adamant about staying here."

She drew in a long breath, then slowly released it. "Last night I...wasn't quite myself."

Suddenly, his features turned to stone and he was gripping the fork in his hand. "So in other words, if you'd been yourself, you would never have invited me into your bed."

The bitter tone of his voice caught her completely off guard and she could only stare at him and wonder.

"You don't have to look so puzzled about it all, Penelope," he said when her silence continued.

"But I am puzzled. I've already told you I don't regret what happened. Why would you even say such a thing anyway?" she asked crossly.

He frowned. "Because you and I both know the woman who sits on the judge's bench back in Carrizozo would never have made love to me. Oh, excuse me," he added dryly, "I mean never have had sex with me."

Her nostrils flared. "You don't have to be so coarse!"

"I'm only using your words," he reminded her. "So why don't you be honest along with blunt and say Judge Parker would never have made love to the sheriff."

Her lips compressed together. He was being a pain in the rear. Why, she had no idea. Lifting her chin, she said coolly, "I don't know whether she would have or not. Judge Parker was never actually given an invitation to go to bed with him. I guess the thought just never entered the sheriff's mind."

Ethan suddenly had the grace to blush. "Don't try to tell me it had never entered yours!"

Her face flaming now, she tossed down her fork. "Actually, it had. But at this very moment, I'm ashamed to admit it!" Before he could stop her, she jumped up from the table and rushed from the room.

He didn't know what in hell had come over him. There wasn't any reason for him to goad Penelope the way he had. But it seemed the more she'd tried to distance herself, the more his hackles had risen. Heaven knew he didn't need or want the complications of a relationship with Penelope. Yet it irked the heck out of him to think she considered him as little more than a bed partner and one whom she could easily dismiss in the cold light of morning.

Penelope was smoothing out the bedcovers when she heard him step into the room. Not bothering to glance around, she continued to tuck the patchwork quilt beneath the edge of the mattress.

"I'll be ready to go as soon as I wash the breakfast dishes," she told him.

"I've already done that."

She straightened to her full height but still kept her back to him. "Oh. Well, I guess it's time to go, then."

"Not just yet."

The quiet steeliness of his voice compelled her to face him. When she did, her heart thrummed against her ribs. There was a look in his green eyes, the same look she'd seen last night just before he'd pushed her back against the bedcovers.

"Why? What is there left to do?"

His lips twisted wryly at her question and then he stepped forward and took her by the shoulders. If possible, Penelope's heart beat even faster. She couldn't make love to him again, she thought frantically. If she did, she'd be lost forever. But, dear God, she wanted him so!

"This," he murmured, then bent his head and found her lips.

Everything inside Penelope wilted as the sweet, familiar taste of his lips infused her mind with erotic images of the night before and tempted her to beg him for more of the same.

Then without warning, he suddenly tore his lips away and set her from him.

Dazed by the unexpected separation, Penelope's fingers lifted to her swollen lips, then she looked at him with wounded confusion. "What was that for?" she whispered hoarsely. "To see if you could make me want you...again?"

The cruel twist of his lips deepened. "No. To see which woman I was taking back to Carrizozo. Judge Parker or the woman who shared her bed with me last night."

"Does it matter?" she asked, her voice quivering.

Ethan had thought so. He'd thought kissing her again would make him feel better. He'd thought it would put her in her place and reassure him that she was no different from any of the women he'd made love to in the past. Yet instead of all that, he was having to fight to keep from tossing her back on the bed and not letting her up until those smooth covers were on the floor and she was in his arms, naked and sweating and sated.

"No," he said gruffly, "I guess it doesn't matter."

He turned and left the bedroom. On shaky legs, Penelope forced herself to follow him.

Three weeks later on the Diamond D Ranch, Ethan stood peering over his sister's shoulder. The chicken pieces Emily was lifting out of the iron skillet were fried to a crisp golden brown and smelled delicious.

"Ethan, I don't know why Cooper has to threaten to put a twitch on your nose to get you out here. You know I'm a good cook."

"I know my visits are few and far between, but I'm a busy man," he countered.

Finished piling the chicken on a platter, the tall, slender blonde turned off the burner, then poked a finger into her brother's ribs.

"Too busy if you ask me. You look scrawny and exhausted."

"Thanks, that's just what I wanted to hear," he said dryly.

"I can't help it if you don't like to hear the truth. You look like you haven't eaten anything in days," Emily scolded as she picked up the platter and stepped around him.

"The last time I checked I still weighed one ninety-five." Actually, Ethan couldn't remember the last time he'd stepped on a scale, and as for eating, it was one of the lowest priorities on his list. He didn't have time to sit down to a leisurely meal. Not with Kirkland still running loose and making even more death threats against Penelope. If it hadn't been for hurting his sister's feelings, he wouldn't be here at the Diamond D tonight. He'd be back at the office trying to piece together any leads that might snag the fugitive.

"Humph! Not even soaking wet," Emily scoffed as she headed toward the dining room.

Once she had disappeared from sight, Ethan walked over to a nearby window. From this part of the kitchen, he could view a collection of barns and working pens situated some fifty yards away. Everything was neat and clean and in top working order. Cooper and Emily were both hard workers and the Diamond D's success was a result of all their efforts. But Ethan could remember a time when the place had been little more than a desolate desert.

Emily's first husband, Kenneth, had slowly turned into an alcoholic and the ranch had steadily decayed along with him. It had been all Ethan and his parents could do to keep from dragging Emily away from him and this place. But one day when he'd been riding out on the range, an outlaw horse had thrown Kenneth. The fall had broken his neck.

Ethan had felt little grief over his brother-in-law's death. The man had dealt his sister too much misery. Then Cooper Dunn, Kenneth's younger brother and Emily's former sweetheart, had come home from the rodeo circuit and he and a pregnant Emily had fallen in love all over again. At first, Ethan hadn't been too keen on his sister's marrying another Dunn. But Coop was nothing like Kenneth. He'd been wonderful for Emily and they had two children to make their family even more complete.

She was well and truly loved now, Ethan thought, as he continued to gaze out the window. As for himself, he seriously doubted his own ranch would ever see a wife or kids. After Trisha had promised her love but left him high and dry, he couldn't imagine any woman devoting herself to him as his sister did Cooper. He wasn't even sure *he* could devote himself to a woman as his father had his mother or as Cooper utterly loved Emily. Bitterness had jaded him, he realized. But he felt safer that way.

Without warning, the image of Penelope drifted into his mind. Thinking of her was something that happened to him on an hourly basis now. And not just because he was concerned for her safety. No, his thoughts of her had grown into a full-blown torment. And no matter how hard he tried, he couldn't keep her or making love to her out of his mind.

Hell, why did he keep referring to the whole thing as making love? he wondered crossly. Penelope had called it sex. Why couldn't he? Because he knew what it was like to just have sex. That's all he'd ever had with a woman. Although he had to admit he hadn't known the difference until Penelope. For some reason he couldn't fathom, she'd turned him inside out. He'd wanted to worship her, give his all to her, commit every moment to memory. And the following morning, he'd even had the terrifying urge to do it over again.

"Mommy! Uncle Ethan's pickup is outside! Where is he?"

Relieved at the interruption of his frustrated musings, Ethan turned his head in the direction of his young nephew's voice. From the clomping sound of little cowboy boots, the boy was making a hasty bolt for the kitchen.

"Whoa, young man," Emily ordered. "Look at your nasty hands. Go clean up. Supper's almost ready."

"But I wanna see Uncle Ethan!" her son said, pouting.

Ethan headed toward the opening leading into the dining room. The moment Harlan spotted him, he shouted and raced to his uncle.

Kneeling, Ethan gathered the six-year-old into his arms. "Well," he told the boy as he planted a playful swat on his backside, "I think your mama's going to have to quit feeding you so much. You're getting way too big for your britches."

Harlan giggled and gazed up at him with adoring eyes. "I am gettin' bigger, ain't I, Uncle Ethan?"

"Don't say ain't Harlan," his mother corrected as she placed silverware around the table.

Ethan tweaked the boy's freckled nose. "Why, I bet you've grown two whole inches in the past month."

The boy's grin stretched from ear to ear, exposing the empty gap where his two front teeth had been. "Daddy got me a bigger pony and he says pretty soon I'm gonna need a bigger saddle, too! And he's teachin' me how to rope! You wanna watch me, Uncle Ethan? I can catch both horns!"

"That's good," he praised the boy. "Every cowboy needs to know how to rope a steer. As soon as we eat, I'll go outside and watch you."

"Oh boy! I better go find my rope right now!" Harlan wriggled out of Ethan's embrace and raced out of the room.

"You can hunt for your rope later, Harlan! Go wash your hands," Emily called after him, then she looked at Ethan with a resigned smile and shook her head. "You're just like Coop. It's probably a good thing you don't come out to the ranch very often. You'd have my children spoiled rotten."

Maybe it was better that he didn't see his niece and nephew all that much. Though he loved them dearly, they always reminded him of just how alone he really was and probably always would be. But Ethan didn't want to think of that now. He was here to enjoy the company of his sister and her family. Not to dwell on his lack of one. "Speaking of children," he asked Emily, "where's my little angel?"

"Melanie is down at the barn with her daddy. She's four years old, but she thinks she's ten. And he lets her try to do anything she thinks she's big enough to do."

"That's good. She'll grow up to be strong and independent."

Emily rolled her eyes, but there was a smile on her face. "She's going to grow up just like me. In a pair of boots and jeans and not know what a dress is until she's thirteen years old."

Ethan walked over to his sister and slung his arm affectionately around her shoulders. "Well, you turned out pretty good, didn't you, Sis?"

Chuckling, Emily patted his flat stomach. "You really are a charmer, Brother. I don't know how you've escaped marriage this long."

Ethan grinned at her. "I've had to work at it."

Frowning, she stepped away from him and headed back to the kitchen. As she went, she called back to him, "I don't know why you can be serious about everything but a woman. If you only knew how much Mother and I would love to see you settle down."

He let out a caustic laugh. "Settle down? Are you crazy, Emily? I barely have time to breathe much less pay any attention to a wife."

"And whose fault is that?" she asked in a raised voice from the other room. "You have a string of deputies to do your bidding. But no, you think you have to personally take care of every problem that crops up."

"I'm the sheriff. That's my job."

She returned to the dining room with a tray full of iced glasses. As she placed them around the table, she cast her brother an accusing look. "Roy was the sheriff for thirty-five years and he had plenty of time for a wife and children."

"Damn it, Sis, I'm not Uncle Roy!" he yelled at her, then let out a disgusted breath. "Sorry, but sometimes I get pretty sick of hearing Roy did this or Roy would've done that. I'm the sheriff now and I wish everybody would remember that."

Undaunted by his outburst, Emily shook her head. "Yeah, you're the sheriff all right. But is the damn job worth it?"

He stared at her with narrowed eyes. "Damn job, eh? Do you think that's all it is to me?"

Seeing she'd offended him, Emily put down the tray she was holding and walked over to her brother. "I'm sorry, Ethan. I didn't mean that the way it sounded. I know how much being the sheriff means to you. But I worry about you, too."

He frowned at her. "Did I come out here for fried chicken or to have my brain picked?"

Emily groaned and went back to tending to the last minute details at the dining table. "I don't need to pick your brain. I know what's inside it. Catching that damn Kirkland!"

Ethan made a hands-up gesture as though to say he was guilty as charged. "He's a crazed, deranged murderer, Emily. I've got to get him locked behind bars again. Before he hurts someone else. Penny trusts her safety to me and my deputies. I just wish to hell she was a little bit more scared for herself."

Emily glanced at him with raised eyebrows. "Penny?

I've never even heard you call her by her first name before.''

''Well, she does have one, you know. She isn't just a judge. She's a woman, too.''

Emily's mouth fell open at her brother's odd outburst. ''I never said she wasn't. What's the matter with you anyway?''

''Nothing,'' he grumbled, then quickly stepped past her. ''I'm going to wash up for supper.''

It was late by the time Ethan drove away from the Diamond D and headed back toward Carrizozo. All evening, he'd desperately wanted to get on the radio and contact Lonnie, but he'd forced himself to visit with Emily and Cooper and the children as though nothing else was on his mind.

Now as he turned west onto Highway 380, the urge to reach for the mike was clawing at him, yet he kept both hands gripped firmly on the steering wheel.

He was letting this whole thing with Penelope get out of hand. She was okay. Lonnie would notify him the second anything out of the ordinary happened. She didn't want Ethan's constant surveillance. Hell, the few brief times he'd seen her since their illicit night at the cabin, she'd barely acknowledged his existence. It was obvious she'd put the whole incident and him out of her mind. And he was going to have to do the same.

The pager hooked to his belt suddenly sounded and all his self-berating was quickly forgotten as he glanced at the number. Swiping the mike off the dash, he tuned the radio to a more private frequency where he knew Lonnie would be waiting for his call.

''I'm east of Hondo, heading back into town. Has something happened?'' he asked the deputy.

"Yes and no."

"What do you mean? Where are you?" he barked the questions impatiently.

"At the judge's house. She's okay. Well, I mean she's not hurt or anything. But she got a phone call a few minutes ago. She's not lettin' on, but I think it's shook her up pretty good."

Ethan's mind began racing. "You mean Kirkland called Penelope's home number?"

"Yeah. About ten minutes ago. She said not to tell you. But…well, you're the boss and she—"

"Penelope's home phone number is unlisted! Where the hell could he have gotten it?" he muttered more to himself than Lonnie.

"I know, sir. She won't tell me what he said. But it must've been pretty bad 'cause after she hung up she looked like a ghost."

Helpless rage roared through Ethan. If he ever got his hands on Kirkland, it would be a struggle not to kill him. But right now, his only concern was getting to Penelope as fast as possible.

"I'll be there in twenty minutes," he told the deputy.

"Sheriff, you're forty miles away! You'd better not—"

"Lonnie, I said I'll be there in twenty minutes! In the meantime, don't let the judge answer the telephone. Or the doorbell! Don't let her do anything until I get there. Savvy?"

"Yes, sir. But she's not going to like it."

"I don't care whether she likes it or not!"

Lonnie let out a dreadful groan. "Well, Sheriff, I guess you can handle her."

No, Ethan couldn't handle her, he thought grimly. But he damn well wanted to. And that was his biggest fear of all.

Chapter Five

Penelope's house was much like the image she projected in the courtroom. Austere and unassuming, but very sturdy. The old pink stucco sitting on the sandy lot at the edge of town was not the type of home a judge might be expected to live in. Ethan knew she made a fairly handsome salary, especially for this area of the state. But she chose to live very modestly.

The fact that she didn't necessarily work for the money only added to her reputation of being "different." Yet when it came to running the courtroom, the people of this county wanted her there. She was formidable and devoted to her job and no one ever doubted or questioned her decisions on the bench. Including Ethan.

But for the past three weeks, he couldn't quit asking himself why she'd made the decision to sleep with him. She couldn't have done it lightly. Penelope didn't do anything lightly. And she'd been a virgin, for heaven's sake.

A woman with her morals didn't just toss her innocence away on a whim!

Ethan pushed the nagging thoughts away as he braked his pickup to a jarring halt behind her little sedan. As he stepped to the ground, he took a quick survey of the place. The yard had little grass to speak of. What there was grew in long, straggly clumps. One tall willow shaded the back of the house. In the front, two large yucca plants flanked the ground-level porch. On this warm May night, nothing was stirring except the fragile leaves on the willow.

As he quietly made his way toward the house, Lonnie came out the front door and onto the porch to meet him.

"Are Powers and Mendoza in place?" he asked in a low voice.

"Yes."

Besides Lonnie's constant vigilance, the other two deputies went on duty each evening to guard Penelope's house from a concealed point somewhere nearby. To avoid being discovered, Ethan ordered the men to change their location nightly. Even he didn't know where the two men were tonight. And as for Penelope, she didn't have a clue there were two more deputies looking after her.

"Any other calls?"

"No. The telephone hasn't rung anymore."

"I don't suppose we were lucky enough to get a caller ID number or any sort of trace?"

Lonnie shook his head. "Kirkland is too smart for that. He must have blocked the number."

Ethan swore under his breath. "One of these days, the man is going to get a little too bold and slip up. When he does, it's going to be all over for him."

Ethan started toward the door. Behind him, Lonnie warned, "I don't think she'll be too happy to see you, Sheriff."

Ethan pulled open the screen door. "I can't help that. This isn't exactly a social call."

He'd never been in Penelope's house. As he stepped into the dimly lit living room, he noticed she'd filled it mostly with old pieces of furniture. Books, candles and plants were scattered throughout the room. A small television sat in an out-of-the-way corner as though it was given little attention. Ethan figured there were only two reasons for Penelope to ever watch television. News or weather.

His boots echoed on the tiled floor, announcing his arrival long before he actually stepped into the kitchen. Penelope looked up from where she sat at a small green Formica table. Other than the blink of an eye, her expression remained unmoved, telling Ethan she wasn't at all surprised to see him.

"I tried to tell Lonnie not to call you," she said without preamble. "But he wouldn't listen."

Ethan walked over to the table and looked down at her. She was clutching a mug with both hands. Her black hair was pulled tightly away from her face and wrapped in a braided chignon at the back of her head. Her cheeks were flour-white, making the dark crescents beneath her eyes even more obvious. She was suffering. No one else might know it, but he did. And the idea tore at him.

"Lonnie answers to me. He might slip up and make a few blunders sometimes, but he never forgets that."

Her lips thinned to a straight line. "Well, everything is fine here. You needn't bother losing sleep."

"I'll be the one to decide if everything is fine here. And from the looks of you, it isn't."

Penelope drew back her shoulders and made sure the button at her throat was still holding the collar of her chenille bathrobe together. Even though she was fully covered with the heavy material, she felt naked beneath Ethan's probing gaze.

"What is that supposed to mean?"

"You look exhausted. Haven't you been sleeping? Or are you too afraid to sleep?"

Her lips parted at his roughly spoken questions. "I— I'm not afraid," she stammered. At least, she hadn't been afraid until half an hour ago. Hearing Kirkland's menacing voice in her ear had very nearly knocked her feet out from under her. When Ethan had walked into the room, everything inside her made her want to run to him and fling herself into his strong arms. Yet she couldn't afford to get that close to him. Hugh had hurt her deeply but she instinctively knew this man had the power to crush her.

"You don't have to pretend with me, Penelope. I don't expect you to be the rock-hard judge every second of your life."

"I'm not afraid," she reiterated.

He cursed openly. "Then you're damn crazy."

Her nostrils flared as she looked up at his set face. "I don't need this from you. Not tonight."

Sighing, Ethan pulled out the chair angled to her right and took a seat. Since their night together at the cabin, he hadn't been this close to her. Just seeing her like this, without her daunting black robes or the sober surroundings of the courtroom, brought back the memory of how she'd been with him even more vividly.

"Neither do I," he said gruffly. "Neither do my men. What did Kirkland say to you?"

Her gaze slanted up to his face and her heart squeezed as she took in the rugged beauty of his chiseled features. "He said nothing that might have given his whereabouts away. There was no background noise. No coins dropping into a pay phone. As to the context of his conversation, he went into great detail describing several ways he wanted to kill me. The only good news is he hasn't decided which one he's going to use yet.''

There was a faint quiver at the corner of her lips and Ethan wanted to drag her onto his lap and hold her tightly to him. But he knew Lonnie could walk in at any moment. And besides, she didn't want that sort of reassurance from him. She didn't want anything from him except the same sort of protection he would give any citizen of the county. But the whole idea left him feeling hollow.

"I'm sorry, Penelope. You shouldn't be going through this," he whispered hoarsely.

"You're no super hero, Ethan. You're just the sheriff."

Just the sheriff. And in her eyes he wasn't even good at that. The rational part of his brain knew any experienced lawman, even Roy, couldn't have done any more than what he had done so far to catch the fugitive. Yet he couldn't help feeling he was falling far short of his duty and, most of all, Penelope's expectations.

"You should leave this place, Penelope. At least until Kirkland is caught."

"That could take months."

He grimaced as her words reinforced what he'd just been thinking. "You really have a lot of confidence in me," he said ruefully.

She shook her head. "I didn't mean it that way. I'm only trying to be realistic. I can't leave my job. I have several important cases coming up. I wouldn't dare allow some other judge to sit in on them."

"You're not the only judge in the state. I know—"

"I know it would make things a whole lot easier for you and your department if I was no longer your responsibility," she interrupted. "But I'm no coward. I won't run."

She quickly scraped back her chair and rose to her feet. Ethan watched her carry the mug over to the kitchen sink and dump the dregs down the drain. Then before he realized what he was doing, he was standing behind her and his hands were gripping her shoulders.

"Then why are you running from me?"

His huskily spoken question caused her eyes to close and she drew in a deep, shaky breath. "What do you mean?"

Her question came out in a shaky whisper and Ethan knew she was bothered by his nearness. "You know what I mean. You make me feel like I've got leprosy."

"That's not my intention."

His gaze slipped over the shiny crown of her hair, the smooth, slender curve of her neck. No matter where his lips had touched her body, her skin had felt like satin. And everything inside him longed to taste her again. "No. You're just trying to keep a wall between us."

Slowly, she twisted around and her eyes were shadowed with torment as she lifted her face to his. "It's not a wall. I only want to make sure we…keep our relationship strictly business."

As his eyes focused on her moist lips, he tried to tell himself she wasn't his woman. He had no right or reason to want her. Still, he did want her. And he didn't know what the hell to do about it.

"Is that what you really want?"

She drew in a deep breath as her gaze fell on the middle of his broad chest. "Of course. And you do, too."

"How the hell can you speak for me? You haven't bothered to ask me what I want."

Pink heat seeped into her cheeks. "I didn't have to ask."

"Why?"

She looked back up at him, then groaned as she met his searching green eyes. "Oh, Ethan, I can see you're not in the market for marriage. Or even a serious relationship. Especially with someone like me. I don't have to ask or be told that."

"What do you mean, someone like you?"

She made a mocking sound in her throat. "Don't be patronizing. You've already said yourself that I'm a strange woman."

"I didn't mean strange in a negative way."

She frowned, then sighed. "It doesn't matter, Ethan. Really. I know I'm not glamorous."

Trisha had been a glamour girl, and for a while Ethan had been blinded by her flashy beauty. Penelope was right, she wasn't the sort of seductress that Trisha had been. But there was a graceful charm about her, a loveliness that drew him to her.

He reached out and touched the tightly woven hair at the back of her head. "Why do you have your hair up? You're not in the courtroom now."

Everything inside her began to quiver. "Lonnie is here in the house. I don't want him to see me with my hair down."

Ethan's brows shot up. "Why?"

"I don't want anyone seeing me with my hair down."

His fingers began to slip the pins from the heavy braid. "You let me see you," he reminded her.

She'd let him see and do far too much, Penelope thought wildly. Now she couldn't get him or that night out of her mind. He'd torn her world apart and she could have told him he was far more dangerous to her peace of mind than Kirkland ever thought about being.

"Please don't," she said in a choked voice as her hair tumbled onto her shoulders like black satin.

In spite of her plea, he threaded his fingers through the glossy strands and tugged her closer. "You're right, Penelope. I'm not in the market for a wife. Hell, I'm already married to the sheriff's department. I don't have much of me to give to any woman. And I figure you and me shouldn't be consorting in any form or fashion. But…" He broke off as he brushed the back of his knuckles against her soft cheek. "I can't forget what it feels like to kiss you, touch you—make love to you."

Her sharply indrawn breath made a hissing noise as his hand covered the small mound of one breast. At the same time, Ethan's lips twisted with self-contempt.

"I came over tonight to talk to you about Kirkland and to reassure myself that you were okay. But now all I want to do is send Lonnie back to the station and stay here with you myself. All night."

"Ethan, you're crazy," she whispered in protest. "Don't—"

Anything else she might have said lodged in her throat as his head suddenly dipped down to hers. She hadn't expected to ever kiss him again and emotions sweet and wild coursed through her as he drew her into the tight circle of his arms and hungrily tasted her lips.

Once he finally lifted his head, he murmured, "If you try to tell me you don't want this, I'll know you're lying. Because your body is telling me you do."

Penelope slowly became aware that her arms had crept around his waist and she was standing on her tiptoes to reach his mouth. "Does it make any difference if I do?" she asked huffily. "This is just sex. And judges do not have affairs with sheriffs!"

With that, she tried to twist out of his arms, but he firmly grasped her by the shoulders. "That's because they're usually men!"

Aghast, she stared at him. "And just because I'm a woman, that makes it okay?"

"That's not what I meant!" He growled with frustration, then shook his head. "And I'm not asking you to have an affair with me!"

Her brows arched mockingly. "Then what are you doing? Trying to make my life miserable?"

Maybe he was, Ethan thought. Maybe he'd agonized over her so much for the past three weeks that he unconsciously wanted to put her through the same torment. "I don't know what the hell I'm doing," he muttered angrily. "If it hadn't been for Kirkland, I wouldn't be here!"

She inwardly flinched as his words lanced a hole right through her chest. There hadn't been any need for his blunt reminder. Just as she'd told him earlier. She knew she wasn't glamorous or desirable. She wasn't the sort of woman he would want to marry or live with the rest of his life. And the idea that he simply wanted to use her to ease a physical ache not only crushed her, it also infuriated her.

"Then why don't you go catch the maniac and leave me alone!"

"That's exactly what I've been trying to do. On both counts!"

"Well, so far you've failed!"

She jerked away from him and hurried out of the kitchen. In the hallway, she nearly crashed into Lonnie, but she kept on going in spite of his effort to stop her.

"What's the matter with the judge?" Lonnie asked Ethan as he entered the kitchen. "Is she afraid Kirkland will get to her before we do?"

Ethan lifted the felt hat from his head and ran a hand through his damp hair. He was hot and tired and more frustrated than he'd ever been in his entire life.

"No. She's got something else on her mind that's bothering her now."

Lonnie cast him a puzzled look. "Oh? What could be worse than a man threatening to kill her?"

A man trying to make love to her, he thought dourly. "I, uh, think I've already done all I can do here. If you don't need me, I'm going to head on down to the office and grab some shut-eye on the cot."

He turned to leave the room, and as he did, he gave the deputy an encouraging slap on the shoulder. "You're doing a good job and I appreciate that."

Lonnie beamed at the praise. "Thanks, sir. And I promise I won't let anything happen to Judge Parker."

"I'm counting on that," he told the other man, but a few moments later when he climbed into his pickup, he had to force himself to turn the key and drive away from the faded pink stucco.

"Penny, as I told you last month, the best thing you could do to put a halt to this disease would be to get pregnant."

From the other side of the desk, Penelope stared at the doctor as if he needed psychiatric attention. "Get pregnant! Doctor, I'm a single woman. And on top of that I hold an elected office. I'm hardly in a position to get pregnant."

His patient, understanding smile made Penelope want to scream with frustration.

"I realize your position in this community," he assured her. "I was speaking strictly from a medical standpoint. In most cases, pregnancy puts an end to endometriosis."

"I'm sorry, but that election of treatment will have to be passed over," she said stiffly.

He sighed. "Tell me, would you like to have a child?

Or am I worrying about your impending sterility unnecessarily? After all, you do have an important job. You might not want the distraction of a baby."

Just hearing the doctor mention the word "sterility" made her sick inside. In a quiet, strained voice, she replied, "I would like a child very much, Doctor. But it appears there's no chance of that happening."

The fatherly man rose from his seat and came around the desk. As he patted Penelope's shoulder, she looked gravely up at him.

"I take it there's no young man in your life?"

She shook her head.

"Well, that might change in the near future. And when it does you'll want to be able to have a child together. As for now, I'm going to have the nurse take you down to the lab for a few tests. When I have the results, we'll discuss how best to treat this problem of yours."

"Doctor, before you call the nurse, can you tell me if this disease I have could make me feel sleepy and tired all the time? I have to push myself to get out of bed every morning and by midafternoon I can hardly hold my head up."

He folded his arms against his chest as he regarded her thoughtfully. "Is this something that's been going on with you for a long time or has it just now started?"

Penelope tried to think back to the point when her exhaustion had actually started. "Sometime during the past month. I'm not exactly sure when."

He studied her thoughtfully. "Well, those sort of symptoms can be a result of many things. You might be a little anemic. I noticed on your chart that you've lost weight since your last visit."

That day she'd learned of her endometriosis seemed like months ago rather than seven weeks ago. "I've had a lot on my mind," she told him. Like losing her virginity to the county's sheriff, being childless for the rest of her life, and then there were Kirkland's threats to murder her. With Lonnie still dogging her every step, she could hardly forget that.

"Worrying is the last thing you should be doing."

He opened the office door and summoned his nurse. When the woman appeared, the doctor handed her a form and promised Penelope he'd see her again in a couple of hours.

Nearly two hours later, evening was approaching and she was still waiting and trying to concentrate on a legal motion she'd brought with her to the clinic.

"Excuse me, Judge Parker, but I'm beginning to think those people back there have forgotten you. Are you sure the doctor is going to see you again today? I think this place is going to be closing soon."

"I'm very sure he's going to see me, Lonnie." She tried to refocus her attention.

"Do you want me to find the nurse? Something must be wrong for them to leave you waiting out here for so long," he went on.

"No. I do not want you to ask anyone anything," she assured him firmly. "If you want to go outside and stretch your legs, then by all means go."

"Can't do that, ma'am. We're in a public place. Sheriff Hamilton would have my hide for leaving you."

Sheriff Hamilton. Dear God, why did he have to mention the man's name? Why couldn't she get him out of her mind? Four long weeks had passed since the night he'd come to her house. In that time, she'd seen him only on the brief occasions when he'd had to appear in court.

The few words they exchanged had been curt and strictly business.

Exactly the way she'd told him she wanted it to be between the two of them, she thought sadly. Yet she continued to relive every moment of his visit over and over in her mind. She could still feel his fingers slipping the pins from her hair and see the glint of pleasure in his eyes as he'd watched it fall to her shoulders. And the way he'd kissed her. Dear heaven, the intensity of it still had the power to send shivers down her spine. But she would eventually forget, she promised herself. She had to. She couldn't keep living on raw nerves and memories.

"Ms. Parker, the doctor is ready to see you."

Relieved more at the interruption of her thoughts than the idea she would finally be able to leave the clinic, she put the folder away in her briefcase and followed the nurse back to the doctor's office.

As she took a seat once again in the large leather chair, she couldn't help thinking the cluttered desk in front of her was beginning to look all too familiar.

"I realize you've had a long wait," he began, "but I'm glad you could stay for the results rather than come back at a later date this week. Especially with the surprising news I have to give you."

He wore such a look of optimism on his face that some of the dread lifted from her shoulders. "News? Do you have a treatment option you think might work?"

Suddenly, he grinned at her broadly. Penelope could only stare at him in bewilderment. She had a disease that was slowly going to ruin her reproductive organs and the man was smiling.

"There's no need for me to order any sort of treatment, Penny. You've already taken care of that yourself. But frankly, I wish you'd warned me earlier that there was a chance you might be pregnant. It would have saved you a lot of time and the expense of unnecessary tests. Actually, I didn't even order a pregnancy test. I thought there wasn't any need for it. But my nurse noticed it wasn't on the list and she thought I'd simply forgotten it. I'm grateful she's so observant and instructed the lab technician to run one anyway."

Penelope continued to stare at him blankly. "I beg your pardon? I don't think I quite understand what you're saying."

He smiled at her again. "In the simplest way I can put it, Penny Parker, you're going to have a baby. From my initial calculations, probably around Christmastime."

During Penelope's term as district judge, she'd seen and heard many shocking things, but none of them came close to this. For a moment, she was so paralyzed by what the doctor had just said she could hardly breathe.

Gripping the arms of the chair, she leaned forward. "But I—I can't be pregnant! I thought... You told me you weren't even sure I could conceive! And it was only that one time..." Her face reddened with embarrassment.

"It only takes one time. And obviously, your fallopian tubes are not yet blocked. The result is a pregnancy. That's why you've been feeling so tired and sleepy. It also explains your weight loss. Have you been experiencing any nausea?"

"I haven't had much of an appetite," she admitted.

While the doctor reached for his prescription pad, Penelope's mind began to whirl. She was pregnant! She was going to have Ethan's baby! It was simply too incredible to believe.

Across town, Ethan poured the foam cup full of strong coffee, then abruptly decided to stir in a spoonful of sugar.

Normally, he didn't like sweetened coffee, but in the past hour the stuff had turned as thick as a campfire brew and he wasn't in the mood to make a fresh pot.

Actually, Ethan wished he could go home to the ranch and use what little daylight was left to saddle Buckeye and see if he could catch sight of his cattle. Thankfully, the summer rains had been steady and most of the ranges were green with grass. He knew the cattle had plenty to eat, but he didn't like too much time to pass without inspecting them close up. Cattle were susceptible to many diseases and the way his luck had been running lately, the whole herd might have pinkeye or hoof rot.

With Kirkland still at large, Lonnie was bound to be feeling the strain of being Penelope's bodyguard. Originally, Ethan had never intended to keep him at the job for this long.

With a weary sigh, he walked over to the open door of his office. "Betsy," he called to the dispatcher, "is Tate Jones anywhere close?"

"I think he's on his way into town. You want to see him?"

"Tell him I'll be waiting in my office."

Ten minutes later, Ethan was staring out the window of his cluttered office, sipping the last of the bitter coffee when a light knock sounded on the door.

"Come in," Ethan called, then glanced over his shoulder to make sure it was Jones. "Shut the door behind you, Tate."

The tall, young man quickly did as he was asked, then walked to the middle of the room. "You wanted to see me, sir?"

Ethan tossed the coffee cup into a trash basket and took a seat at his desk. "Sit down," he instructed, motioning toward the chair in front of his desk. "I want to discuss something with you."

Tate Jones had been on the force for three years, and so far he'd been a dependable deputy for Roy and Ethan. He was the only man, other than Lonnie and himself, whom he'd want watching closely over Penelope.

"Is something wrong, Sheriff? I—"

Ethan waved a hand at him. "No. Quit worrying—"

"I know I was late serving those warrants, but—"

"You don't have to explain. I realize we're stretched thin around here. And you got the job done. That's all that matters."

The young deputy visibly relaxed, and for a brief moment Ethan wondered if his men were beginning to regard him as a tyrant. If they were, he could hardly blame them. He was well aware he'd been rough on the whole department, demanding time and energy beyond their normal duties. Yet he never asked them to do more than what he asked of himself.

"What I wanted to discuss with you," Ethan went on, "is Judge Parker."

Jones looked at him with anticipation. "Oh. Has something new come up on the Kirkland case?"

Ethan grimaced. "Not since yesterday's briefing. As for Judge Parker, you know Lonnie has been guarding her since day one."

"Yeah. I imagine he's getting cabin fever being cooped up in the courthouse and her home day after day. I heard he had to sit for hours with her down at the health clinic today. He was probably needing a doctor himself by the time they left there."

Ethan's brows puckered as he glanced at the deputy. He hadn't been aware that Penelope was at the clinic today. But since the night he'd gone to her house, Ethan had made every effort not to keep up with her every move. It was hard enough to get her off his mind without having Lonnie giving him a detailed agenda of her daily activities. Yet the idea that she'd had to see a doctor unnerved him. He could only hope this whole thing hadn't made her ill with stress.

"Then you can understand he needs a break?"

The deputy's mouth fell open. "Me! You want me to guard the judge?"

Ethan leveled a stern look at him. "Yes. Do you have a problem with that? If you do, spit it out now."

"Well, because I know how much importance you've placed on the judge's safety, I wouldn't think you'd want to make changes in midstream."

Ethan nodded. "You're right. I don't want to make changes. But this damn thing has gone on too long. I don't have any other choice."

"We're going to catch him, sir. Any day now."

Ethan appreciated the deputy's confidence. "I realize all you men are weary of this whole thing. But I also know you won't let up until Kirkland is caught."

Jones nodded. Then after assuring Ethan once again that he'd be ready for the assignment, he left the office.

Once he was gone, Ethan glanced at his watch. It was already growing dark. By the time he reached the ranch, it would be too late to do anything except take a shower and fall into bed. He might as well go over and talk to Lonnie tonight.

And Penelope. She wouldn't want to see him. But what he had to say to her would only take a few minutes. And anyway, he wanted to find out for himself why she'd spent hours of her busy day at the health clinic. If the worry and fear of Kirkland's threats were making her ill, then he might just be able to talk her into leaving Lincoln County. At least until it was safe for her to return.

Chapter Six

Twenty minutes later, Ethan sat behind the wheel of the squad car and tried to hide his impatience while Lonnie continued to argue. He'd thought the young deputy would be thrilled to finally be getting out from under Penelope's long, trying schedule. Instead, he was pleading with Ethan to leave him on the job.

"Judge Parker isn't going to like it."

Ethan scowled at the deputy. "Seems to me you're always saying Judge Parker isn't going to like something or other. I don't know what in hell difference you think that's going to make in my decision. If it was left up to Judge Parker, she'd send you home and tote that revolver of hers under her robes."

"Well, she's not like other women, Sheriff. She's different."

Ethan was still trying to forget just how different she'd been that night in the cabin. And not because she'd been a virgin. Though, heaven only knew how few of them were left around. But Penelope had made *him* feel different and he still couldn't figure out why.

Ethan sighed as he tried to push the thoughts away. "I remember a time not long ago when you said Judge Parker wasn't a woman at all."

A sheepish expression stole over Lonnie's face. "I know. But that was before I got to know her a little bit."

A quirk of a smile moved Ethan's lips. "Oh. So the two of you are chummy now?"

"No. She still keeps pretty much to herself. But I…well, I guess I've been able to see more of what she has to do on the job. I don't think people understand how hard she works. I didn't. Until now."

Ethan supposed he'd always known her workload was heavy, yet he'd never bothered to think how it might affect her or her personal life. Up until a couple of months ago, he'd always thought of her as being more robot than human. She ruled the courtroom with an iron hand and in her chambers she was steady, cool and emotionless. It was still difficult for Ethan to connect that Judge Parker to the warm, passionate Penelope who'd made love to him.

"Jones informed me you were down at the health clinic nearly all day. Is Penelope ill?"

Lonnie shrugged his shoulders. "I don't know. And I sure as heck wasn't about to ask her what was wrong."

"Well, her health isn't our business, Lonnie. Only her safety." He reached for the door handle and slid out to the ground. "I'm going in to tell her about Jones. So I don't want any more arguing out of you. You'll make the change with him tomorrow."

"Watch out, she was in an odd sort of mood. I'd handle her carefully if I was you."

Ethan didn't need to handle Penelope in any way. But

he knew the moment he saw her, he'd want to get his hands all over her. It was disgusting and he was beginning to get very annoyed with himself because he couldn't get this little woman with the big job out of his system.

He left the deputy on the porch, then searched through the house until he found a room at the back with the door closed and a dim streak of light beneath it.

He knocked, then waited.

"I don't want anything else to eat, Lonnie. So quit trying."

Ethan's brows lifted and his lips twisted. Apparently, his decision to take Lonnie off this assignment had been the right one. The boy was becoming too attached to Penelope. But then, wasn't he?

"This isn't Lonnie. It's Ethan."

A few seconds later, he could hear a rustle of papers, then the door opened and she was standing before him.

"Hello, Penelope."

Her lips parted as though she was surprised to see him and her gray eyes searched his face. "Ethan," she finally replied.

"If you're not too busy, I'd like to talk to you a moment."

A flicker of hesitancy crossed her face, but then she stepped out of his path and said, "Come in. I was just—"

"Working after hours," he finished for her.

"Aren't you?"

How odd that he'd never thought of his tireless hours as work. It was simply his life. And suddenly, his sister's words drifted through his mind. *Roy was the sheriff for thirty-five years and he had plenty of time for a wife and children.*

"It's a necessity these days," he told her.

Along one wall was a deep leather couch scattered with

throw pillows. Penelope gestured for him to take a seat, then stood tensely in the middle of the room while he made himself comfortable.

After Ethan had crossed his boots at the ankles and laid his Stetson on the floor by his feet, he looked at her questioningly. "Aren't you going to sit down?"

"I've been sitting all day."

"Yes. I know. At the clinic. I hope you're not ill."

A hysterical laugh bubbled up in her throat, but she somehow managed to choke it down. What would this tough man with a badge pinned to his chest think once she told him he was going to become a father?

"No. Not really."

Actually, Ethan thought she looked off her feed. There was absolutely no color to her face. Even her lips were pale. She was dressed in a pair of slacks and matching blouse of pale blue silk. The soft material fluttered against her body, and as his gaze traveled over the jut of her breast and the indentation of her waist, he was certain she'd become even thinner since he'd last seen her.

"I can't imagine sitting for hours in a doctor's office just for the heck of it."

She turned and walked over to the high arched windows that looked out over the barren backyard. Across the way, she could see the old woman's house. Her name was Josephina, but Penelope knew most everybody simply called her the old woman. She was the only person Penelope socialized with. Although you could hardly call talking over a cup of coffee or glass of tea socializing.

Since Kirkland had jumped parole, however, Penelope had only talked to the old woman on two brief occasions. Right now she wished she was over there in Josephina's warm kitchen rather than in this small room with Ethan's eagle eyes measuring every inch of her body. He was a lawman through and through and he missed no detail.

"Doctors are like us law people," she told him. "They're overworked."

"You don't look like you've been eating at all. Are you worried about your safety? If—"

Her heart pounding nervously, she said hastily, "Ethan, I'm not worried. I'm not ill."

He grimaced. "You wouldn't tell me if you were."

She turned around to face him. "Is this why you came by tonight? To question me about my health?"

She sounded both vexed and amazed. "Partly," he admitted.

Her gray eyes narrowed with speculation. "What's the other part?"

"To tell you Lonnie won't be guarding you after tonight."

Penelope was totally taken aback by his announcement. Quickly, she walked over to the couch and took a seat at the opposite end from him. "Why?" she asked. "You've caught Kirkland?"

"It's not that. To be frank, I think Lonnie's becoming too attached to you."

Her brows arched with disbelief and then, to Ethan's surprise, she chuckled. "You really get some odd notions, Ethan. There isn't a man in this county, or beyond, who would get attached to me."

Ethan didn't reply immediately. Instead, he allowed his gaze to slip over her pale face, shadowed eyes and sleek black hair coiled at the back of her neck. At first glance, she appeared nondescript. But Ethan hadn't forgotten the image of the woman he'd seen that night at the cabin. Now, when he looked at Penelope, he wanted more than

ever to see the vibrant, glowing face he knew was underneath the somber mask she presented to the world.

"You deliberately want to make yourself plain and un-
attractive, don't you?"

She glowered at him, then ran her palms nervously
down her thighs and over her knees. "Where...what has
that got to do with anything?"

"It just hit me now more than ever that you've been
living in disguise."

A laugh of harsh disbelief escaped her lips, then she
rose from the couch and walked back to the window. "I
realize you're the sheriff and have to be able to see
through people. But you're not seeing me clearly. This is
who I am," she said as she gestured at herself.

"No," he said, then easing to his feet, he walked over
to her. "Maybe you have everyone else fooled, Penny.
But not me. I know there's another woman inside Judge
Parker. I saw her that night at the cabin. I made love to
her. She was attractive and desirable. Why do you want
to hide her?"

"Why do you keep bringing that up, Ethan?"

The raw huskiness of her voice told him she was remembering, too, and all of a sudden he felt everything
inside him being drawn to her.

"I honestly don't know," he answered roughly. "I'm
sure I'd be a lot better off if I could forget you and that
night."

Forget that night! It was going to be impossible to forget now, Penelope thought wildly. A baby was already
growing inside her. His baby! Dear God, how was she
ever going to tell him? She could already see the shock
on his face. But it was his anger she couldn't deal with
tonight. And he would be angry. There was no doubt in

her mind that he wasn't going to be pleased about any part of it.

"You're a good-looking, sexy man, Ethan. I'm sure you've had your share of one-night stands before and you forgot those, didn't you?"

He frowned. "I haven't hopped in and out of bed with a string of women, Penelope."

The idea that she had only been a one-night stand was crushing something inside her, but she couldn't let herself think otherwise. To do so would only be asking for more heartache. Calling on every ounce of strength she possessed, she turned to him and looked up into his strong, handsome face. "But the ones you have, you've forgotten. The only reason it's taking longer with me is because I'm an oddity."

In the blink of an eye, his fingers were clamped around her shoulder and his hard gaze was boring down on her shocked face. "What is it with you, Penelope? You have every confidence in yourself as a judge. But as a woman, you want to put yourself down. Why do you want me to see you as a quaint old maid?"

She tried to shrug away from his grasp, but her efforts didn't budge the grip of his fingers. "I'm at home in the courtroom, Ethan. I'm comfortable there. I know what I'm doing there. With men, I…well, they don't fit in with my life."

"Because you don't want them to."

She groaned. "You told me not so long ago that you were married to the sheriff's department. You don't have room in your life for anything else. That's what you said, wasn't it?"

When the only answer he gave her was a frown, she went on, "Well, that's the way it is with me, Ethan. Being a judge doesn't leave room in my life for anything else, either.''

But now she was going to be a mother. *A mother!* She wanted to laugh and cry. She wanted to shout to the world that Penny Parker wasn't going to be alone in the world for the rest of her life. A child was going to love and need her.

"And is that the way you want it?"

His question caught her completely off guard. So much so that it took a while before she was finally able to answer. "What I want and can have are two different things, Ethan. Besides," she added as she turned and slowly moved away from him, "none of this really matters to you. For the life of me, I don't understand why you've brought any of this up."

"Yeah, I agree it's pretty stupid of me. I damn well don't know why it should bother me if you're ill or lonely or scared. You like to flaunt the fact that you're independent and don't need help from anybody. Or even companionship. Why the hell would I want to offer mine?"

As he turned to go, she could see his face was rigid with anger, and all at once Penelope couldn't bear to see him walk away thinking all those things about her.

"You're wrong, Ethan. I have needed help before. And there've been plenty of times I've been lonely. Desperately lonely. But I learned a long time ago that men and sincerity do not go together."

He stopped in his tracks but didn't turn to face her. "And you think I'm not sincere?" he asked with a measure of disgust.

She groaned as though his question was absurd. "I think that maybe you'd like to be sincere with me. But you just don't have it in you. And I think what you really want is…"

When she didn't go on, Ethan turned and was instantly shocked motionless as he watched Penelope tearing the pins from her hair. "What are you doing?" he finally managed to ask.

With a strange sort of smile on her face, she shook her hair free, then slowly and deliberately leaned over and switched off the lamp on the desk. The room went dark except for the faint glimmer of light coming from the windows. It was enough for Ethan to see her unbuttoning her blouse and moving toward him.

"Penelope, what…"

Like a vamp from an old movie, she put her hands on his arms and snuggled her body up against his. "You don't seem to know what you want, Ethan. So I think it's time I made it clear. You want to have sex with me again so you can get the urge out of your system."

Slowly, his hand came up to push the tumbled hair from her forehead, and as he stroked his fingers through the silken mass, he wondered how such an angel could speak so crudely. And yet the hell of it all was that she was half-right. He did want to make love to her. He did want to get her out of his system. And since staying away from her hadn't seemed to work, maybe being with her would.

"Is that so bad?" he asked gently.

Her soft lips twisted. "No one likes being used, Ethan."

"Did I make you feel used that night in the cabin?" he whispered.

She groaned, then her fingers tightened on his arms as the pleasurable memories of that night washed over her. "No," she admitted. "But this time, it—"

"This time, it would be even better," he promised, his voice thickening with desire.

She was already carrying his child in her womb. It

seemed so right and natural to make love with him again. As far as her body was concerned, it had chosen its mate. But what would it do to her heart once he had his fill of her?

"Ethan, you're not thinking—"

"You're right, I'm not. Not when you're near me like this." He pushed the fronts of her loosened blouse apart and cupped his hands around her breasts. "And you shouldn't be, either," he added. "It's all right not to think sometimes, Penelope. To just let yourself feel this and nothing else."

Without any more words, her hands flattened against his chest, then she stood on tiptoe and offered her mouth to his.

He took it with a vengeance, and as his fingers gripped her and his lips consumed hers, she realized she was lost to this formidable man. She and their baby were at his mercy.

Ethan was certain he'd never wanted any woman so frantically. The need to have Penelope was consuming him, turning his insides to rampant flames. His arms tightened to pull her even closer, and then without warning, he felt her body go limp and her lips slacken beneath his.

"Penelope?"

Her head rolled lifelessly to one side at the same time her body became dead weight in his arms. Quickly, he swept her up, carried her over to the long couch and laid her gently down.

The blue silk fell away to expose her lacy bra. He pulled her blouse back together and placed his hand on her brow. It felt warm but not feverish. My God, what had he done to her? What had happened? She was out cold! His fingers were searching for a pulse at the base of her throat when she began to moan softly.

"Penelope? Do you hear me?"

His face was hovering just above hers. She tried to focus on the vision swimming before her eyes. After a moment she began to make out the chiseled outline of Ethan's mouth and nose, the lock of hair falling over his forehead as he bent over her.

"Did—did I faint or something?"

She tried to rise, but he pushed her shoulders back against the couch. "Don't move," he ordered. "I'll be right back."

Wasting no time, Ethan found a bathroom at the end of the hallway. He dampened a washcloth with cold water, then hurried back to her.

By the time he'd sponged her face, she was well and truly awake. "This is…terribly embarrassing," she said weakly. "Please let me up."

"You're not going anywhere until I call your doctor," he informed her. "Give me his name and number."

Icy fear clutched Penelope's stomach. "No! There's— there's no need for that. I only fainted. I'm fine now."

He scowled at her. "People don't go around fainting without reason. And though I'd like to think it was my kiss that made you swoon, I seriously doubt I affected you *that* much."

He couldn't possibly know just how much he'd affected her. In more ways than one, she thought ruefully.

"The doctor said I'm a little anemic," she hastily fibbed. "He gave me a prescription for an iron supplement. I'll be fine once I get a few of them in my system."

Ethan's eyes narrowed to slits as he made an even closer inspection of her face. He could certainly believe she was anemic. She didn't look like she had a drop of blood in her. But he also got the feeling she wasn't telling him everything. "Are you sure that's all? Was something else wrong with you?"

He sounded so truly concerned, Penelope had to look away from him when she answered, "That's all. Now please let me up."

He gave her enough room to sit up but remained close enough to grab her in case she swooned again.

"I didn't mean to upset you. Or—or scare you," he said as he watched her smooth her hair back over her shoulders.

She glanced up at him and her heart squeezed with pain. Maybe it was a good thing she'd fainted, she thought sadly. Making love to Ethan now would only make it worse when she finally had to tell him about the baby.

"You didn't. Honestly."

To her surprise, he squatted on his boot heels and began to button her blouse back together. Her heart beat fast and strong as she allowed her gaze to glide over the lines and angles of his striking face. He was like no man she'd ever known. Both tough and tender. Strong but bending. Even before she'd found out about the baby, she'd felt connected to him. Now that connection was even stronger.

"I guess I should apologize to you," he said.

The buttons were finally fastened on her blouse, yet his hands lingered against the soft silk and the warmth of her breast.

"No. I was behaving shamelessly."

"I provoked you."

Her tongue crept out to moisten her lips. "I believe we provoked each other."

The urge to gather her back into his arms was so strong he had to force himself to rise and step away from her.

"That's an understatement," he muttered. He jammed his hands into the pockets of his jeans and walked over to the windows. With the light still off in the small room, he could easily see the backyard and the neighboring house some forty feet away. "That's where the old woman lives."

"You know Josephina?"

"I know everybody." He glanced at her. "It's my job."

And his job always came first, she thought. Just like hers. What would things be like, she wondered, if he wasn't the sheriff of this county or she the judge? If they were just two ordinary people, he might actually be glad about the baby. As it was, she didn't have any idea what her pregnancy would mean to his career or hers. They were both elected officials, both carefully watched by the public. For them to have a child out of wedlock together was going to be scandalous.

But the woman inside Penelope didn't care what the public thought. For one night, Ethan had loved her and she was going to have a child. No one was going to take that blessed gift away from her.

He walked back over to her then. "Are you feeling better? Do you want me to get you something to drink? Ice water? Coffee?"

She shook her head. "No. I'll help myself in a little while."

"Would you like me to help you to your bedroom? Your legs might still be a little shaky."

It suddenly struck her that this man might actually care about her. Not in a romantic sense, but simply as a person he'd come to know, and somehow that made the pain in her heart even worse.

"I don't..." She shook her head as she realized how foolish it was to try to avoid him at every little turn. Sooner or later, she'd have to confront him head-on with the news of the baby. She might as well start getting used to him. "Yes. Maybe it would be better if I had your arm to lean on. I'm still feeling a little giddy."

He fetched his Stetson from where he'd left it on the floor. After he'd clapped it back on his head, he reached down and helped her to her feet. She swayed momentarily and his hard arm quickly came around her back.

"I could carry you," he suggested.

"No. Let me walk. It will help me get my feet back under me," she told him.

They left the study and walked slowly down the darkened hallway until she stopped at another closed door not far from the bathroom.

"This is it," she said.

He opened the door, then paused on the threshold with her. "Will you be all right?"

Penelope wasn't sure if anything would ever be all right in her life again. But for herself, and most of all for her baby, she had to hope and continue on.

"Yes."

"Do you want Lonnie to check on you later?"

"No." She glanced up at him in the darkness. He was very close and the warmth of his body was both comforting and exciting. Tonight she needed him more than ever. But it was tomorrow she had to think about.

"I'd better go," he said finally.

She nodded, but her hand remained on his arm. "Ethan, the body found over near Fort Stanton, do you think…was it a homicide?"

He let out a long breath. "The man was found facedown in a cattle pen. Apparently trampled to death. The coroner's report isn't back yet. But my feeling is that he was knocked on the head, then thrown in with the cattle."

She tried not to shiver. "My memory isn't short. The

victim turned state's evidence against Kirkland for a suspended sentence.''

Ethan nodded while thinking how odd it was that he wanted to shield her from such evil. Yet, in the end, she was the sole person who had to make final judgment on such murderers. He couldn't shield her from anything.

"They were stealing cattle together, remember? Those two and the first man Kirkland murdered.''

"I remember.'' Her gaze clung to his face, and without realizing it, she tightened her grip on his arm. "The first man. You say that as if you know he killed this one, too.

"Oh, Ethan,'' she breathed, then buried her face against his chest. "I'm frightened.''

Surprise and wonder filled him as he gazed down at her head pressing against the middle of his chest. He'd never expected to hear her admit any sort of fear, much less reach out to him.

"It's all right, Penelope,'' he whispered. "I won't let anything happen to you.''

The promise rang hollow in his ears. For weeks now, the man had been playing cat and mouse with him, while everyone watched and wondered why the sheriff and his men couldn't get the job done. That bothered the hell out of Ethan. Especially when he knew the majority of the public expected him to fall far short of their beloved retired sheriff, Roy Pardee. Yet none of that mattered nearly as much as failing in Penelope's eyes.

Penelope wasn't just afraid for herself, she was also afraid for Ethan. But she couldn't bring herself to voice the words to him. Not for anything did she want him to think she was starting to cling to him out of fear or need.

Clearing her throat, she moved back from the warm comfort of his chest. "I know I'm protected. And

I'm...really not falling apart. It just seems that way tonight.''

Tonight, she was more like the woman he'd made love to and he was finding it damn hard to resist her.

"You have every right to be frightened, Penelope. And every right to rail at me for not catching Kirkland before this.''

She gently shook her head. "I don't want to rail at you, Ethan. You've hardly been lying down on the job. And covering Lincoln County isn't like taking a walk in a city park. It's rough and rugged terrain—with a thousand isolated places a man might hide."

Ethan grimaced. "I don't think he's been hiding in the rough. At least, not all the time. He somehow manages to get to a phone. That's when we should have already caught the bastard.''

The angry resolution in his voice frightened her almost as much as Kirkland's running loose. From her experience in the law, she knew how much this whole thing was eating at Ethan. And she feared his anger and frustration might eventually make him reckless.

"What's going to happen, Ethan? If the coroner rules the death a homicide?''

His face like a piece of granite, he answered, "It's going to be all-out war."

Another shiver of dread ran down her spine. Once Kirkland was located, Ethan had several deputies he could send after the fugitive. But she knew he wouldn't. He would go after the man himself. Or die trying.

"This is going to sound trite, Ethan, but please be careful."

Ethan couldn't remember the last time a woman, other than his mother, had urged him to keep himself safe. There had been an occasional shouting match where a woman had cursed at him and called him a few choice names for not quitting a job that put his life on the line for a small amount of pay. Trisha had even called him stupid and selfish. Maybe he was. But at this moment, Penelope's simple encouragement was a balm to his soul.

"I will." He pressed the back of her hand to his lips, then turned and headed down the darkened hallway.

Penelope sagged against the doorjamb while her heart silently cried. *Please keep yourself safe, Ethan. Our baby needs you. And so do I.*

Chapter Seven

Tate Jones was not Lonnie. The young deputy was so polite and indiscreet that Penelope rarely noticed he was around. And though the past week of relative quiet should have been a relief, she realized she was actually missing Lonnie's brash forwardness.

Dear God, pregnancy must be doing something to her, she thought as she glanced up from the civil case she was reading. A thousand things were on her mind. She didn't need to be constantly interrupted by a chatty deputy.

"Jones, have you heard from Eth—the sheriff this afternoon?" she asked.

The tall deputy rose from a chair and walked across the judge's chambers to Penelope's spotless desk. "Yes, ma'am," he answered.

"Is he still gathering evidence on the Fort Stanton homicide?"

"Uh...yes."

She knew the deputy was reluctant to talk about department business. And she didn't blame the man. Ethan would more than likely fire anyone who talked when he shouldn't. But she was desperate to know what Ethan was doing and she couldn't bring herself to call his office. Even though it was perfectly proper and not unusual for the judge to need to speak to the sheriff, she didn't want to raise any eyebrows. Especially Ethan's.

Jones turned to go, then paused and looked back at her. "Judge Parker, if you need to talk to the sheriff, I'm sure the dispatcher could reach him for you on the two-way."

She quickly shook her head. What could she possibly say to him? she wondered wryly. Don't get yourself killed, Ethan. You're going to be a daddy! All the privately owned police scanners in the area would explode with the news.

"No. It's quite all right, Jones. I'll speak with Sheriff Hamilton later. Right now, I'm sure he has his hands full."

"He sure does, ma'am," he told her, then surprised her with a brief smile. "I'm really glad you understand he's doing all he can. A lot of folks around here are—"

"Yes?" she urged.

"Well, I think they like to compare him with Sheriff Pardee. And that's not right."

Her expression grim, she said, "No. It isn't right. Sheriff Hamilton has been in office for only a year. Roy Pardee held the job for thirty-five. And who's to say he would've caught Kirkland already? But I'll tell you, Jones, when you're an elected official, you're a target for all sorts of gossip and criticism."

He nodded in total agreement. "Judge Parker, I can truly say I would never want to be in Sheriff Hamilton's boots today. Or any time. The walking would be too damn rough for me.''

And now she had one more burden to throw on Ethan's shoulders, Penelope thought. She just couldn't do it. Not until this mess with Kirkland was over. She didn't want him to be distracted with thoughts of her or the baby. And in the end, she didn't really see what difference it would make if she told him a few days or a few weeks from now. She fully expected to raise the child alone as a single parent. If Ethan wanted to acknowledge his role as father, she would be very glad. But she would never demand or expect anything more from him.

Ethan lifted the Stetson from his head and swiped at the sweat trickling down his forehead. The sun had set more than an hour ago, but the heat lingered, baking the rocks and brush and every other living thing that happened to be in the deep arroyo. The air was still. Not even the delicate white blossoms on the yucca plants were stirring.

The six deputies gathered around Ethan all spoke in hushed tones. But every now and then, one of the bloodhounds tied in a nearby shade would bark, the sound echoing through the small canyon like a cannon shot.

''Sheriff, if you wait till morning, we could get a chopper in here to help us,'' one of the deputies spoke up. ''If he runs, we could track him by air.''

For the past week, events had taken place at a blurring rate of speed. The minute the coroner's report hit his desk, Ethan had hardly slept or ate. He and his deputies had worked night and day to gather every shred of evidence they could find. And now, thanks to a rancher's report, it looked as though they were finally homing in on Kirkland.

Ethan had no intention of waiting until morning or even one more hour to go after the killer.

"No. I don't want a damn chopper around here alerting the bastard. Besides, there's too much timber on the mountains in this area for a chopper to be much help. If he runs, the dogs will catch him. But I don't anticipate that happening. If he's in the line shack the rancher told us about, he'll more than likely try to shoot it out."

The deputies all looked at each other, then at Ethan. "None of us has ever been in a shoot-out, Sheriff," one of the men said. "I can't imagine this guy would actually try to kill us. He ought to know he'd be much better off if he gave up and turned himself in."

"Get the dogs and your rifles," Ethan ordered the group of lawmen. "You already know the plan and we've got a long hike ahead of us."

By the time Penelope left the courthouse that evening, the news about the manhunt was buzzing everywhere.

The sheriff and a posse of deputies were combing the mountains. The killer was holed up in a sheepherder's shack with an arsenal of weapons. But by damn, the sheriff was a sharpshooter. One good aim and he'd take the SOB down.

The snippets of talk had left Penelope shaking with fear. As soon as Tate Jones drove her home, she switched on the television, but to her disappointment all she could find was regular programming.

Rising from the couch, she switched off the television. "I'm going over to Josephina's," she told him. "If you hear anything, please let me know."

He nodded. "I'll be in the backyard."

Penelope left the house and walked across the parched earth to the old woman's back door. Josephina quickly answered her knock and smiled broadly when she saw the visitor was Penelope.

"*Chica*, come in!" The large Mexican woman stepped out of the way and motioned for Penelope to enter the kitchen.

"I hope I'm not bothering you, Josephina. Were you having supper?"

The old woman laughed and pointed at a small round table sitting in one corner of the room. On it, a plate of steaming-hot enchiladas was waiting to be eaten. "You're just in time."

"I'm not hungry, really. You go ahead and eat and I'll talk."

"No. No. There's too many enchiladas. Even for a fat woman like me. You can help me eat them."

Penelope hadn't been able to keep much food down earlier and she wasn't sure she could eat anything now. But the baby needed nourishment and the food smelled heavenly.

Penelope took a seat at the table. "All right," she conceded. "I'll eat a little."

Beaming, Josephina went to the cabinet and took down another plate and glass, then fetched silverware from a drawer. After she'd filled the glass with sweetened iced tea, she placed everything in front of Penelope.

"You haven't come to see me in a long time."

Penelope sighed. "Yes, I know. A lot has been happening."

"I see the deputy staying at your house. Where is he now?"

"He's watching in the backyard."

The old woman frowned as she took her place across from Penelope. "You must be very tired of that. Having a man follow you around." She took a bite of cheese enchilada, then grinned. "Unless he's the right man."

The right man was out in the mountains tracking down a killer. The very thought made her ill.

"Josephina, you know I'm not in the market for a man."

The old woman clucked with disapproval. "Such a waste for a beautiful woman like you."

"We can't all be like you, Josephina. You were married to a good man for sixty years and you have lots of children and grandchildren who adore you."

"And so will you, *chica*. Just wait and see what Josephina tells you."

Penelope sighed. At least she was going to have a baby. As for the good man, he was already married to his sheriff's badge. He didn't want any woman in his life on a permanent basis. Much less a drab woman who knew nothing about pleasing a man.

"Well, right now, a man wants to kill me," Penelope said.

The old woman made a scoffing noise and waved her hand through the air. "The sheriff will keep you safe. He'll get the man. Maybe tonight. And soon it will all be over."

Penelope looked at her neighbor's wrinkled brown face. "So you've heard the news?"

Josephina nodded. "My daughter has a police scanner. She hears everything that goes on."

Just then, a gray tabby cat wandered into the room. He meowed loudly up to the old woman and she placed a bite of enchilada on the floor for him.

"There was nothing about it on television," Penelope said, then tried her best to concentrate on eating. But all she could think about was Ethan facing a madman with a deadly weapon.

Eventually, Josephina must have noticed her lack of appetite. She motioned to Penelope's plate and shook her head. "You worry too much, *chica.* Eat."

Penelope put down her fork and pressed her fingertips against her furrowed brow. "I can't help it, Josephina. I feel very responsible for all this. And if something happened to Ethan—I mean, Sheriff Hamilton—or his deputies, I would never forgive myself."

Josephina was quiet for a moment, then she said, "You like the sheriff."

Penelope dropped her hand and glanced over at the other woman. "What do you mean, like him?"

Josephina's brown face crinkled with a sly smile. "You *like* him."

If everything didn't seem so tragic, Penelope would have laughed. She liked Ethan so much she was having his baby. But she could hardly tell her neighbor that. Ethan had to be the first to know. But now he was somewhere out there with bloodhounds and rifles, and God forbid, bullets flying by him. Maybe she'd been wrong in keeping the news to herself these past few days. Maybe he would never know he was going to have a child.

"Yes. I like him," Penelope said in a half whisper.

Josephina nodded with approval as though she could read every line of worry on Penelope's pale face and knew they were all for the handsome sheriff. "Ethan Hamilton is a good man. You could not do better."

Penelope frowned at her. "Josephina, the man doesn't belong to me."

The old woman simply smiled at her.

"I don't want him to belong to me," she said, her voice

rising with each word. "Men are demanding and heartless. They only bring a woman trouble and pain."

"Not all of them."

Penelope was an educated woman. She'd already seen more in the courtroom than most people ever saw in a lifetime. She realized all men were not like Hugh. Still, she couldn't forget how she'd trusted him. She'd planned to devote her whole life to him, but in the end he hadn't loved her at all. He'd loved only himself. He'd cared only about his own wants and needs. She'd been so crushed she could never imagine putting that sort of trust in another man.

"Like I said, Josephina, not all of us women are as fortunate as you have been."

The old woman solemnly shook her head, then dropped the tabby another bite of food. "The sheriff is a good man," she repeated. "And his mama, Rose, is a fine woman. She was a Murdock. She's got money, but she don't act like it. None of them do. You know her?"

Penelope shook her head as she realized she'd never formally met any of Ethan's family. What would they think about this child she was carrying? she wondered. Would they accept him or her as a part of the family? Or see her child as an illegitimate embarrassment? Either way, she couldn't think about that now. The whole situation was too much for her worried mind.

Eventually, she finished the food on her plate, and after several more minutes of small talk, she said goodbye to Josephina and left.

Tate Jones was at the back of the house waiting for her. As he escorted her across the sandy yard, he said, "I think they might've gotten Kirkland. The radio transmission was breaking up and the dispatcher could only catch bits and pieces of the message."

Her heart beating wildly, she looked at the deputy. "Was anyone hurt? Are they bringing him in now?"

The deputy shrugged. "I don't know. The posse was several miles up in the mountains. It might be a while before they get back to town."

Penelope hurried into the house and switched on the television. This time, a news crew had gathered somewhere on Highway 70 between Hondo and San Patricio. There was no sign of Ethan or any of his deputies. The reporter was saying the information they had so far received was very sketchy and could not yet be confirmed. But it was believed that Kirkland had been captured. Shots had been fired. However, it wasn't yet known if there were any injuries.

An icy lump of fear settled in her stomach and she turned a desperate glance on Tate Jones, who'd been standing a few steps away, watching the telecast with her. "Would you please see what you can find out down at the station? I know it's probably chaos there, but try anyway."

He nodded and left the room. Penelope sank onto the edge of the couch and tried to still her racing heart. Though she tried to assure herself that Ethan was trained and experienced, all she could think about was the horror and loss she'd felt when her parents were killed. She couldn't bear to go through such an ordeal with Ethan. And as the black thought swirled through her mind, it dawned on her just how much she'd come to care for the man. He was in her heart, and if something happened to him, a part of her would die along with him.

Hours ticked by before Penelope finally caught a glimpse of Ethan on the newscast. He appeared to be transferring the captured convict from a four-wheel-drive vehicle to a waiting patrol car.

The moment the reporter spotted the sheriff, he broke off in midsentence and hurried over to attempt to get a comment. The camera and lighting crew followed and for a few seconds Penelope caught a clear view of Ethan as he pushed the handcuffed Kirkland into the back seat of the car.

"Sheriff! Sheriff Hamilton!" The reporter shoved his microphone in Ethan's direction. "Can you tell us a little bit about the hunt? Did Kirkland give you any resistance?"

Ethan spared the man a weary look. "He didn't exactly turn himself in. That's all I can say. You can get the rest tomorrow."

The reporter, who by now had been joined by newscasters from two other stations, continued to throw questions at Ethan, but he ignored them as he skirted the vehicle and climbed into the driver's seat.

"Well, it looks as though Sheriff Hamilton is going to personally haul the prisoner back to jail," the reporter began saying to the television audience. "I'll see if I can stop one of these deputies long enough to get some details of what happened up there in the mountains."

Penelope didn't wait to hear more; she aimed the remote at the television and switched off the power. She didn't want the details. She'd seen enough.

Ethan's face had been haggard. His khaki shirt and blue jeans were covered with dirt and sweat and a stain on his sleeve looked suspiciously like blood. But he was safe. Right now, that's all that mattered.

When Penelope woke the next morning, the sun was high in the sky. She bolted straight up in bed, aghast that she was going to be late for court. Then she remembered it was Saturday. There would be no trial or work today.

And last night, Ethan had captured Kirkland. Thank God that nightmare was over. Before she'd gone to bed, Tate Jones had been given the word he could go on home and Penelope finally had her house to herself again.

Her spirits lifted at the thought and she quickly swung her legs over the side of the bed. Yet before her feet hit the floor, nausea washed over her in sickening waves.

Carefully, she eased back down on the bed and reached for the crackers she'd left there from past episodes of morning sickness. As she slowly nibbled on the saltine, the nausea began to fade and hunger took its place.

She ate another cracker, then eased her feet onto the floor. This time, she felt she could safely remain upright, and after a visit to the bathroom, she pulled on a robe and pattered down to the kitchen to make a pot of coffee.

Because of the baby, Penelope only kept decaffeinated in the cabinet now. From the moment the doctor told her she was pregnant, she'd tried to be conscious of everything she ate or drank. More than anything, she wanted this baby to arrive healthy.

As she stood waiting for the coffee to drip, the palm of her hand settled protectively against the lower part of her stomach. How long would it be before her waist thickened? she wondered.

Since she normally wore her judge's robe at work, it would be easy enough to conceal her pregnancy for a while. But by the midtrimester, her growing figure would become obvious even beneath the folds of her black robe. She didn't know what she was going to tell people if they dared to ask her. Other than her secretary, Julie, and of course, Josephina, she honestly didn't believe anyone would question her about her condition. They would do all the talking behind her back.

With a small sigh, she poured herself a cup of the coffee, then laced it heavily with half-and-half cream. While she sipped, she walked over to the back door and opened it to the fresh morning breeze. It was going to be a beautiful New Mexico day and she should be dancing a happy jig around the kitchen. Kirkland was safely behind bars and when he returned to prison this time, there would be no chance of parole. Penelope would make sure of that. And then there was the baby. She was finally going to have the child she'd always wanted. The threat of endometriosis taking away her chance to be a mother was over.

Yet in spite of all those good things, she couldn't dance around the kitchen with a big grin on her face. The time had come to face Ethan. There were no more reasons to put off telling him about the baby.

After a light breakfast, she dressed in a thin cotton dress, and in a daring last minute decision, left her hair down. She'd never stepped out of the house that way before, and as she walked to the car, she felt rather foolish and naked. But with a faint measure of humor, she realized seeing her hair loose on her shoulders wasn't going to be nearly as shocking to the people of the community as seeing her stomach grow to massive proportions with Ethan's child.

Penelope had never been to Ethan's ranch, but she knew where it was located. She drove east of town for several miles, then turned off the main highway, where a wide cattle guard was marked with an etched metal sign that read Bar H Bar Ranch.

She drove slowly through the open range. Blue sage, creosote bush and grama grass covered the mesa floor. Then farther into the ranch, hills gradually began to rise. On their slopes, piñon pine and twisted juniper grew between great slabs of rock. Here and there, a yucca stood in bloom and once in a while a cholla cactus graced the edge of the road with its bright pink and yellow blooms.

Penelope tried to relax as she took in the beauty of the land. Yet every few minutes she would have to remind herself to ease the death grip she held on the steering wheel. Driving out here to see Ethan was not an easy thing to do.

The house was an old, square-shaped ranch house with a wide porch bordering three sides. The weathered structure was nestled in a grove of cottonwoods and willows and overlooked a deep arroyo.

As Penelope pulled to a stop beside Ethan's four-wheel-drive vehicle, she couldn't help thinking how the place had a rugged charm that somehow matched its owner.

A blue heeler stock dog was lying on the porch by the door. The moment Penelope stepped out of the car, the animal was on its feet standing sentinel beside the steps. She had no idea whether this particular breed of dog was a biter, but with Ethan nowhere in sight, she had no choice but to chance making it to the door.

Thankfully, the dog turned out to be female and friendly. Penelope gave her several affectionate pats before she climbed the steps and crossed the porch. The house was open, but she could see no sign of Ethan through the screen door.

She rapped her knuckles against the doorjamb several times, then waited. When there was no response, she called Ethan's name, and the dog, who'd planted herself at Penelope's heels, began to whine with anticipation.

"I don't think your master is around here, lady," she said to the dog. "Maybe he's at the barn?"

Penelope walked around to the right side of the house and peered across the hundred or so yards to a collection of barns and cattle pens. There were several horses milling inside the dusty pens, but Ethan wasn't in sight.

Returning to the front of the house, she found the dog was whining even more loudly and scratching at the screen door.

"Are you trying to tell me Ethan is in the house?" she asked the dog.

The heeler gave a happy yip, then whirled around in a circle. How dandy, Penelope thought dryly. Now she was having conversations with a dog. Ethan was changing her in more ways than one.

With a cautious tug, she found the screen door was unlocked, so she stepped quietly inside. "Ethan?"

The living room had a high ceiling and a cool linoleum floor. The furnishings were sparse and basic and the room was cluttered with dirty dishes and all sorts of papers and magazines. Across a breezeway, she found the kitchen. More dirty dishes were on the round wooden table and stacked on the counters. Obviously, Ethan didn't have a cleaning lady to take care of his messes.

She left the kitchen and crossed the breezeway again. This time, she walked to the opposite end, then stopped in her tracks when she came to the last open door.

Ethan was in bed and, from the looks of him, still sound asleep. His long, lean body was sprawled facedown on the queen-size mattress. A white sheet was the only thing covering him and it had slipped dangerously low on his hips. As her gaze took in his tousled rusty hair and bare torso, heat burned her cheeks. She'd never seen a naked man in broad daylight—and Ethan was quite a specimen.

"Ethan."

His name came out as a hoarse whisper, so she cleared her throat and stepped into the room.

"Ethan?"

Her voice reached him this time. He bolted awake instantly and snatched the sheet to his waist. "Penelope! What in hell are you doing out here?"

Her first instinct was to run from the room and never look back. But it wouldn't be fair to the baby. Nor to Ethan, or so she kept telling herself.

"I...there's...I wanted to talk to you," she said, summoning up her best courtroom voice.

He sat up on the side of the bed, swiped a hand over his face and through his hair, then squinted at her. "What time is it?"

His voice was still husky with sleep and the sound was somehow as erotic as the sight of his bare chest. She took a deep breath and glanced at her wristwatch. "Eleven-fourteen," she announced.

He groaned. "I had no idea it was so late. I must have died when I fell into bed this morning."

"What time was that?"

"Somewhere around five."

"I'm sorry I woke you," she said, and meant it. Ethan hadn't just put in a hard night. He'd pushed himself for many weeks running. "I know you must be exhausted. But I was already here and your door was open."

His narrowed eyes studied her face and then she felt his gaze slipping over her loose hair and down the length of her gauzy dress.

"It was cool this morning when I got home. I didn't need the air conditioner," he explained.

"You aren't afraid someone might walk in on you?" she asked.

"Like you?"

The pink color already burning on her cheeks turned a shade darker. "I know Kirkland is behind bars. But you probably have other enemies."

His lips twisted wryly. "I usually sleep with one ear open. And Goldie always barks," he said, then quickly frowned. "By the way, how did you get by her and into the house?"

"You mean the dog?"

"A blue heeler. Wasn't she out there?"

"Yes. But she was very sweet. She told me you were in here."

His brows shot up. "Sweet! Hell's bells, Goldie tries to tear anybody's leg off who comes into the yard!"

It was too late for Penelope to be frightened. Anyway, she couldn't imagine the dog was anything but a lovable puppy. "I don't think you know your dog," she told him.

At the moment, Ethan didn't know much of anything except that he felt like he'd ridden a horse for twenty hours, then slept four on the hard ground.

"If you're here to ask me about Kirkland, I've got him in my jail right now. Since he was captured in Lincoln County, the paperwork to get him back to prison will have to go through your court."

"I know. And believe me, no matter what happens in this next murder trial, he'll never have another chance at parole."

Ethan should have known he couldn't tell Penelope anything about the legal necessities of the case. She was a judge who knew her law. And as Trisha had told him long ago, he was just the peon who enforced them.

"That will ease both our minds," he said.

"I'm very glad that it's all over for you. I know this business was wearing you down. The people—"

"To hell with the people," he barked. "*You* were the one being threatened. Now you won't have to put up with a deputy following your every move. Or having me show up on your doorstep."

So he hadn't planned on seeing her again, she thought. At least, not outside the courtroom. The idea shouldn't hurt or disappoint her. She'd known all along that once the ordeal with Kirkland was over, Ethan would put her out of his mind. And yet she felt wounded that he now considered everything between them severed and done with.

"It wasn't that bad," she said, though she had to push the words through her tight throat. "I was getting used to it."

She didn't say more and once again he began to study her shrewdly. "So," he said after a tense silence, "you want to tell me something else, or was that it?"

She opened her mouth to speak at the same time as he bent forward to pick up a pair of dusty jeans lying on the floor at his feet. It was then Penelope saw the deep gash on his upper arm. Dried blood was crusted around the outer edges and smeared nearly to his elbow. Along with the caked blood, the skin around the wound was purple and red.

"Ethan, your arm. You've been hurt!" She rushed over to him and leaned forward for a closer look. "Were you shot?"

He rose just as her hand came down on his shoulder. The soft touch of her fingers against his skin pushed all thought from his mind. She was so close he could feel her warmth, smell her, and if he wanted to, touch her. And he wanted to like hell.

"No. I wasn't shot," he said with a tight grimace. "Kirkland and I had a little scuffle inside the line shack. I raked my arm on something. I didn't have time to look with the barrel of a shotgun about to be pointed in my face."

She swallowed as the image he was painting formed in

her head. "You're telling me you had to physically take him down?" she asked in disbelief. "Where were your deputies?"

"In the positions I told them to hold."

Her head swung back and forth. "You mean you ordered them to stay behind and out of danger."

His green eyes cut up to hers. "Don't try to make me out a hero, Penelope. I'm far from it."

She frowned at him. "I don't know whether you've very brave or very foolish."

"Try very mad."

She looked away from him and tried to focus on his wounded arm. "This needs to be cleaned and dressed. If you'll get out of bed, I'll do it for you."

"Is that why you came to see me? To nurse my wounds? I don't know whether to be surprised or flattered."

His voice was right at her ear and she knew as soon as she turned her head that her face would be a breath away from his.

"I didn't know you were injured," she said, her voice beginning to shake as her heart throbbed at a runaway speed. "I came out here for another reason."

Suddenly, his hands were in her hair, his fingers threading tightly through the silken strands. She turned toward him, and the next thing she knew, her back was pressed against the mattress and Ethan's face was hovering just above hers. "Was it this?"

He didn't give her time to answer. His hungry mouth covered hers and for the next few moments all she could do was cling to him and wonder what it would be like to have him kissing her out of love.

"Ethan," she breathed once he finally lifted his head, "I didn't come out here to…go to bed with you."

The grin on his face was purely sexual and taunted her just to try to resist him. "Yeah. But somehow you wound up in my bed anyway."

His face began to dip back to hers, and she planted her hands against his warm, naked chest in an effort to halt his downward descent. "Ethan, I'm trying to tell you something."

His gaze savored her face as his hand fumbled with the buttons between her breast. "I know. You've decided you want to make love to me and get me out of your system. Well, I'm here for the taking."

She squeezed her eyes shut as tears began to sting her throat. "I can't get you out of my system now, Ethan. I'm going to have your baby."

Chapter Eight

Shock froze Ethan's features and his hand stilled against the buttons on her dress.

"My baby!"

She nodded as her heart threatened to beat right out of her chest. "That's what I came over to tell you."

"My baby!" he repeated as though the words were too foreign for him to comprehend.

"I know it's a shock to you," she said quietly. "It was for me."

He moved away from her and reached for his jeans once again. "Shock, hell! I can't believe it." She jumped up from the bed and scurried past him. Behind her, Ethan jerked the jeans up over his naked hips. "Where are you going?" he called as he noticed she was headed out the door.

"To the kitchen. I think you need some coffee."

"Coffee," he muttered to himself. It sounded like he needed a damn sight more than coffee.

In the bathroom, he splashed cold water on his face and head, then raked his hair back with his fingers. As for shoes or a shirt, he didn't take time for either. He headed toward the kitchen with long, purposeful strides.

He found Penelope at the sink, dropping dirty dishes into soapy water. The coffee was nearly finished dripping and the strong aroma reminded his empty stomach it had been long hours since he'd eaten anything.

She turned to look at him. "Would you like for me to cook you breakfast?"

"No," he lied. "I want to know…"

Taking a deep breath, he muttered a curse and Penelope waited while he took down a cup from the cabinet and filled it with coffee. After he'd taken two careful sips, he sidled up to her at the sink.

"Penelope, are you certain you're pregnant? You told me…that night, you said you were protected."

Her face was so hot with color she hardly dared glance at him, but she forced herself to meet his steely gaze. "I thought I was. I mean, I wasn't using birth control. But I thought there was no need."

His narrowed eyes snapped wide open. "No need! You were about to make love to a man and you thought there was no need?"

"I realize how foolish that sounds, but there were other circumstances that…" She was unable to go on and stepped away from him.

He followed and grabbed her by the arm. "What circumstances? What are you talking about?"

Her lips tightened. "Does it matter, Ethan? What's done is done. The how it happened is rather insignificant now, don't you think?"

His fingers tightened on her arm. "I don't like to think you lied to me, Penelope."

Anger shot through her and she jerked her arm free of his grasp. "I didn't lie. That day...the doctor told me I was more than likely sterile! Does that sound like I needed to be worried about birth control?"

His features crumpled into a confused frown. "Sterile? Why?"

She let out a heavy breath as she tried to compose herself. "Because I had endometriosis."

"That doesn't explain anything to me. I don't know anything about a woman's health problems."

She made a helpless gesture with her hands. "Normally, a woman passes the uterine lining every month, but with endometriosis it stays inside her body and attaches itself to the outside of her reproductive organs. After a while, it destroys them and the woman is unable to conceive. I didn't know I had it until the day I went to the cabin."

Ethan's mind began to whirl as he thought back to the night he'd found her there. After what had transpired between them, he'd almost forgotten that she'd been crying and upset about something.

"That's why you were upset that night? That's why you fled to the cabin in the first place?"

Penelope nodded. "The doctor told me if I didn't conceive within a year, it was likely I would never have a child. He wasn't even certain I could conceive now. But somehow by a miracle from God, I did."

An odd look of dawning spread over his face. "Am I hearing you right? The doctor said if you didn't get pregnant within a year, you could never have children?"

"That was his initial diagnosis."

His dark features turned to rock as his gaze raked an

accusing path over her pale face. "So in other words, you needed stud services and I just happen to be handy." Before she could make any sort of reply, he turned his back to her and lifted his gaze to the ceiling. "I thought I'd learned my lesson about you women. But I guess I'm just a big sucker. Obviously, none of you are above using a man to get what you want."

Furious now, Penelope marched around in front of him. "I didn't use you for stud services! There is such a thing as artificial insemination!"

"Sure," he sneered. "But you were thinking why not do it the pleasurable way. The good ole sheriff is handy and available."

Penelope gasped. "I didn't invite you to my cabin that night! Or into my bed!"

"Oh, no? Well, I didn't see you pushing me away, either!"

With a sickening jolt, Penelope realized she was wasting her time. It didn't matter what Ethan was accusing her of. He wasn't a happy man. He was furious at being implicated in any sort of way. As far as this baby was concerned, she was truly on her own.

"No. I guess I wasn't pushing you away," she said quietly. "Maybe I should have. But unlike you, I'm not sorry I'm going to have this baby."

She was almost out the door before Ethan was aware she'd moved at all. "Where are you going?" he asked incredulously.

Where did he think she was going? Penelope wondered. The only places she ever went were home or the courthouse and sometimes to her cabin. And God help her, she couldn't face that place now.

"Home," she said wearily.

"So you're just going to drop this bombshell on me, then leave?"

Lifting her chin, she turned back around to face him. "Look, Ethan, I just wanted you to know I'm carrying your child. I thought you had a right to know. That's all. If you're worried that I want or expect anything out of you, I don't."

He quickly closed the space between them and Penelope winced as he snagged some of her hair between his thumb and forefinger. "It sure as hell looks like you didn't want anything from me. I'm not a total idiot, Penelope. You came here with your hair down and that see-through dress on for some reason. Maybe you thought you could trick me into marrying you."

His earlier anger had hurt her, but this was too much for her fragile heart. One man had already denigrated her and nearly smashed her self-esteem in the process. She couldn't let Ethan stomp on what was left of her. "I wouldn't marry you if you were the last living man on this planet," she said icily.

The sight of his mouth falling open was the last thing Penelope saw as she hurried out of the kitchen. As she rushed down the steps, she was vaguely aware of the blue heeler tagging along at her ankles, but she didn't stop to pat the dog. She wanted to get off the Bar H Bar as quickly as she could and forget she ever knew the man who owned it.

The dirt road leading away from the house was as dry as powder. Dust boiled behind her little car, but even if the brown cloud hadn't been there, she wouldn't have noticed Ethan speeding up behind her. When she walked out of the kitchen, she'd been determined not to look back.

The sound of the horn caused her to jump and clutch

the steering wheel even more tightly. Then before she could glance in the rearview mirror, Ethan's four-wheel-drive vehicle came storming past on her left. It shot in front of her, then stopped in the middle of the road, blocking her path.

Penelope jammed on her brakes and waited for him to come to her. As he stalked to her car, she could see his temper hadn't cooled. His jaw was locked and his eyes were shooting daggers straight at her.

Penelope started to roll down the window, but he jerked open the door before she could finish.

"What are you doing?" she cried as he climbed in beside her.

"You're not leaving this ranch until we get this matter settled!"

Her breast heaved with anger as she fought the urge to slap him. "This matter! Can't you even say the word 'baby'?"

"All right. Baby. What are we going to do about it?"

Her delicate brows arched in disbelief. "Do? *We* aren't going to do anything. You needn't involve yourself."

"So you're just going to have the baby all by yourself? You're going to raise it alone?"

She nodded. "Exactly. Thousands of women do it every day. No one ever has to know you're the father. I doubt anyone will even dare to ask me. And I'm sure they would never guess it's you."

It was becoming clear to Ethan that she truly meant to dismiss him from the whole thing. It didn't matter that he was the father. And that made him even more furious than the idea of being used.

"And do you honestly think I'd want a son or daughter of mine to grow up that way? Not knowing who his father was?"

"Ethan, you don't want a son or daughter. Period. So don't try to make me believe otherwise now. It would ring pretty damn false."

He'd never heard her use anything close to a curse word and he was taken aback. "You're going to have to marry me, you know."

If Ethan thought she was going to fall at his feet weeping with relief, he was crazy, Penelope thought angrily. "I don't *have* to do anything, Ethan Hamilton. No man is ever going to make demands on me. Not ever! Now get out of my car!"

Ethan opened his mouth to tell her he wasn't getting out of anything until he had his say. But as his gaze searched her face, he could see she'd closed herself off to him.

Slowly, he climbed from the car and closed the door behind him. "We'll talk about this later, Penelope. After you've had time to cool off."

She glanced at him, then with a harsh laugh she pulled away from him and around his vehicle. This time as she picked up speed, she carefully watched her mirror to make sure he wasn't following. But she needn't have worried. It was obvious Ethan was finished with her. And she with him.

When she reached her house back in town, her anger had drained away and in its place a cold resolve had settled over her. Inside her bedroom, she stood in front of the bureau mirror and stared at her image as if she were seeing it for the first time. And she couldn't believe her eyes.

She'd been stupid, stupid, stupid! She'd let her hair down and worn the only feminine fluttery dress she owned because she'd had the notion that she was different now.

She was pregnant. A man had made love to her. She *wanted* to be different.

Fighting back the acid tears burning her eyes, she quickly coiled her hair tightly at the back of her neck and pinned it securely. Then she stripped off the dress and crammed it into a drawer she used for dusting rags. Ethan would never have reason to think she was trying to beguile him. From this day on, he would see her as Judge Parker and nothing else.

He was going to be a daddy! Three days had passed since Penelope had given him the news. But the passage of time had still not adjusted him to the idea. Every few minutes, he was struck with an episode of disbelief alternating with the silly urge to grin.

What in hell was he going to do? he asked himself for the hundredth time. Penelope was still furious with him. He'd called her office several times and each time her secretary had put him off. In the evenings, he'd tried her home, but she never answered. No doubt as soon as she spotted his name on the caller ID, she walked away.

Ethan pulled Buckeye to a halt a few steps from the shallow stream and dismounted. He and the horse had been traveling a good two hours this morning, and though the summer sun wasn't sizzling yet, it was already hot.

He led the gelding over to a shady part of the stream and gave him enough rein so he could drop his head and drink. Once the horse got his fill Ethan lay on his stomach and drank thirstily.

Back on his feet, he asked the horse, "Buckeye, you ready to go home?" The animal turned his head and nudged his nose affectionately against Ethan's shoulder. "I know," Ethan said as he patted Buckeye's neck. "You like it out here. Well, so do I, boy. It's quiet and peaceful and pretty. But we have to go back sometime.''

Ethan had ridden away from the ranch this morning at sunrise with the excuse of checking the cattle. He'd found the whole herd not far from the ranch, all of them fat and sound. He could have turned back then. Instead, he'd kept on riding across the mesa and up into the far hills on the edge of his property. He'd hoped the quiet would allow him to think and decide what to do about Penelope and the coming child. But so far, he'd found no easy answers. He only knew he would not allow his child to be born out of wedlock. His parents had raised him with strong moral values. Whether he wanted to be a husband or not, it was his duty, his obligation, to be there for the child.

Penelope believed he didn't want a son or daughter. But that really wasn't true. Deep down, he'd always hoped one day he would have children by a woman who truly loved him, and he her.

It hadn't happened that way. But he would live with it. He had to.

He rode back to the ranch at a quicker pace. After a shower and a short talk with his hired hand, he drove into town and entered his office through the back of the building.

''Thank God you're here, Sheriff,'' Lonnie exclaimed the moment he saw Ethan. ''Those reporters are back out front having a fit. They want to talk to you about Kirkland's return to prison.''

For the past week, Ethan had been badgered by newspeople and he'd had his fill of them. He understood the fugitive's flight and capture was of interest to people in southern New Mexico, but it was over. He had other arrests to think about now.

"Lonnie, I'm appointing you spokesman for the Lincoln County Sheriff's Department."

The young deputy gaped at him. "Really? I didn't know there was such a position."

"There is now." Ethan went over to the coffeepot. Someone had seen fit to make a fresh pot before he arrived, so he poured himself a cup. "And I want you to go out there and tell those reporters only what they need to know."

Lonnie straightened his shoulders and tugged at the brim of his straw hat. "Okay, Sheriff. What do they need to know?"

Ethan sat down at his desk. "Tell them Kirkland will be going in front of Judge Parker next week. And after she gets through with him, you expect he'll never see the light of day."

The deputy's eyes bugged out. "You want me to tell them that! Don't you think that's a little bit, well, rough?"

Ethan swallowed a sip of the coffee. "Hell, yes, tell them that! We're not running a nursery school here. This is a rough business. Besides, they're going to dramatize whatever you say anyway."

Lonnie rubbed his hand across his stomach as though he'd suddenly developed indigestion. "Sheriff, sometimes I think you deliberately give me the hardest jobs in the department."

In spite of the troubling thoughts on Ethan's mind, he actually chuckled out loud. "That's because I know you can do them, Lonnie. Now get out there and get those newspeople off the steps."

Lonnie hurried out of the room and Ethan reached for the phone. He'd dialed Penelope's office enough to remember the number. Her secretary answered after the first ring.

"This is Sheriff Hamilton. I'd like to speak to the judge, please."

"I'm sorry, Sheriff, but Judge Parker is in court right now. I expect she'll probably break for lunch just before twelve, if you'd like to call back then."

"No. I'll leave a message. Tell her I'll see her tonight."

The secretary suddenly cleared her throat. "Will she know where or should I write that on the message, too?"

"She'll know."

The secretary assured him she would give the judge his message and Ethan thanked her and hung up. He was wondering whether it might have been better to surprise Penelope by showing up on her doorstep without warning, when someone knocked on his office door.

"Come in."

The door opened and Ethan was surprised to see his uncle walk in. Immediately, he got up from his desk and came around to greet the older man.

"Roy! This is a nice surprise." Roy offered his hand and Ethan gripped it warmly with both of his.

"I'm not going to ask you if you're busy," his uncle began. "Because I know you are. I was in town and thought I'd stop by and congratulate you on getting Kirkland back behind bars."

Ethan shook his head while motioning Roy to take a seat. "I don't deserve congratulations. I should've caught the bastard far sooner. Especially before he killed again."

Roy took a seat and crossed his legs in the same easy manner that he'd run the sheriff's department for thirty-five years. Ethan envied his ability to be so laid-back, but try as he might, he could not still the nervous drive inside him and be more like his uncle.

"Son, you did just fine. I wouldn't have done anything different. Sometimes being the sheriff isn't so easy. I know you were getting a lot of flak from people while the man was on the loose. But now they're singing your praises from Roswell to Alamogordo.''

Ethan gave him a sheepish grin. ''I realize public opinion is fickle.''

Roy laughed. ''That's an understatement. One minute you're a hero and the next you're a sorry so-and-so. You have to let all that roll off your back and go on and do your job.''

Ethan shrugged. ''I guess I've been harder on myself than anybody.''

''That's what I figured. Have you talked to your folks?''

''The night I caught Kirkland. I knew Mom would be worried.''

Roy nodded. ''She was. I guess she's never quite gotten over you being shot.''

''Yeah. But this is what I have to do. You know how it is. You chose to do this job for a good many years.''

Ethan went over to the coffeepot and poured his uncle a cup. As he handed it to him, Roy chuckled. ''Many years,'' he repeated, then added, ''Justine never did actually like me being the sheriff. But she accepted it. And I love her for that.''

Propping one leg over the corner of his desk, Ethan smiled dryly at his uncle. ''You loved her because she was one of the most gorgeous women around these parts. Along with Mom and Aunt Chloe, of course.''

Roy laughed loudly this time. ''What are you talking about *was?* Justine is still a hell of a looker. I guess she'll excite me 'til I go to the grave.''

A few months ago, Ethan wouldn't have really understood what his uncle meant. But now, since Penelope, he knew for himself what it felt like to be excited by a woman. He didn't have to touch her. He didn't even have to be near her. All he had to do was think about her and longing coiled deep inside him.

"Uncle Roy, can I ask you something personal?"

"Since when did you think you had to ask to ask? I like to think I'm your second daddy. Not your uncle."

Ethan smiled at that. Because truthfully, Roy had been like a second dad to him. Harlan was a wonderful father. He'd always loved and supported Ethan through thick and thin and Ethan adored and admired him. But Roy was a lawman and that had given him a special connection with the other man. Thankfully, Harlan had never resented their closeness.

"I…well, this is not something…oh, hell, I don't even know where to start."

Roy looked concerned now. "Why don't you just put it in simple words."

Ethan let out a long breath. "All right. I was curious about when you first found out you were Charlie's father. How did you feel?"

Roy's brows shot up at the unexpected question. "Mad as hell. I wanted to strangle Justine because she'd kept him from me."

"She had good reason."

"I know. But I was still mad. I felt cheated and betrayed. And I couldn't bear the thought of Charlie going all those years without his father. Without me being there for him."

"Do you think Charlie ever thinks back and remembers when you weren't around?"

After a long sip of coffee, Roy balanced his cup on his knee. "Sure he does. But he doesn't blame me. Now if I'd known about Justine's pregnancy from the very beginning and turned my back on her, then that would've been another matter. The boy would've probably hated me. But I never would've turned my back on Justine. Good Lord, I've always loved that woman."

Love. Roy mentioned the word often. Maybe that's where the difference lies, Ethan thought. If he loved Penelope, he might know exactly what to say to her, exactly what to do. But he wasn't even sure he knew what it was to love a woman. Or maybe he wouldn't let his heart feel that much connection. God knows, he didn't want to make himself that vulnerable to Penelope or anyone.

"Would it be nosy to ask why you were wondering about all this?" Roy asked.

Ethan glanced at him. "Damn nosy."

Roy laughed and rose to his feet. After he tossed his empty cup away, he gave Ethan an affectionate slap on the shoulder. "I take it you've got a little woman on your mind?"

Ethan grimaced. "I've got a lot on my mind."

Roy patted him again, then headed for the door. "Oh to be a young lawman again," he said with a winsome sigh.

"You've got everything you want," Ethan reminded him.

With his hand on the doorknob, the older man glanced over his shoulder and grinned. "Yeah. And so do you, son. You just don't know it yet."

When Penelope first read Ethan's message, she seethed for a good ten minutes. But then she decided it was probably all for the best he was going to take it upon himself to meet with her. She couldn't continue to avoid him. And perhaps once she'd let him have his say, he would leave her alone and let her get on with her life. And that was what she wanted. She'd told herself that so many times now she had to believe it.

When Penelope arrived home later that evening, she changed into a comfortable pair of slacks and a huge blouse that was anything but attractive, then headed to the kitchen to prepare herself supper. She was still suffering from early-morning nausea, but by evening she was always ravenous.

Spaghetti was simmering on top of the stove and garlic bread was toasting in the oven when she heard Ethan's knock on the door. She hastily checked the food to make sure it wouldn't burn, then put her hand to her hair to assure herself it was still tightly bound in its knot.

If she'd been expecting him to be standing at the door with his hat in his hand and an apologetic look on his face, she would have been sorely disappointed. His gray Stetson was riding low on his forehead and he hadn't even bothered to change out of his khaki uniform shirt. But Penelope knew better than to expect any such thing from Ethan. That day at the Bar H Bar when she'd told him about the baby, she'd learned he was a hard man. Too hard for her.

"May I come in?"

She stepped out of his path and gestured for him to enter. "You'll have to excuse me. My supper is cooking and I don't want it to burn," she told him, then quickly walked away in the direction of the kitchen.

Ethan followed and sniffed with appreciation when he entered the room behind her. "Smells good. What is it?" he asked.

"Spaghetti and garlic bread. Would you like to join me?"

The invitation took him by surprise, especially since she hadn't talked to him for three days.

"Well, I was planning to grab a burger once I left here," he said.

She shrugged and bent to open the oven. "Suit yourself."

So she didn't care one way or the other whether he ate or not, he thought dourly. But then, he couldn't rightly blame her. She'd offered to cook him breakfast that morning at the ranch. Instead of accepting gracefully, he'd done nothing but yell at her. Even now, days afterward, he wasn't quite sure what had made him say all those things to her. In her eyes, he figured, he'd gone a little bit crazy. But at the time, Ethan had never felt so manipulated in his life.

With the oven door open, Penelope reached for a pair of quilted mittens. The tempting aroma of the toasting garlic bread escaped into the kitchen and Ethan's stomach gnawed in protest at the idea of eating another hamburger. "Are you sure you have plenty?" he asked.

She lifted the tray of bread from the oven. "You can't make just a small amount of spaghetti. There's enough here for several people."

"Then I accept your invitation."

Without saying more, she began to set the table for two. He started to offer to help. But he didn't know where anything was in her kitchen and he decided he'd only be in the way.

"I'll just go wash up," he told her, then hung his Stetson on the back of a chair as he headed out of the room. When he returned a few moments later, everything was on the table and ready to eat.

"Would you prefer iced tea or water?" she asked.

"Water will be fine," he answered.

She filled both glasses with water, then motioned for

him to take a seat. She said nothing as they filled their plates and began to eat.

As the silence began to stretch between them, Ethan's gaze slid covertly over her bound hair and stern expression. It was obvious to him that she'd reverted back to being only the judge. The pretty woman with the gorgeous black hair on her shoulders, pink color on her lips and cheeks and fluttery dress swirling around her calves was gone. He'd killed her, he supposed. But damn it, he'd been bowled over by her looks and her announcement that she was pregnant. And anyway, he wasn't good with women; he'd learned that a long time ago.

He wasn't like his father, Harlan. Even now, in his sixties, the man could simply smile at a woman and she'd be like putty in his hands. It didn't matter if she was nine or ninety. Without asking, he knew precisely what they needed and wanted to hear. He could soothe them when they were distraught or make them laugh when they were down. And yet the hell of it all, Harlan Hamilton never used his innate charm with women for his own gain. He would die before he ever cheated on his wife. He simply knew how to handle the opposite sex. And compared with his father, Ethan had always felt very lacking.

"I really didn't expect you to feed me this evening," he said, breaking the silence.

"I have to eat anyway."

And she was eating with a healthy appetite, he noticed. That much he was glad to see. "You've been ignoring my calls."

She chewed some more spaghetti before she spoke, "I had to remind myself this isn't a conventional pregnancy. You're not my husband. You're not my lover. I'm not sure you're even my friend. You're simply caught in this situation because you're the father of my child. I had anticipated your being angry. And I was right about that. But I foolishly believed once the anger was over, you would show a little bit of happiness or excitement or—or concern for me. But I was wrong to expect those things.''

He put down his fork. ''You're trying to make me sound like a heel.''

She shook her head. ''No. I'm simply stating the facts. I'm a judge, Ethan. I know all about facts. How to examine them, weigh them and decide how they'll eventually affect a person or persons.''

Now she was viewing the two of them as she would a pair of defendants in her courtroom, he thought with disgust. ''So you're going to regard this whole thing coolly and clinically. I take it Judge Parker is going to make the decisions concerning this baby. Not Penelope.''

Judge Parker was far more capable, Penelope thought. It was when she was out of the courthouse and with him that she blundered. ''You should be glad, Ethan. As a judge, I don't make mistakes.''

He picked up his fork and stabbed at the food on his plate. ''Well, as you said a moment ago, I'm the father. So I will have a say about this child. And the first thing that's going to happen is that you and I are going to be married!''

Chapter Nine

Her nostrils flaring with temper, Penelope glanced at him. "Please don't ruin my supper. I've been starving all day."

Ethan wanted to yell at her, but he didn't. She'd grown so very thin in the past few weeks. She needed to eat. In spite of what she believed, Ethan was concerned about her. He wanted her to be healthy. But most of all, he wanted her to be happy. And he didn't have a clue as how to make her that way. Or even if he should try.

Except for a few comments about the weather and the court docket, they ate the rest of the meal in silence. When she got up to clear the table, Ethan felt obliged to help her.

"I can wash the dishes later," she said stiffly as he began to scrape the food scraps from the plates.

"I don't mind."

"All right. If you want to do that, I'll make a pot of coffee," she told him.

While she worked a few steps down the counter from him, Ethan washed the few dishes. It was something he'd never done for a woman before. But it seemed Penelope had the strange ability to make him do things out of character.

He was finished with the task by the time she was pouring the coffee. He took it and thanked her, then glanced around the long room.

She started to make her way out of the kitchen and Ethan followed. "Would you like to go out on the back porch?" She tossed the question over her shoulder. "It's cool there beneath the willow."

"That's fine," he agreed. At least outside, he wouldn't be as apt to try to put his hands on her, he thought wryly. Which was something that was continuing to eat at him. He'd had the notion once he'd learned of her pregnancy, all of his desire for her would fade away. But he'd found out how horribly wrong that idea was the moment she'd opened the door and he looked into her serious but charming face. For some insane reason, he wanted her even more.

The sun was sinking and a breeze was blowing from the west. There were two webbed lawn chairs on the ground-level porch. After they sat down, Ethan glanced across the way to the old woman's house. Though he'd talked to Josephina on occasion and liked the woman, she seemed like the last person Penelope would be close to.

"This may sound like an odd question, Penelope, but what made you become friends with the old woman?"

Penelope blinked at the mist of tears burning the back of her eyes. She realized being pregnant was causing extra hormones to flood her body and make her emotional over every little thing. But Josephina held a soft spot in her heart.

"*She* made me become friends. It didn't matter to her that I was the district attorney or later the judge. She just thought I was a lonely person whom she wanted to take under her wing. She has seven children, you know. Being a mother comes naturally to her."

"Is that how you see her? I mean, you told me your parents were dead. I guess you must miss having a mother."

Especially now, Penelope thought. There were so many things she would have liked to ask her mother about being pregnant, raising a child, loving a man.

"I wish my parents were alive so I could tell them about the baby."

Something winced inside Ethan's chest. It wasn't right for anyone to be as alone as Penelope.

"What would they think about your having a baby?"

"Probably that it was about time."

He wanted to smile at her dry humor, but she said it so seriously he was afraid it might anger her. And he never wanted another fight with Penelope like the one they'd had at his ranch.

"I'm not sure how my folks will react," he replied. "Shock, mainly. Then I expect they'll be happy about it."

She glanced at him, unaware that her fingers were fiercely gripping her coffee cup. "You haven't told them?"

"No. I think we should do that after we get married."

Penelope took a deep breath and shifted in her seat. "You keep bringing that word up, Ethan. But I've already told you I'm not going to marry you."

Sighing, he set his coffee cup on the floor beside his

chair, then with his elbows planted on his knees, he leaned toward her. "Why?"

The simple question caused her to splutter with disbelief. "Do you really have to ask? I might seem like...like a desperate spinster to you, but I do have my pride. I don't want a husband who was forced into marrying me!"

"No one is forcing me."

"Oh, hell, Ethan!"

He grimaced. "That's the second time I've heard you curse now. Am I corrupting you or something?"

He was doing *everything* to her! Twisting her emotions until they were little more than raw, dangling threads.

She sighed. "You vex me like no other person I've ever known."

"Believe me, I'm not trying to. I'm only trying to make you see reason. I won't let a child of mine be born a bastard!"

Her gaze hardened on his face. "You would look at it that way," she said with disgust. "I view it as a child born to a single mother."

"There's no difference!"

"I didn't know you were so old-fashioned," she muttered.

His lips twisted. "I hardly think you're the swinging, to-hell-with-ethics type."

No, he was right about that. She was probably even more old-fashioned and moralistic than Ethan. But she had to make him believe she could have this baby on her own. She didn't need or want his forced concern. It was too humiliating. "You know I'm not. But I..."

She couldn't go on. Not with his green eyes searching her face and her heart begging her to give in to him.

Doubt flickered in her eyes and Ethan seized her hands from her lap and squeezed them tightly. "Penelope, you said earlier at supper that you had to face the fact that this wasn't a conventional pregnancy. Well, you're going to have to look at this marriage the same way.''

If his words had hurt her before, he was killing her now. She quickly rose from her chair and hurried away from him. Beneath the willow, she rested her forehead on the trunk and allowed hot tears to flow down her cheeks.

Only a few moments passed before Ethan's hands came down on her shoulders and his husky voice sounded next to her ear. ''Why are you so upset? Is the idea of marrying me that repulsive?''

He didn't understand. He couldn't know that from the very first moment she met him, she had fantasized about him and wondered what it would be like to love him, to be married to him and be the center of his world. Now here he was insisting she marry him, but not for any of the reasons she'd ever dreamed about.

''It isn't that, Ethan,'' she said in a choked voice, then desperately twisted around to face him. ''Don't you understand a woman wants more? You don't love me. You don't even want to marry me. Not really. If it wasn't for the baby, the idea of marrying me would never have entered your mind!''

He threw up his hands in total frustration. ''Well, what do you want from me, Penelope?'' he asked. ''Would you want me to lie and pretend I'd fallen suddenly and madly in love with you? Would that make marrying me any easier?''

Her lips quivered as she looked up at him. ''I would never want you to pretend anything with me.''

The sight of her wounded face tore at Ethan. Hurting her was the last thing he wanted to do. Yet it seemed as though that was all he'd managed to accomplish since that fateful night at her cabin.

He cupped his hand against the side of her face. "I'm sorry, Penelope. For your sake, I wish things were different. I wish I was the romantic guy of your dreams. I wish I could give you all the things you wanted and expected from a man. But I can't. So we're going to have to make the best of it for the baby."

For the baby. Where Ethan was concerned, it would always be for the baby. She might as well face the fact. Because it was something she was going to have to live with for the rest of her life.

"Yes. I guess you're right," she murmured, then reached up and wiped the tears away from her cheeks.

"Then you're agreeable? You've decided to marry me?"

There was such a hopeful sound to his voice, she wanted to burst into another fresh rain of tears. "Not really."

He closed his eyes. "Why? Because I'm just the sheriff? Because you think a better man will come along?"

A better man! Did he honestly think she could ever want anyone but him? she wondered, then mentally kicked herself. Of course he did. He didn't have any idea how she felt about him. And from the looks of things, she could never let him know.

"Your being the sheriff has nothing to do with it. Well, it might bring up problems in the courtroom from time to time," she admitted. "But as for a better man, I was never looking for a man in the first place. And anyway, are you a sorry catch?"

His lips twisted. "Some women might think so. I don't make a lot of money. I'm never off duty. My job is dangerous. And the public is always going to gossip about me, whether it be good or bad."

Penelope wasn't like those "some women" he'd

known. Though she feared for his safety at times, she admired the devotion he gave to his job. "You don't understand, Ethan. It isn't any of those things. Marriage is such a final step and—"

"If that's what you're worried about, we'll put a limit on the marriage. Would that make you feel any easier about it?"

Puzzled, she studied his face. "A limit?"

He shrugged as though he was trying to be casual about the whole thing, but Penelope got the impression he was anything but nonchalant. He truly wanted her to marry him.

"A time limit. If you find you don't want to be married to me after a year. Then we'll end the marriage. But the baby will have been born to married parents."

His suggestion wasn't necessarily what her heart wanted to hear, but the sensible side of her brain thought it was a good solution. At least this way, she wouldn't be tying Ethan down to a loveless marriage. After a year's time, he'd be able to go on with his life and find someone else.

"So in other words," she said quietly, "it would be a marriage of convenience."

"If you want to call it that."

She looked away from him as her heart clenched with pain. "And what's your family going to think of your marrying a woman for that reason?"

His hand deserted her cheek and wrapped tightly around her shoulder. "Do they have to know?"

Her gaze whipped back to his face and she stared at him in disbelief. "What do you mean? Are you suggesting we pretend we're a normal, loving couple?"

"Would that be so hard?"

"It would be deceitful!"

"Sometimes a little deceit is kinder than the truth."

A small cry sounded in her throat as she twisted her back to him. "Do you know what you're asking?" she whispered. "And besides, your family is going to realize you haven't been dating me. They'll think the whole thing strange."

"If we told them the truth, it would sound even stranger," he reasoned.

He was right, Penelope thought dismally. No one was going to believe that Ethan had impulsively shared one night of passion with Judge Parker, the result being a baby on the way.

"When the baby is born, they're going to know I was pregnant before the wedding," she argued.

"By then it won't matter."

She drew in a deep breath and tried to collect her scattered emotions. "Your family's opinion must mean a great deal to you."

"My mom's not only a wonderful mother, Penelope. She's a wonderful person. Her heart is as big as a house. And she truly believes the only real happiness people have on this earth is through the love they give to each other."

"I understand she's talking about love. Not lust," she said quietly.

"Mom's not a prude by any means. She just happens to think the two go together."

"And you don't?"

Penelope wished she'd kept the question to herself. Especially after long moments passed and he said nothing. Finally, she turned back to face him and was surprised to find him staring off at the darkening horizon rather than frowning down at her.

"I'm not a loving kind of man, Penelope. So don't get to thinking you might change me."

''I wouldn't dream of it,'' she said curtly, then quickly stepped around him and walked back to the porch.

She picked up their empty coffee cups and entered the house. By the time she'd reached the kitchen, she could hear Ethan following her. She was rinsing the cups in the sink when she felt his presence moving up behind her.

''Have I made you angry?'' he asked her.

She closed her eyes. ''No.''

''Then you've decided to marry me?''

''Yes.'' Her throat was so tight, getting the word out was like trying to cough up a nail.

She heard his sigh and was somewhat bewildered by his obvious relief. She'd tried to give him the easy way out. Instead, he apparently intended to go to great lengths to make it appear as if they were a pair of lovers who were longing to get married and spend the rest of their lives together. Was it really all for the baby and his mother? she wondered. Or was a part of this pretense to be undertaken for the sake of his position as sheriff of Lincoln County?

His motives for marrying her and pretending it was a love match really didn't matter, Penelope fiercely argued with herself. *She* wasn't the reason. And that was all she needed to remember.

''Good. I'll pick you up tomorrow evening after work and we'll drive out to see my parents.''

Her eyes widened with shock. ''So soon! I've just now agreed to this—this marriage! I'd like to get adjusted to the idea myself before we start springing it on anyone else.''

Frowning, he shook his head. ''If you think we're going to have a long, drawn-out engagement while your belly swells to the size of a ripe watermelon, forget it.''

She stared at him as if he were someone she'd just met

and wished she hadn't. "For your information, my *belly* won't be growing for a while yet." Her back ramrod straight, she skirted around him and headed to the living room.

Ethan followed on her heels. "What's the matter now?"

"You really know how to say the nicest things to a woman," she muttered. "Or is it just me that brings the barbarian out in you?"

"I've never professed to be a sweet-talker," he said crossly. "So if you're expecting a bunch of mushy words from me, you might as well forget that, too."

She whirled on him. "All I expect from you is polite respect. If you can't give me that much, then this whole marriage deal is off. Now. Before it's even started!"

He rolled his eyes toward the ceiling. Damn, but he didn't know how he always managed to get off the tracks with this woman. "I wasn't trying to insult you! I was just trying to make you see sense."

"Listen, Ethan, if the idea of my swollen figure is going to cause you embarrassment, then you'll never make it as a husband for a year. Much less a father! So why don't you just stick with being a sheriff? That's all you really want to be!"

She turned and left him standing in the hall. Ethan swore under his breath, then headed to the kitchen for his hat. He jammed it on his head and went to find her.

She was sitting on the couch in the living room, staring straight ahead. He knew he'd managed to offend her. Again. But hell, it was like he'd always known. He wasn't good with women. And God knows he didn't have any experience in how to treat one who was pregnant with his child.

"I'll pick you up at the courthouse tomorrow evening," he promised curtly.

Penelope glanced his way. He was already at the door, his hand on the knob as though he couldn't wait to leave. She supposed she was being a little hard on him, but he wasn't exactly making things easy for her.

"I don't know when court will recess," she told him. "Several witnesses are lined up to testify tomorrow. And I can hardly make up an excuse to recess without good cause."

"It doesn't matter. I'll wait," he assured her, then quickly stepped outside the door and closed it behind him.

The silence was deafening. Then she heard his pickup roar to life and pull away from the house.

She'd just agreed to marry a man. And yet there'd been no kiss. No ring or flowers. No I love yous. Not even a gentle goodbye. It was all going to be convenient and covert.

She went over to lie on the couch, buried her face in the cushion and cried bitter tears.

"I'd like for you to get a search warrant, Sheriff. I have a hunch that place is infested with dope."

Ethan looked up from the papers he was signing. "What makes you think that, Jones? You have to have good probable cause to go in with a search warrant. And Judge Parker isn't going to give you one unless you do."

"Well, we've got plenty of witnesses stating there's traffic going in and out of the place day and night. With out-of-state plates."

"Not enough."

"Jim Barnett swears he saw the back end of his stolen four-wheeler parked in a barn out back of the house."

"What was Jim doing over there? Trying to get himself

killed?'' Ethan asked as he pushed one set of papers aside and proceeded to sign and initial another set.

''Then you do think something is going on there, sir?'' Jones asked hopefully.

''Yes. I just had to see where you'd gotten your deductions. But as for a search warrant, I want to wait. When we do go in there I want to make certain we don't have a dry run. Right now I want you to go out and find out all you can about those people and their contacts.''

The deputy frowned with confusion. ''But, Sheriff, if they find out the law is asking questions about them, they're liable to run. Or hide all the evidence. Wouldn't it be better to take them by surprise.''

Ethan grinned at him. ''We will take them by surprise, Jones, if you do your job right. The trick is not to let anyone know you're asking questions.''

He shifted his gaze to encompass both deputies. ''Is there anything else?''

Both men assured him they understood his orders, then left the room. Once they were gone, Ethan finished signing the papers, then reached for the telephone.

He'd put off calling his parents all morning. A few times, the notion had struck him not to call them at all and simply show up this evening with Penelope. But he never knew if they'd be home or having company. And he didn't want the drive to the Flying H to be wasted. He wanted this whole marriage thing with Penelope to be over and done with before she had the chance to change her mind.

Rose answered on the fifth ring. Ethan could tell she was out of breath and from the sound of the radio in the background, he knew she'd answered the phone in the horse barn.

''Hi, son!'' she exclaimed the moment she heard

Ethan's voice. "What's going on? It's not like you to call in the middle of the day."

"I'm sorry for interrupting your work, Mom. I know you're busy."

"Not nearly as busy as the sheriff. And I'm never too busy to talk to my son," she said, love warming her voice. "Are you coming out tonight?"

His lips twisted wryly. There had been many a time his mother seemed to anticipate his actions before he could say a word. "How did you guess?"

"We haven't seen you in a while and from the sound of your voice I don't think this is an emergency call."

As far as Ethan was concerned, it was an emergency. Penelope was going to have his baby.

"Well, I was thinking about driving over. That is, if you and Dad were going to be home."

"Of course. And I've already got pot roast cooking. Come in time for supper."

"I'm going to bring someone with me. I don't know if we can make it that early. Just don't go to any extra trouble."

"All right, honey. I won't pull out the good china or put flowers on the table. It'll just be plain ole ranch grub," she assured him.

"Thanks, Mom."

She laughed and told him goodbye.

After Ethan had hung up, he left his desk and walked over to the window. As he looked out at the sunny day, a word his mother had said drifted through his head. Flowers. Had Penelope ever received flowers from a man? he wondered. Would Penelope even want any flowers from him?

Oh, she'd agreed to marry him. But she wasn't the least bit happy about it. And maybe that shouldn't matter to him, he argued with himself. As long as the baby was legally born with his name, he should be satisfied. But the sight of Penelope's tears were still haunting him.

When Penelope spotted Ethan entering the back of the courtroom, the district attorney was cross-examining the last witness of the day.

Once he'd taken a seat, she allowed her gaze to briefly meet his to let him know she'd seen him arrive, then she forced her mind back on the trial. Though it was very difficult to concentrate on the testimony with her heart dancing in anticipation of being near him again.

"Your Honor, since I expect my questions for this witness to take at least another hour, would you rather we recess for the day and continue fresh in the morning?"

Penelope felt like kissing the D.A. She glanced at her wristwatch, then reached for her gavel. "If you think you're going to need that much time, I do agree. The jury has already had a long day."

"But, Your Honor," the defense attorney loudly interrupted, "my witness has had a trying day, too. It would be putting undue stress on her to ask her to return to court tomorrow."

The only stress Penelope could see it was going to put on his witness was to give her more time to forget her coached answers. She glanced warningly over her glasses at the young attorney. "Mr. Jamison, is it going to upset your mental balance to return to court tomorrow?"

"No, Your Honor, but—"

"Then it shouldn't upset your witness. She's not the one on trial." Penelope glanced at the young woman in the witness box. "Miss Gryder, will you be able to testify in the morning?"

The young woman nodded. Then realizing she needed

to announce it verbally, she leaned forward and spoke into the microphone. "Yes, Your Honor."

"Good. Then court is recessed for the evening and we'll resume at this same point in the morning at nine o'clock." Penelope dropped the gavel, and as she left the courtroom, everyone on the other side of the bench rose to their feet.

In her chambers, she removed her robe and was hanging it in a small closet when a knock sounded on the outer door.

"Come in," she called, then turned just in time to see Ethan entering the room.

"Hello," he said.

She walked toward him, adjusting the tiny white collar on her gray dress as she went. "Hello," she replied, amazed that she suddenly felt shy with him. But it wasn't every day a man asked her to marry him and invited her to meet his parents. In fact, this was a first since all those years ago with Hugh and she could only wonder if this engagement would end as drastically as that one had.

"Is there anything else you need to do?" he asked. "Or are you finished here for the day?"

She glanced at him as she reached for her purse and briefcase. He was out of uniform this evening. The sleeves of his blue oxford shirt were rolled back against his forearms and the stained gray Stetson he usually wore had been replaced with a cleaner cream-colored one. His looks were devastating. But tonight he looked especially nice. An extra effort for his mother, she figured. It certainly wasn't for her sake.

"No. I'm finished here. Just let me make sure I have all my notes in here before we leave."

She glanced inside the leather briefcase, and as she flipped through the corners of the pages, Ethan said, "You aren't going to work tonight, are you? It might be late before you get back home.''

Satisfied all her papers were in order, she closed the case and jammed it beneath her arm. "It doesn't matter what time I get home, Ethan. I have court in the morning. I have to be prepared.''

Ethan opened his mouth to tell her she couldn't nurture a developing baby while working such long hours. But after a second thought, he decided to keep the opinion to himself. Tonight of all nights, he didn't want to get started off on the wrong foot with Penelope.

"Here, I'll carry that for you," he said, and reached for the briefcase under her arm.

She handed it to him, then lifted a hand to smooth her hair away from her forehead. "Am I presentable enough to meet your parents?" she asked him.

Since she asked, he deliberately made a slow perusal of her appearance. Her hair was in its usual tight chignon. Tiny pearls were fastened to her earlobes and a faint pink gloss colored her lips. Her gray dress could only be described as severe. It was straight and shapeless with narrow white cuffs buttoned at the wrist and a small white collar fastened high around her neck. She looked like she was headed for a convent rather than a night out with her fiancé.

"What happened to the dress you were wearing that day at the ranch?"

Her features tightened. "I threw it away."

Ethan wasn't surprised. He was beginning to see that underneath her cool, stern exterior was a temper like a volcano. "Well, I wouldn't mind if you wanted to let your hair down," he suggested.

Her brows slowly inched upward as though he were treading on dangerous ground. "But I would mind.''

He groaned aloud. "Penelope, you look fine. But my parents are expecting to meet a woman in love. Not a judge on a mission."

"But that's what I am," she pointed out.

"We're supposed to be faking it," he felt compelled to remind her.

Her eyes narrowed on his face. "Faking it! Since that night we spent together at the cabin, I think that all you've done with me is fake! Your concern! Your desire! I'm—oh—what are you doing?" she demanded as she watched him toss the heavy briefcase onto her desk.

"You think I was pretending the night our baby was conceived? Do you think this is phony?"

He snatched her up against his chest. Before she could reply to either question, his hands cupped both sides of her face and his lips swooped down on hers.

Having his lips next to hers again was like getting a drink after nearly dying of thirst. She hated herself for responding. She tried her best to keep from clinging to him. But in the end, she went as limp as a sunflower in the blistering heat and her hands gripped his forearms to keep herself upright.

"There," he murmured with satisfaction as his dark gaze roamed her face, then settled on her puffy lips. "Now you look like a woman who's been kissed."

"Ethan…"

He ignored her protest as he began to pull the pins from her hair. "Your hair is beautiful, Penelope. At least let me see it loose for this evening."

How could she tell him no when it was all she could do to keep from snuggling back in his arms and begging him to kiss her again? Would she ever be able to refuse him? she wondered bewilderedly. It was indecent. Especially when she knew he had no love for her at all.

"All right, for this evening," she murmured. After all, it was just her hair. Her heart was the thing she was going to have to keep safely bound and tucked away where he couldn't touch it. And she would hide her heart away, she promised herself. She had to. Or a year of marriage to Ethan would crush her.

Chapter Ten

The Hamilton ranch was located several miles east of the community of Hondo. Once they turned off the main highway and headed into the rolling desert hills, Penelope tried to relax and enjoy the scenery. It was not often she got out this way and never off the highway. This was all new country for her. Yet she could scarcely keep her mind on anything but Ethan and the idea of giving his parents the news of their upcoming marriage.

Penelope seriously doubted his family was going to be happy. They were affluent and highly thought of in the area. No doubt they expected their son to marry well. And she figured they would consider the daughter of a rich rancher far more suitable for Ethan than a staunch judge.

The Blazer rolled to a stop, pulling Penelope out of her deep reverie. She glanced around to see they were at the entrance of the Flying H Ranch. Two rock pillars flanked a wide cattle guard. Suspended overhead was a board with the words "Flying H" burned into it. Prickly pear grew thick around the base of the rocks and was presently in vivid yellow bloom. On each side of the entrance, stretching away for some distance, enormous poplar trees lined the fence and cast a protective shade over the loamy ground. Beneath one of them, a lone red bull grazed at the grama grass hidden between the clumps of sage.

"Why are we stopping here? Isn't this the entrance to your parents' ranch?"

He killed the engine, then turned toward her. "Yes. But I have something to give you and I wanted to do it before we got there."

Surprise flickered across her face. "Something to give me?"

He reached back over the seat and Penelope was stunned when he handed her a bouquet of cut flowers wrapped in pink cellophane. "Consider them a peace offering," he said with a sheepish little grin. "And a thank-you for agreeing to marry me."

Penelope didn't know what to say as she unwrapped the huge collection of daisies, carnations and cornflowers with baby's breath mingled in between. The colors were bright and cheerful and made her lips tilt into a soft smile.

"I accept the flowers as a peace offering. But I don't want you to thank me for marrying you. I'm doing that because…I believe it's the right thing for the baby."

"I believe it's right, too," he murmured. To see she was pleased with the flowers made him very glad he'd gone to the trouble of getting them. The sight of her smile was so rare and beautiful he wished he could see it a thousand times and even that would not be enough.

"There's something else," he said, then reached behind him once more.

This time when he lifted a small velvet jeweler's box

from behind the seat, she drew in a sharp breath of shock. "Ethan! I didn't——"

"Expect an engagement ring," he finished for her. "I'm sure you didn't. Last night, we talked about how unconventional this all was, but that doesn't mean...well, I want to do things as right as I can. And you deserve a ring, Penelope."

He popped open the lid and turned the box around to face her. Penelope stared at the glittering pear-shaped solitaire set on a white-gold band as if she'd never seen a diamond in her life. And especially one that was meant for her.

"See," he explained, "the little band beneath it will be your wedding ring. But we can get a wider one if you like. Or maybe you'd like a different stone, better."

Awed beyond words, she touched her fingertip to the glittering stone. It was like a glistening teardrop caught forever in time. She couldn't imagine him giving such a thing to her.

"It's very beautiful, Ethan. But don't you think...much too expensive? I mean, I'm not a real fiancée."

She hadn't yet taken her eyes off the ring and Ethan could see she was overwhelmed by it. Or perhaps she was more bowled over by the simple fact that he'd gotten her one. He couldn't deny that most of the time these past few weeks, he'd resembled the back end of a horse. In fact, he figured, Penelope had seen the very worst side of him. But this whole situation had thrown him like an angry bronc.

"You're going to marry me, aren't you?"

She lifted her head and nodded as she met his gaze.

He smiled as though that solved everything. "Then you're a real fiancée."

"But, Ethan, a diamond of this quality is...well, a fake one would have served the purpose."

He chuckled under his breath. "We just had a little round back in your chambers over faking it. Let's not get into it again."

He pulled the ring out of its velvet nest and reached for her hand. A blush stole over Penelope's cheeks as he gently slid the ring onto her finger.

"Well, I'm sure your parents would think it odd if I didn't have a nice engagement ring," she said. "And the public, too."

He was still holding on to her hand, his thumb pressed into the knuckle of her ring finger as his green eyes caught hers. "Penelope, this ring isn't to impress my parents. Or the public."

Her gray eyes darkened with shadows. "I'm not the love of your life, Ethan," she said softly. "You don't have to pretend just because you think it will make me feel better."

Maybe she wasn't the love of his life, Ethan thought. But she'd become an important part of it. And try as he might, he couldn't ignore the overwhelming desire he felt for her or his need to protect her.

"The ring isn't just for appearances, Penelope," he said once again. "It stands for something between you and me. A bond to signify the night our child was conceived. Understand?"

She nodded, but underneath, Penelope was more confused and torn than she'd ever been in her life. This was supposed to be a marriage of convenience between them. Yet he wanted it to be like a love match minus the love. How could she do it? she asked herself. It was going to be torture. But she couldn't think of that now. She had to remember the baby and how all of this was going to eventually affect him or her.

"Thank you, Ethan. For the ring. And the flowers."

"You're welcome, Penelope," he said with a grin, then

settling back behind the steering wheel, he drove the vehicle onto Hamilton land.

The family ranch house was a rambling brick-and-lumber structure with no certain shape or style. Ethan explained how years ago his mother had refused to tear down the old ranch house in order to build a new one, so Harlan simply began adding rooms on as they needed them.

"You're going to see my mother is sentimental, Penelope," he said as he parked the truck beneath a grove of piñon pine a few yards away from the house. "In fact, she's a whole lot like you. Or you like her. Whichever way you want to say it."

Penelope glanced at him with surprise. "Really? Why do you think so?"

Before he answered, he came around the front of the vehicle and helped her down to the ground. "She's basically quiet and shy until something gets her riled. Then she has a temper. Though it's not nearly as hot as yours."

She shot him a dry look. "Maybe you haven't given her the irritation you've given me."

"Humph," he snorted with amusement. "Maybe I haven't."

He took her by the hand and Penelope allowed him to keep it as they walked to the front porch. Then before Ethan had the chance to knock, the door swung wide and a tall redheaded woman stood smiling at the two of them.

"Hello! Come in!" she exclaimed, her warm smile encompassing both her son and Penelope.

"Hi, Mom. I hope we're not putting you out this evening," he said, then brushed a kiss against her cheek before the two of them stepped into the cool house.

Rose grasped his hand and patted the top of it as though he were still her little boy. "Of course you're not putting us out. Your father is in the den and I've just taken a pitcher of lemonade in there. Why don't we join him while the last of my dinner cooks.''

''Fine,'' Ethan told her, then reached for Penelope, who was standing quietly to one side. ''Penelope, meet my mother, Rose. Mom, you might recognize Penelope better as Judge Parker.''

Penelope extended her hand to the tall, gracious-looking woman. Her hair was red with only a few threads of gray showing at one temple and brushed her shoulders in loose, soft waves. Her cotton skirt was a gold-and-turquoise Southwest print and her blouse was cinched at the waist with a silver concho belt. She looked young enough to be Ethan's sister. ''It's very nice to meet you, Mrs. Hamilton.''

Rose smiled as she shook Penelope's hand. ''I'm glad you could come tonight, Penelope. I may call you Penelope?''

''She doesn't expect you to say Your Honor every time you address her, Mom,'' Ethan teased.

Rose laughed and shook a finger at her son. ''I'd forgotten just what a sweet thing you are,'' she said, then motioned for the couple to follow her.

Harlan Hamilton was a familiar figure to Penelope. He'd sat on two different juries since she'd been judge. He was as handsome as Rose was beautiful and Penelope could see where Ethan could only have been born with striking good looks.

The older man left his easy chair the moment he spotted the three of them entering the room. ''Hello, son. And Judge Parker, it's especially nice to see you again.'' He reached for Penelope's hand and squeezed it warmly between the two of his.

Ethan cast Penelope a wry glance. ''I didn't realize you knew my father.''

''I've been a juror in her courtroom,'' Harlan explained, then beamed another smile at Penelope. "You're the best damn judge we've ever had in this county."

"Thank you, sir."

"There are no sirs or ma'ams used around here," he warned her with an easy laugh. "Just Rose and Harlan."

"Well, now that everybody knows everybody," Rose spoke up, "why don't we get some lemonade and sit down for a few minutes?"

"Not yet," Ethan told her. "We—Penelope and I— have something to tell both of you."

Rose and Harlan glanced expectantly at each other, then back to their son. Rose's eyes were wide and worried. Harlan's brows were cocked into suspicious question marks. Penelope could feel embarrassing heat rising from her feet all the way to the roots of her hair.

"Are you two planning some sort of fund drive for the sheriff's department? Or a political event?" Rose asked.

"Why don't we let them tell us, honey. It would be easier than guessing," Harlan told his wife.

"Actually, it's nothing of that nature," Ethan said, then wrapped his arm around Penelope's slender shoulders and smiled down at her as though she was the most precious thing he'd ever laid eyes on. "We're going to be married."

Like the eerie stillness before a tornado, the room went deathly quiet. Then just as Penelope dared to draw a breath, Rose squealed and Harlan began to chuckle.

"Married! I can't believe it!" Rose cried.

"Well, if this isn't some good news!" Harlan reached for Ethan's hand and gripped it tightly. "Congratulations, son! I'm very glad for you. You couldn't have picked a finer woman."

To Penelope's surprise, Rose came to her first and her throat stung with tears as the older woman gently touched her cheek. "My dear," she said softly, "I've prayed my son would find someone like you. You can't imagine how happy you've made me.''

"What about me, Mom? I hope I've made you happy, too,'' Ethan teased.

Rose looked at her son and she suddenly began to weep and laugh at the same time. He gathered her in his arms and patted her shoulder, and in that moment, Penelope realized she'd been all wrong about Ethan. He wasn't really a hard man. He was only hard where she was concerned.

"Let's break out the spirits, Rosie!'' Harlan exclaimed cheerfully. "Do we have any of that champagne left over from our anniversary party?''

Ethan gently drew back from his mother and she smiled and shook her head as she dabbed at her eyes. "No, dear,'' Rose answered. "All we have is that homemade wine Justine and Roy's neighbor sent us.''

"Well, get it! We've got to toast this young couple!''

Penelope had never felt like a hypocrite or a liar. She'd never been deceitful about anything in her life. But for the next few minutes as Ethan and his family celebrated their engagement, she decided this was the way a defendant must feel when he's on trial and lies through his teeth in an attempt to save himself. And yet, strangely, she had to agree that Ethan had made the right choice not to tell his parents the whole truth of the matter. They believed Ethan was happy and in love. Penelope didn't want them to know their son was being forced into a marriage of convenience. A marriage that in all probability might ruin his future happiness.

"When is the wedding going to take place?'' Rose asked later as they all sat around the dinner table enjoying the last bites of pot roast on their plates.

Penelope glanced questioningly at Ethan. A wedding date had never been discussed.

"Two weeks from tomorrow," Ethan stated as though he had the date firmly etched in his memory.

Penelope's mouth fell open, but Rose didn't notice. She was too busy trying to deal with her own shock.

"Two weeks! But you've just now gotten engaged! And you can hardly get the preparations for a wedding ready in two weeks! What are you thinking, Ethan?" Rose quickly glanced at Penelope. "Do you have a dress or anything ready?"

Color burning on her cheeks, Penelope shook her head. "No. Your son has rather jumped the gun on me. I thought I was going to have a little more time."

Across the table, Harlan chuckled. Rose glared at him. "This isn't funny, Harlan. We're talking about your son's wedding. He is the only son we have, you know. If we don't get to do this one right, we won't have another chance."

He grinned at his wife. "Don't worry, there'll be some grandsons to come along. You can dress them up in tuxedos and marry them off in grand style. But I expect Penelope would just as soon have a nice little ceremony without all the fuss."

Penelope glanced across the table at the older man and thanked him with her eyes.

"Well, it's a cinch we can't go to the judge for a civil ceremony," Ethan offered. "Penelope can hardly marry herself. I guess we'll have to drive to Alamogordo or Roswell."

"Ethan!" Rose softly scolded. "You know you want to be married in Our Lady of Guadalupe."

"Penelope might not be Catholic," he warned his mother, then cast a questioning glance at Penelope.

"I am," Penelope answered while wondering what the Hamiltons were thinking. Probably that she and their son didn't know anything about each other. They hadn't even discussed their religious preferences. Well, in a sense, they'd be right, Penelope thought sadly. She and Ethan didn't know each other the way true lovers should.

"Good," Rose said. "Then that settles where to hold the ceremony. What about your parents, Penelope? Is your mother helping you with the plans?"

"Mom, Penelope's parents both passed away a good many years ago. She has no family. Not around here."

Harlan frowned and Rose looked terribly contrite. "Oh, I'm so sorry, Penelope. My mouth got to running ahead of my brain. Please forgive me if I hurt you."

"You couldn't have known," Penelope assured her. Her gaze dropped back to her half-empty plate. "And anyway, I was already thinking about them. Wishing they could be here. I believe...they would be very happy."

Rose cast her a gentle smile. "Well, honey, you're marrying into a big family. Pretty soon you'll have more relatives pouring out your ears."

Dinner lasted only a few more minutes, then Penelope automatically began to help Rose clear away the dishes. But Harlan quickly stepped in and took the stack of plates from her. Handing the plates to his son, he said to Penelope, "Ethan can help his mother while I show you around the place."

"Dad, Penelope isn't a cowgirl," Ethan warned as the older man began to lead Penelope out the back door. "She's a judge."

His father laughed. "I know what Penelope is without you telling me. Besides, who says she can't be both?"

"I'm in trouble now," Ethan muttered as he carried the plates over to the counter.

Rose squirted liquid soap beneath the spray of hot water rushing into the sink. "Why?" She glanced up at him with an amused smile. "Can't you be without your sweetheart for a few minutes?"

Ethan grimaced. "A few minutes with Dad and she'll be eating out of his hand."

"Don't you want the two of them to get along?"

He walked back to the table to fetch more dirty dishes. "Of course I want them to get along. But next to Dad, well, all of us other men pale. She'll be expecting me to be like him now."

Rose laughed softly. "What a silly notion. Oh, I know Harlan has his charm. But, honey, so do you in your own way. And I'm sure Penelope knows what a fine man you are. If she didn't, she wouldn't be marrying you."

She doesn't want to marry me, Ethan felt like saying. But he couldn't utter the words now. His mother would be devastated. She deeply believed in true love between a man and a woman.

"And by the way, why didn't you tell us you've been seeing Penelope?" Rose asked. "You've really floored us. We didn't know you'd been dating anybody."

"Well, actually, Penelope and I haven't been courting in the way you're thinking. We...well, that whole thing with Kirkland sort of bound us together. I had guards posted on her night and day and sometimes it was me." At least, that one time he'd been her guard and more, he thought wryly. "Since then, we've come to know and respect each other. And—"

"To love each other," Rose finished for him.

"Yes. To love each other," he murmured, then cleared his throat. "Where do you want me to put this bottle of ketchup?"

Rose walked over and plucked the bottle from his hand. "You make coffee and leave the rest to me. Harlan and Penelope will be back in a few minutes and then we'll have dessert."

Ethan busied himself with the coffee. Across the room, Rose began to load the dishwasher.

"I'm greatly relieved about your bride-to-be."

"Hell, Mom. You make it sound like my taste in women has been horrible."

"Oh, they were all pretty and fashionable. But they weren't the kind of women you needed. Especially Trisha. She was a vulture and nothing but. I feel like I can say that now that Penelope has come into your life," Rose pointed out.

Rose Hamilton rarely said anything negative about anyone. She always tried to look for the good qualities in a person rather than dwell on the bad. Ethan was more than a little surprised to hear her say even one word against Trisha.

"I tell you, Mom, after Trisha, I really didn't care if I ever got involved with another woman."

She reached over and patted his shoulder. "I know. But now you have, and it's obvious Penelope is going to make you very happy."

"You just met her. How could you know that?" he asked with a crooked grin.

"Because I can see she loves you."

He'd never known his mother to be wrong about anything. But this time she was, and Ethan suddenly felt a sadness fall heavily onto his shoulders. All his life he'd wanted to make his family proud. The Murdock's were a strong, hearty bunch. His cousins, Adam and Charlie, were both highly successful in their jobs—Charlie as a prestigious Texas Ranger and Adam as an oil mogul.

Ethan sometimes wondered if his ambition to be sheriff had fallen far short of what his parents had expected of him. And now he was going into a pretend marriage. He didn't know whom he was letting down more—himself or his family. Or was Penelope the one he was really shortchanging? he asked himself.

Outside, Penelope strolled alongside Ethan's father as

he pointed out some of their favorite horses grazing beyond a board fence. "You have a beautiful place," she told him. "How long have you lived here?"

"Many years," Harlan confided. "Ethan's sister, Emily, was six at the time I bought this place. We'd lived back in east Texas and her mother died after a short illness. I wanted to make a new beginning, and when I found this land, I fell in love with it."

"So you lived here before you married Rose?"

He smiled with fond remembrance. "Oh, yes. I was determined to remain a widower until she came along and changed my mind. In fact, you remind me a whole lot of her back in those days."

"That's what Ethan's told me."

"Then he paid you a compliment," Harlan returned warmly. "Rose is quiet and reserved, but underneath she has a lot of spunk. Before me, she'd decided she hated men. She had good reason for feeling that way, too. And she had it in her head she wasn't going to like me, either. She rode horseback all the way over here from the Murdock ranch just to order me to keep my cows off her land." He stopped and chuckled. "Lord, that was a long time ago. But you don't ever forget moments like that—when you know you're looking at someone special, but you don't know what to do about it."

"I guess you could say I moved to Carrizozo for a fresh start, too," she found herself telling him. "I'd lived in California for several years while I was in law school. I didn't like the congestion or the fast-paced life of the city." Or the relatives who'd reluctantly taken her in after her parents' deaths, she thought. Since they'd finished raising their own children, they'd regarded Penelope as a burden and an intrusion in their lives. Once she'd earned her lawyer's degree and began to earn a nice salary, she'd sent her aunt and uncle a hefty check to pay them back for the room and board they'd given her. And to further prove she'd been right about their feelings, they had cashed the check and never so much as given her a thank-you.

"Is that where your parents were from?" Harlan paused to prop his arms over the top board of the fence. Penelope leaned her shoulder against the white fence and gazed out at the horses. Talking about her parents had always been difficult. Time had merely dimmed the grief and bitterness she felt over losing them. The years hadn't taken those emotions away. But Harlan was an easy man to talk to.

"No, my parents were from Colorado. That's where I grew up. I have an aunt and uncle in California."

"Maybe they'd like to come to the wedding?" he suggested.

"No. We don't get on very well. You see, they took me in after my parents were killed. But they didn't want to, if you know what I mean. If it hadn't been for having their friends and neighbors think badly of them, I'm certain they would have sent me to a foster home."

"Sounds like a real loving pair," Harlan commented. "You say your parents were killed? How did that happen?"

"They were walking across the street and run over by a hit-and-run driver."

Harlan shook his head regretfully. "That's a hell of thing."

She breathed deeply and was surprised to find she felt a little better for telling him. "Yes. The driver was never caught. That's the main reason I went into law. There are too many victims out there."

As soon as she finished speaking, she heard the crunch of footsteps behind her. She turned to see that Ethan had walked up behind them, and from the odd look on his face, she couldn't help but wonder if he'd heard at least part of the conversation.

"Mom asked me to come fetch you two," he said. "She has dessert ready."

"Good!" Harlan exclaimed. "I think it's going to be blackberry cobbler. Do you like cobbler, Penelope?"

She glanced away from Ethan to smile at her soon to be father-in-law. "Yes. Very much."

Before she could turn her attention back to Ethan, she felt his fingers close around her upper arm. Trying to hide her surprise at his touch, she glanced at him. He wasn't smiling and she wondered if she'd somehow angered him. But then she had to remind herself that Ethan Hamilton was a man who rarely smiled. Especially at her.

The three of them returned to the house and gathered for dessert in the den. Once their cobbler and coffee were finished, Ethan announced he and Penelope had to get back to Carrizozo.

"But you haven't been here that long," Rose exclaimed. "And I need to discuss more of the wedding plans with Penelope."

"Penelope has work to finish tonight and court early in the morning," Ethan told his mother.

"Oh. Well, I don't want her to have to work late," Rose assured her son, then turned her gaze to Penelope, who was sitting beside him on the couch. "I'll call you and we'll set up a time to meet. Okay?"

Penelope smiled at the older woman. "I'll look forward to it."

A few minutes later, the four of them said their good-byes on the front porch. Penelope was surprised when both Rose and Harlan hugged her and kissed her cheeks. She hadn't expected such warmth or affection from Ethan's family. It felt so nice, she was actually scared.

Any time she'd ever believed she was loved or wanted, she'd wound up on the losing side.

Ethan had driven several miles before he spoke. Penelope had been equally quiet, her mind churning with all that had happened that evening.

"What do you think now?" he asked.

She turned her head toward him. "About what?"

"My parents. Our getting married."

She glanced at the diamond on her finger. "Your parents are wonderful, Ethan. I never expected them to be so kind. I just wish...I didn't feel so deceitful. They think we love each other. But I guess..." She glanced away from him and swallowed. "I can see it would only hurt them if they knew the truth."

He didn't say anything and Penelope finally lapsed back into her own thoughts.

"I heard you talking to Dad about your parents."

The accusation in his voice startled her far more than his words. Her gaze scanned his shadowed profile. "Was that wrong?"

He grimaced. "No. I'm just curious why you couldn't tell me. I asked you that night at the cabin. You deliberately avoided the subject."

She dropped her head. "That night...I was very troubled. And it...would've hurt even more to start explaining to you about their deaths."

"But I guess it didn't hurt you to explain it to Harlan," he stated flatly.

Her head shot back up and she stared at him in disbelief. "Why, Ethan! You sound...almost jealous! Of your own father!"

He wasn't jealous, damn it! He was hurt. But he couldn't tell Penelope that. He wasn't supposed to care. So why did he?

"I'm not jealous. I just felt stupid. You're going to be

my wife and I don't even know the most basic things about your life. And you don't seem to want to tell me. I realize I'm not the easiest man in the world to talk to, Penelope. But—''

''It isn't that, Ethan. I didn't tell you about my parents because...'' She shook her head. ''This is probably going to sound foolish. But I've always known you were from a strong, close family. I knew you took pride in that. After I was orphaned, my upbringing was...well, I was fed and clothed, but not much more. It's not easy to admit that your own relatives thought of you as a nuisance. I didn't want to explain all of that to you and have you...looking down on me.''

He glanced at her, and in spite of his intentions to keep his heart frozen, he could feel it melting like a pat of butter. ''Do you honestly think I'm that sort of man, Penelope? I realize I've been blessed with a wonderful family. I don't think less of others who haven't been. And in your case, you could hardly help it because your parents were killed.''

''I know. It's just...even though it's been years since their deaths, it's still very hard for me to deal with emotionally.''

''How did you manage to go to college and law school? Did your aunt and uncle help you with any of that?''

She let out a caustic laugh. ''Not hardly. Once I graduated from high school, they were relieved to see the last of me. I put myself through college by working at odd jobs and with scholarships I received for good grades.''

''You must have wanted to become a lawyer very badly.''

''Oh, I didn't want to be just a lawyer. I knew shortly after my parents were killed that I wouldn't stop until I became a judge. I wanted to have that power. I wanted to be able to point my finger and say you will pay for hurting this person, for taking this person's life, for stealing and lying. My job won't ever bring my parents back. But it does give me some sense of retribution."

By the time she finished speaking, her voice was quivering. Ethan wanted to stop the vehicle and take her into his arms. He wanted to tell her it wasn't good for her to keep seeking revenge for their deaths. He wanted to tell her that she was no longer alone.

But he couldn't make his foot hit the brake. Penelope didn't love him or need him. He wasn't even sure she trusted him. The only connection they had was the baby growing inside her. And he doubted that would be enough to hold her past a year of marriage.

"Being a judge must be the most important thing in your life," Ethan said quietly.

Tears ached in her throat as, once again, she gazed down at the sparkling diamond on her finger. It was truly fitting that the stone was cut into the shape of a teardrop, she thought sadly.

"It always has been," she answered huskily. Until you and the baby, she wanted to add. But the words just wouldn't find their way past the fear in her heart.

Chapter Eleven

The next two weeks passed in a blur. Between court and the preparations for the wedding, Penelope barely had time to draw a deep breath. And then all at once before she knew it, the morning of her wedding day arrived and she was fighting the constant urge to throw up.

Thankfully, Rose and Emily, Ethan's sister, put her queasiness down to last-minute wedding jitters and kept bringing her glasses of lemon-lime soft drink to settle her stomach. Penelope kept wondering what the two women would think if they knew she was already pregnant with Ethan's child. Maybe they would shun her the way she'd been shunned for most of her life. But she couldn't let herself dwell on the matter. It was her wedding day, and even if it wasn't a real union of love, she wanted to savor as much of it as she could.

"I don't know what I would've done without you and your mother," Penelope said to Emily as the other woman fastened a row of tiny pearl buttons at the back of her dress.

Rose had purchased the dress for her in an expensive boutique in Albuquerque. Penelope had never seen, much less owned, anything like it in her life. The cream colored batiste fabric was fashioned in Victorian style with yards of antique lace adorning the skirt, leg-o'-mutton sleeves and high collar. The part of the bodice above her breasts was made of fine lace netting and was partially see-through. When Penelope had first tried on the dress, she'd been a little shocked because she'd never worn anything so daring. But Rose and Emily had thought it perfectly beautiful, and after a second look, Penelope had to agree. She looked like a different woman in it. And she was secretly glad that pregnancy had already plumped up her breasts so that she filled out the alluring bodice.

Emily laughed. "I wouldn't have missed one minute of these wedding preparations. My brother's getting married is a miracle. I still have to stop and remind myself it's actually true."

Emily finished the last button, then motioned for Penelope to sit down at the dressing table. As the blonde began to search for a hairbrush, Penelope eased down on the brocade-covered seat.

"Ethan must have really been off the idea of marriage for a long time," Penelope remarked.

"Oh, 'off' isn't the word," Emily assured her. "After Trisha left him, I think he actually hated women. I didn't think he'd ever look at another one. At least not seriously."

Ethan had never mentioned any woman's name or the fact that one had left him. As far as that went, Penelope couldn't envision any woman leaving Ethan. He was one of the most gorgeous, sexy men she'd ever seen in her life. But perhaps the woman had come to realize he didn't love her. Just like Penelope knew he didn't love her.

"I just thank God you came along and made him realize that all women aren't man-eaters," Emily went on.

Penelope's lips parted to ask Emily about this Trisha, but the door to the bedroom opened and Rose rushed in all out of breath.

"I've finally gotten the bouquet from the florist! Doesn't it smell heavenly?" She handed the cluster of white gardenias to Penelope, then looked at the two younger women's reflections in the mirror. "My gracious, hurry and finish her hair, Emily! The limo is waiting and we only have fifteen minutes to get to the church!"

"All right, Mom. Just calm down. We'll make it." To Penelope she said, "I thought I would twist it all up on top of your head and let a few tendrils hang loose. What do you think?"

A hesitant look on her face, Penelope reached up and touched a hand to her black hair. "I don't think I should put it all up. Ethan doesn't like it that way."

"Oh, Lord," Emily said with a laugh, "you're not going to start letting the guy tell you what to do even before the wedding, are you?"

Judge Parker would never have let any man tell her what to do. But something had happened to Judge Parker since Ethan had come into her life. "Well, I do want him to think I look nice," Penelope said doubtfully.

"Okay, I won't argue. I'll let the back hang loose and we'll pull the front part away from your face and secure it beneath your veil. How does that sound?" Penelope nodded in agreement. Smiling, Emily quickly leaned down and gave her a peck on the cheek. "Penelope, you're going to look better than nice. You're going to look ravishing!"

Our Lady of Guadalupe was a small church near Hondo

that had been in existence for more than a hundred and fifty years. Rose and her sisters had all been christened and married there, and down through the years, all of the Murdock offspring had been married within its sacred walls. This afternoon, friends and relatives overflowed its pews until many well-wishers were forced to stand outside in the hot afternoon sunshine.

Ethan's cousin, Charlie, had managed to get away from his duties as a Texas Ranger long enough to drive up from Austin to serve as best man while Emily had happily agreed to be matron of honor. Ethan's uncle, Wyatt, the oil baron of the family who was married to Rose's sister, Chloe, had been called upon to walk Penelope down the aisle and give her away.

Wyatt was as equally charming as his brother-in-law, Harlan, and he managed to keep Penelope's nerves soothed until they began the long walk to the altar. After that, everything took on a surreal quality. Once Ethan took her hand and she looked into his eyes, she hardly heard the priest speak the solemn words of the marriage service. She was only aware of the flickering candlelight, the scent of the gardenias in her hand and the quiet, sober expression of conviction on Ethan's face. It was not a look of love, but rather a mission accomplished. And when he slipped the wedding band on her finger and pressed his lips to hers, she forced herself to think of the baby and remember it was all for him or her.

The reception was held at the Bar M, the original homestead of the Murdock sisters. Penelope had never been there until a few days ago when Rose and Emily had taken her to okay plans with her about the reception. The ranch was as fabulous as the rumors she'd heard. It was a stucco structure with a red tiled roof and built in the old Spanish tradition of a square with a courtyard in the middle.

This afternoon, the courtyard was overflowing with

people. The surprise union of the sheriff and the judge had caused quite a stir all over the massive county. Acquaintances of Ethan's had shown up for the wedding along with a slew of his relatives. A few of them had driven long distances to attend, such as his cousin, Caroline, who lived in Santa Fe. And the twins' younger sister, Ivy, who was now working as a doctor in Arizona but planning to return to Ruidoso.

Back at the church, the young redheaded beauty had caught Penelope's bouquet and the attention of one of Ethan's young deputies, it also appeared. Now as the reception began to wind down, Penelope watched the couple sharing a glass of punch together and she could only hope once Ivy did marry it would be for love and no other reason.

She felt an arm slide around the back of her waist and looked up to see that Ethan had rejoined her. Throughout the afternoon, he'd been swallowed up by friends and relatives. Yet he'd given Penelope far more attention than she'd expected. They'd even danced several times to the live band Justine and Roy had hired as part of their contribution to the wedding.

"Would you like to dance again?" he asked. "Or are you getting too tired?"

A slow song had just begun, so she nodded in agreement and Ethan led her onto a part of the patio that had been cleared for dancing. Fortunately, a nearby willow shaded it from the July heat.

"I can't believe there are so many people here," Penelope remarked as she followed Ethan's smooth steps. "I thought this was going to be a small wedding."

He chuckled. "This is small by Murdock standards. If we'd given my mother and two aunts any more time, they'd have invited at least two hundred more guests."

It was still difficult to believe that Penelope had married

into such a prominent, wealthy family. Not that Ethan was rich by any means, but he did stand to be very wealthy one day. Yet Penelope had never attached much value on money. It was nice to have. Certainly nicer than being poor. But she'd always lived modestly, even after she'd begun making a handsome salary. No, Penelope was more concerned about what was inside Ethan than what he owned on the outside.

This afternoon, he truly seemed to be a happy groom, a man in love with his new wife. But as much as Penelope wanted to believe in appearances, she knew it was only an act for his family and friends.

"How much longer do we need to stay?" she asked. "I don't want to appear rude, Ethan, but I am getting a little tired."

He glanced at her sharply. "Are you all right? You haven't overdone it, have you?"

The concern on his face was real and it comforted her to know he did care about the baby. "No, I'm fine, really. Just feeling the effects of a long day."

He let out a breath of relief. "Actually, I've been ready to leave this shindig for more than an hour. Why don't we change clothes and head out of here?" he suggested. "And don't worry about my family. Our leaving won't stop them from celebrating. This party will probably last until midnight."

His hand was in the middle of her back, pressing her close against the long, hard length of his body. The closeness reminded Penelope that she had no idea where they were going from here. But wherever it was, the two of them would finally be alone. The idea sent a shiver down her spine.

"Where are we going, Ethan? To your house?"

His brows lifted as though her question had taken him by complete surprise. "I guess we've been so busy these past couple of weeks, neither one of us thought about a honeymoon. Where would you like to go?''

Just the mention of the word ''honeymoon,'' put a blush on her face. Which was silly. She was already pregnant with Ethan's child. It wasn't like she was a virgin anticipating her wedding night. It wasn't like Ethan planned to make love to her at all.

''I…haven't thought about it. Since I only have four days before I have to be back in court, that doesn't give us much time to go anywhere.''

''Well, we're not staying at the ranch house or your place. We're newlyweds. People are expecting us to take off somewhere. We could drive up to Colorado and stay in the San Juans or charter a plane and fly to Galveston Island or Lake Tahoe. Anywhere. Just name it, Penelope.''

Her gaze dropped to the middle of his chest. ''I…it doesn't matter to me, Ethan. But I'd really rather just stay at the cabin. It's always nice and cool there and we could take a few groceries with us.''

A smile slowly spread across his face and he bent his head and kissed her long and hard.

''Let's get out of here,'' he whispered.

It was well after dark by the time the newleyweds had packed everything they needed and driven to the secluded cabin. Penelope had not returned to the place since she and Ethan had left it more than three months ago.

For a long time, Penelope had thought it would trouble her to revisit the place where she'd lost her innocence and conceived Ethan's child. But now that they were man and wife, it somehow seemed right that they should spend their honeymoon or the facsimile of a honeymoon here.

With nightfall, the cool mountain air had settled around the small cabin. Penelope sat curled up on one end of the porch swing, her arms wrapped around her to ward off the chill. To the right of the cabin, sage and piñon pine clung to the craggy slope of the mountain rising far above. To the left, the ground began to slope gently downward to a grove of tall ponderosa pine. If she stopped the slow movement of the swing with her toe at just the right moment, she could see a part of the mesa far below through a break in the huge trees. She couldn't think of a prettier place to be at this moment.

The screen door creaked open and she glanced around to see Ethan carrying two cups of coffee.

"I thought you might like a cup after that delicious meal of sardines and crackers," he teased.

"I like sardines," she said. She took the cup he offered, then thanked him. "And anyway," she went on after a careful sip, "I was still stuffed from all that food at the reception."

"Mom did go rather overboard on the food," he said with a wry grin. "I almost made myself sick on those smoked ribs. And they were pork! And me a cattleman. My whole family has made their fortune in cattle for more than seventy-five years and she serves pork! But I have to admit it was delicious."

Penelope smiled. It was the first time she had ever seen him so relaxed and it gave her hope that perhaps this marriage wouldn't make him as miserable as she'd first feared.

"Maybe you should start raising hogs, too."

He laughed. "This country is too dry for hogs. It's more suited for scorpions, sidewinders and coyotes. You have to be tough to survive around here."

Like him, Penelope thought. He was a tough man. Inside and out. He'd already survived a gunshot wound that would have killed a lesser man. Penelope had felt the scars on his shoulder and no one had to tell her the wound had been dangerously close to his heart. He might have been wounded again the night he'd set out to capture Kirkland. If all had not gone well she could be sitting here on the porch alone, her baby half-orphaned before it was ever born.

When Penelope thought of things in those terms, maybe having Ethan love her wasn't so important after all. Maybe just having him should be enough.

She finished her coffee, then went inside to get ready for bed. She was in her nightgown, sitting at the dresser brushing her hair, when Ethan came back inside the cabin.

Her heart beat fast and heavy as she heard his footsteps head into the kitchen, then slowly approach the bedroom. When he came up behind her, she gave him a tentative smile in the mirror.

"I hope you're not sorry you agreed to come here," she said gently. *And most of all, I hope you're not sorry you married me, Ethan.*

He reached down and took the brush from her hand, then slowly began to draw it through her long hair. "I'm not sorry. I think we both need the peace and quiet. The only person who knows where we are is Dad. And it would take a major earthquake or something worse for him to tell anyone. The department is going to have to do without me for the next four days. And the courthouse is going to have to survive without the judge."

He put down the brush, but his hands remained in her hair, stroking its length, his fingertips testing the texture of the long, silky strands. Penelope's heart beat even faster and her breaths grew short and shallow.

"I will never forget walking into this cabin and seeing you with your hair flying loose around your shoulders," he said softly.

The corner of her mouth lifted in an expression that

was both wry and sad. "Up until then, I could've been bald and you wouldn't have noticed."

"Oh, I knew you had hair. I just didn't know it could look like this." He lifted the heavy mane and brought it up to his face. "It smells like your wedding bouquet."

"Gardenias," she whispered, surprised that he'd noticed and even more surprised that he was touching her so tenderly.

He let her hair fall against her back and then he eased down beside her on the edge of the bench. Penelope began to tremble with longing as his finger came up to brush the soft skin at her temple. "Penelope, I know we both agreed this marriage of ours is one of convenience. But that doesn't mean I've stopped wanting you. Since the night we made love, I've never stopped wanting you. And I may be wrong, but I believe you still want me."

She closed her eyes and swallowed as her heart continued to pound wildly inside her chest. "Ethan, if you want us to share a bed like a regular man and wife, just say so. We are married now."

"That's true. But I don't want to mislead you in any way. I don't want you to get the wrong idea. If we—"

"You don't want me to start thinking it's more than sex," she interrupted.

His gaze dropped from hers. "I guess that's what I'm trying to say. Spoken aloud, it doesn't sound very good, either, does it?" he mumbled.

Her hand closed over his forearm and brought his gaze back up to hers.

"At least you're being honest, Ethan. And there's no need for you to worry. I know how you feel about me. I didn't come into this marriage with stars in my eyes."

Tomorrow he might look back on her words and wonder what they really meant to him. But for now, tonight, all he could hear in her voice was a yes and that was all he wanted or needed.

"Oh, Penelope," he groaned, then before she could say another word, he gathered her up in his arms and carried her over to the four-poster bed.

Still fully clothed in jeans and a short-sleeved shirt, he lay facing her, his head propped on his hand. He smelled of the outdoors. A spicy mixture of sage and piñon mingled with the masculine scent she'd come to recognize as completely his.

As he leaned his head over hers, a wave of rusty-brown hair fell over his forehead. She reached up and brushed it aside with her fingertips and his eyes glinted down at her.

"You look beautiful tonight," he said as his fingers slid seductively along the low neckline of her gown. "Even more beautiful than you did today at the wedding. And I hadn't thought that would be possible." His compliment flushed her cheeks with color and he smiled gently as he traced a finger over the smooth skin near her lips. "You find that hard to believe, don't you? You don't think of yourself as beautiful."

She shook her head. "I've always been more concerned about filling my brain with knowledge than the way I look."

He chuckled softly. "Well, as far as I can tell, you've filled that brain of yours up to the brim. And you haven't done too badly on the outside, either."

"This gown isn't very sexy," she said, glancing down at the pale blue satin and lace. "But I didn't want you accusing me of trying to seduce you."

He groaned and bent his head down to hers. "It doesn't matter," he murmured against her lips. "You've already seduced me anyway."

He kissed her then, hungrily devouring every sweet

curve of her lips. Penelope's hands gripped his shoulders as her head began to reel with sweet pleasure.

Eventually, he tore his mouth away long enough to slip the silky gown up and over her head. After he'd tossed the garment to the floor, he eased back to look at her.

Penelope wished to heaven she'd never turned on the small lamp at the head of the bed. Even though it was only shedding a dim, soft glow, she felt sure Ethan could see every flaw she possessed.

A strand of her long hair had fallen over one breast. He pushed it aside, then gently traced the outline of her nipple with his forefinger. Her breasts were much fuller now, the nipples changed to a dark chocolate color. He cupped the weight of one in the palm of his hand, then bent his head to taste it.

The gentle tug of his teeth, the moist laving of his tongue against her breast sent an ache of desire spreading through her loins. Just as she began to groan with desperate need, his head finally lifted and his hands began a slow, teasing search down the rest of her body.

His fingers had almost reached the triangle of dark curls when he discovered the swell of the growing baby. The mound was small but obvious. For a moment, he went very still, and Penelope began wondering if the sight had somehow repulsed him.

"The baby is growing," she said softly.

"The baby," he murmured. His fingers trailed gently back and forth across her lower belly. And then he stunned her by lowering his head and placing a kiss on the precious bulge of her body. When he looked back up at her, Penelope's eyes misted over. "You should always look just like this," he whispered.

The corners of her soft lips curled faintly upward. "You mean naked and pregnant."

"And in my arms," he added with a groan, then scooping her close, he rolled onto his back and took her along with him.

The hard bulge beneath the heavy fabric of his jeans pressed against her, telling her how much he already wanted her, and the fact gave Penelope a heady sensation to know she had that much effect on him. She had never thought of herself as desirable to any man. Yet every touch, every glance, from Ethan made her feel she was truly longed for. He made her feel bewitched and beautiful and wanted. And she wanted to give everything to him in return.

Dropping her head, she found his lips. He clasped her to him, his hands roaming her back, tangling in her hair, clutching the soft cheeks of her bottom.

Finally, he held himself away from her long enough to shed his clothes. When he rejoined her on the bed, she almost asked him to turn out the light. But once he took her in his arms, she decided it didn't matter if he saw the look of longing on her face. It was the hunger in her heart she had to keep hidden in the darkness.

When his fingers found the moist heat between her thighs, he looked into her drowsy eyes. "Will it hurt the baby if we—"

"No. He's safe in his own little cocoon."

He sighed with relief, then his lips twisted self-recrimination. "It's shameless to want you this way. To want you so much," he said huskily. "But I do."

Her fingers reached up and traced the ribbon of white scar leading from his collarbone down toward his heart. "I know you've made love to other more sexy women than me, Ethan. And I don't know much about this."

As his fingers delved deeper into the moist heat of her body, he watched her eyes widen, then her hips lifted in response. Groaning, he lowered his head to the valley between her breasts.

"I'm glad you don't know, Penelope," he said, his voice tight with desire. "I'm glad I'll be the one to teach you."

After that, there were no more words. No more waiting. He straddled her and entered her body with one hungry thrust. Penelope was instantly transported to the heavens, and after a moment or two she realized her hips were moving rhythmically with his, her hands desperately clutching his back.

Ethan's fire for her was fueled even more strongly by her eagerness, and all the weeks of wanting her, needing her and not having her were coming to an end. The softness of her body, the touch of her lips against his skin, the scent of her hair and taste of her tongue all merged together until he wanted to absorb every fiber of her being. He wanted to hold her to him, keep himself inside her forever.

But, finally, it became impossible for him to hold back, and as he spilled his warm seed inside her, he knew nothing in his life had ever been like this. Nor would it ever be. Unless Penelope was with him.

When he rolled away from her at last, she was so spent she could do nothing but lie there. The rapid pounding of her heart throbbed in her ears, sweat glazed her body and her lungs continued their greedy gulps for air.

Beside her, Ethan rose and leaned over her. "Are you okay, Penelope?"

His fingers touched her cheek, then moved down to the baby. As his palm cradled her there, a heavy weight settled in the region of her heart. She would never have been Ethan's wife if it wasn't for the baby. The two of them would never have been here like this again.

Foolish tears pooled in her eyes. She quickly turned her head from him and desperately tried to blink them away.

"Yes. I'm fine."

His fingers stroked her hair away from her cheeks. She bit down on her lip and swallowed at the fiery lump in her throat.

"I didn't hurt you?"

"No."

His arm curled around her waist and pulled her up against him, then he buried his face in the side of her neck. "Good. Because I never want to hurt you, Penelope."

Oh, Ethan, don't you know you already have? She wanted to cry. Instead, she turned and pressed her cheek against the beat of his heart and tried not to think about tomorrow.

Chapter Twelve

The days at the cabin passed all too quickly for Penelope. Returning to Carrizozo was a sudden jolt back to reality. Her honeymoon was over and life had to go on.

In her absence, work had piled up at the courthouse. She did her best to handle all the warrants, subpoenas and trial motions during the day. At night, she slowly packed her belongings for the move to the Bar H Bar.

Ethan tried to help her as much as he could. But his work had backlogged even more than hers and he rarely made it home until eleven or twelve at night.

Eventually, he hired two young men to do the actual moving, then left it up to Penelope to find space for her belongings in his ranch house. Emily came over and helped her on several occasions. Together they managed to turn the sparsely furnished house into more of a home. Yet try as she might, Penelope was reluctant to think of his place as hers, too. Even though she was legally his wife, she felt more like an interloper who'd come to stay for an indefinite length of time.

Nonetheless, she couldn't say she was entirely unhappy. As the weeks passed, her pregnancy continued on a healthy course. Emily was the first to notice her increasing girth, and before long the whole family knew she and Ethan were going to have a child. If they were shocked at the Christmas due date, no one showed it. In fact, Rose and Harlan seemed utterly thrilled to be having a new grandchild. Penelope assumed that Ethan's parents believed the pregnancy was a result of a deep love that couldn't wait.

As for the townspeople, Penelope realized her sudden marriage to Ethan had brought about both good and bad gossip. For the first few weeks after their marriage, cards of congratulations and well wishes had landed on her office desk. But since then she'd also received letters from citizens expressing their concerns over the fact that the judge was married to the sheriff and it would be impossible for any defendant to get a fair trial in Lincoln County.

In her heart Penelope knew the concerns were unwarranted. Her love and admiration for Ethan would never take precedence in the courtroom. With her, it was nothing but the facts. Both sides had to present evidence within the strict legal guidelines of the law or a jury would not be allowed to hear or see it. And in the past months since her marriage to Ethan she'd taken extra care to make sure no rules were bent in her courtroom.

Still, the critical letters had hurt. Especially because it cast doubts on Ethan's performance as sheriff, too. That was the main reason she'd chosen not to mention the complaints to him. She and the coming baby had already intruded into his life and she didn't want to cause his job to be any harder than it already was. Yet in the back of her mind, Penelope feared more complaints could very well crop up in the future. Especially if a major trial was scheduled on the court docket. If that happened, she would be forced to let Ethan know what some of the people in this county were thinking about the two of them.

With a weary sigh, Penelope pulled off her reading glasses and put them, along with a stack of legal motions into her briefcase. Even though she still had work to do before a hearing in the morning, it was time for the courthouse to close and Penelope was more than ready to go home and put up her feet. She'd had a long day of phone calls and hearings.

As she buttoned a coat over her growing tummy, Penelope caught the sound of loud giggles coming from the closed door to her secretary's office.

A small frown tugged Penelope's brows together as she walked across her chambers to Julie's door. The young woman was always very careful about keeping her office quiet. It wasn't like her to allow this much noise to go on.

Penelope was about to turn the doorknob to investigate the racket when she heard a female voice and instantly recognized it as that of Susan Brewer's, the court clerk. And what the woman was saying froze Penelope in her tracks.

"I can't believe that Penny Parker's pregnant! All I can say is Sheriff Hamilton must have really wanted a big favor from the judge to take a woman like her to bed. I always thought she was frigid anyway. Maybe the sheriff considered her a challenge."

"Susan! That's an awful thing to say!" Julie responded sharply.

"Well it must be true," the other woman retorted, then giggled again. "Why else would Ethan Hamilton have made her pregnant! The man could've had his pick of women!''

"But he chose Judge Parker," Julie pointed out none too kindly to the court clerk.

"That's right. And God knows it couldn't have been for love or even sex. He—"

"It was more than sex," Julie interrupted. "He made her his wife."

The other woman snorted, then laughed. "Well, we all know why, don't we? As sheriff he could hardly go around as a bachelor while the judge carried his illegitimate baby. No, the way I see it, Sheriff Hamilton wanted the hanging judge to favor his department and marrying her was the way to do it."

Penelope closed her eyes and drew in a sharp breath. In the back of her mind, she'd expected there would be nasty talk about Ethan marrying her. It was always that way when a good looking man married a dowdy spinster. But this was the first time Penelope had heard it first hand and the hurt sliced right through her chest.

"I'm sorry, Susan, but you'd better go. It's quitting time and I have to see what Judge Parker needs done before she leaves her chambers."

Penelope forced herself to move away from the door, but the moment Julie entered the room and spotted her white face, the secretary knew she'd overheard the court clerk's comments.

"Oh, I'm so sorry, Penny," she said, rushing over to her. "You shouldn't have had to hear that. I kept trying to get her out of the office, but the woman wouldn't shut up."

Her throat tight with pain, Penelope said, "Don't apologize for her hateful words, Julie. She was only saying what she thought. And I heard you defending me. Thank you for that much."

Julie glanced with disgust back toward her office door. "Susan was gossiping! Plain and simple! And she was only doing that because she's jealous."

Penelope cast a puzzled frown on her secretary. "Jealous?"

"Of course! Because you got Sheriff Hamilton instead of her."

When Penelope continued to frown with bewilderment, Julie went on, "Penny, don't you know lots of women around here would have liked to snare Sheriff Hamilton into marriage?"

Penelope let out a long, painful breath. It didn't matter what they said about her, but to hear Ethan degraded in any way, crushed her. "I didn't *snare* Ethan. He wouldn't allow any woman to do that to him!"

Julie smiled reassuringly. "I know. That's why you should feel very special."

As the summer heat began to fade and autumn approached, Ethan and several hired cowboys began rounding up the cattle on the Bar H Bar to drive to market. Ethan had taken three days off from the sheriff's department to get the job done and every night he'd returned to the house, dusty and exhausted.

Although a cleaning woman did the heavy work, so far, Penelope had done her best to be home in time to cook him a good meal. She tried to have it ready by the time he finished in the evenings, but tonight she was still standing at the cookstove, turning fried chicken, when he entered the back door.

Glancing over her shoulder, she watched him hang his work-stained gray Stetson on a peg by the door, then join it with his jean jacket.

"Supper's not quite ready yet," she told him. "I was a little late getting home."

"Don't worry about it. I'm too tired to eat anyway." He walked over to the sink and washed his hands, then splashed water on his face.

She handed him a clean towel. "Did you have trouble today?"

He wiped his face dry, then tossed the towel onto the counter. "Buckeye crippled his ankle. I had to haul him out to the vet and leave him at the clinic. A calf ran down into a dry wash and got his leg stuck between two rocks. By the time we got him out, the leg was broken. I had to put him down. Other than that, I guess my day went fine."

She turned her attention back to the skillet full of chicken and Ethan couldn't help but notice her hand pushing tiredly at her back. She had to be exhausted from putting in a long day at the courthouse. And yet she never complained to him. Even as the baby grew heavier, she'd never failed to have something nice cooked for his meals. She'd turned the house into a home with colors and flowers.

Before he'd married Penelope, he'd never thought about what a wife might mean to his life. Mainly, he'd put the whole idea of having a wife out of his mind a long time ago. And when he did think of one, he more or less had the image of a bed partner and little more. But Penelope had made him see that a wife was much more to a man. Much more to him. She did little things for him he never expected or counted on. And just knowing she'd be there at the end of an exhausting day soothed him in a way he could not understand.

"Did you have a busy day?" he asked as he went over to join her.

"I had a doctor's appointment late this afternoon. That's why supper is running late," she explained.

His hand reached up and stroked the long, dark hair hanging down her back. She still continued to wear it up in a tight knot in the courtroom. But she always wore it down at home. It was a concession she made just for him. "What did he say?"

"He performed an ultrasound to make sure the baby was developing properly and was on schedule. He said everything looked great. But the position the baby was lying in made it impossible to tell about the sex. Actually, I was glad. I don't want to know if it's a boy or a girl until I have it. Do you?"

A faint smile curved his lips. "Oh, I don't know. It might be nice to be forewarned. Then I'd know whether to go out and start buying him saddles and horses and spurs. But I guess I could get those things for a little girl, too. All the women in my family like them."

All except her, Penelope thought. She often wished she could be like his mother and aunts and cousins, who were all ranch smart and were as comfortable on a horse out on the range as they were in the kitchen. But she'd never had the opportunity to live an outdoor life. She knew she could learn, but she never mentioned to Ethan that she wanted to. It was hard for her to plan for any sort of future when she didn't know how long her future was going to be here with him. Once their year of marriage was up, he could very well say he wanted to end it. So far, he hadn't told her otherwise. And the word "love" had never been mentioned at any time.

"I'm sure you could make her into a real little cowgirl," Penelope murmured as she tried to shake away the dark thoughts.

"By the way," Ethan said as he quickly set the table with plates and silverware, "did the doctor mention anything about your working?"

Penelope placed the platter of chicken in the middle of the table. "No. Why?"

She looked at him and his brows lifted as though he considered her question inane.

"Why?" he repeated. "Because you're getting pretty far along and I know working is wearing you out."

"I'm doing all right. If I hadn't been, the doctor would have told me so."

Ethan grimaced. "The man doesn't see you every night like I do, Penelope. You come home exhausted."

"The doctor said I could work right up until labor."

He looked shocked and affronted. "Is that what you want to do?"

She went back to the cookstove to collect the rest of the supper. "Of course," she said. "I am the people's judge, Ethan. I'm the one they elected to serve them. I don't want to let them down."

Disbelief marred his face. He'd always figured her job meant more to her than him. But he'd never dreamed she would put it before the baby. "Even if it harms our baby?"

She frowned at him. "You know I would quit before I let something like that happen."

He threw up his hands. "How do you know it won't happen? My brother-in-law, Cooper, never knew his mother because she died giving birth to him. Is that what you want to happen to you?"

Penelope calmly placed the dishes on the table, then laid her hand on his forearm. "Don't you think you're getting a little overdramatic, Ethan? My work in the courtroom isn't going to kill me. I'm sitting all day."

"But it's stressful. And you're nearly seven months pregnant. I think it's time you quit and stayed home. In fact, I'm telling you. I want you to make arrangements for a leave of absence."

Her mouth fell open. She didn't mind the notion of staying home. It was the idea of his demanding her to do it that instantly heated her blood. "You're not going to order me to do anything, Ethan! I'm not one of your deputies!"

She went back to the counter and filled their glasses. Hers with milk, his with iced tea. As she placed them on the table, he said, "You're damn right you're not one of my deputies. You're my wife! And I don't want anything happening to you or the baby! Is that so terrible?"

"Look, Ethan, my job as judge is just as important to me as being sheriff is to you. Would you want to give it up?"

"You're a woman. A very pregnant woman. That makes it all different," he argued.

"Where did you get such antiquated notions, Ethan? Your father isn't like that."

If possible, he looked even angrier. "I am not like Harlan! Don't ever expect me to be!"

Her breasts heaved as her gray eyes raked accusingly over his face. "No, you're right. Harlan has a heart!"

Not even noticing she'd yet to place one bite of food on her plate, much less eaten it, Penelope pushed herself to her feet and hurried out of the room.

In the living room, she pulled on her coat and slammed out the front door. Goldie was instantly at her side and the blue heeler followed her as she walked away from the house and toward the creek.

The night air was brisk but not uncomfortable. She was dressed in wool slacks and a heavy sweater and her coat was lined with fleece. But even if she hadn't been dressed warmly, she doubted she would've felt the cold for the hot anger pouring through her.

Once she reached the creek, she sat down on a large boulder and tried to calm herself. Goldie waded into the water but quickly decided it was too cold for an evening swim. Back on dry ground, she shook herself and trotted back to Penelope.

She rubbed the dog's head, then hugged her up close to her thigh. "Silly girl, you know the water's too cold."

The dog looked up at her and whined and Penelope smiled in spite of her anger. Goldie had become her dear pal and oftentimes it seemed the dog was trying to talk to her.

"Your master says you're a killer," she said to the dog. "He doesn't know either one of us, does he?"

The dog whined again, but this time Penelope couldn't find it in her heart to smile. Instead, tears stung her eyes. But she refused to let them fall.

"Penelope! Damn it, what are you doing down here? It's dark. You could have stumbled and fallen."

She turned to see Ethan picking his way over the stony path. He'd put on the hat and jacket he'd left in the kitchen and she tried not to let herself feel guilty because he was down here searching for her instead of eating his supper.

"You're supposed to be eating," she said.

"So are you."

When he reached her, she turned her head and kept her gaze firmly on the shallow water rushing over the rocks and boulders of the creek bed. "I'll eat later."

"When I'm not around? Penelope, I want to know why you've gotten so angry about this. I thought you wanted this baby."

Her head whipped around and she stabbed him with furious eyes. "I love my child! This isn't about the baby. It's about you! You—"

"Penelope—" He broke off with a shake of his head. It was obvious he should have discussed this with her a long time ago. Before her pregnancy became so advanced it encumbered her physical activity. But it seemed that both of them deliberately avoided speaking of anything that would ultimately affect their marriage. Ethan's reason was mainly born out of fear. He didn't want to give Penelope any reason to announce she'd be leaving after their year of marriage was up. As for Penelope's reluctance to talk of anything deeper than the weather or the local news, Ethan figured she simply didn't care about developing their relationship to anything more than what it was.

"How would you like it if I demanded you quit your job as sheriff?"

His nostrils flared as he digested her question. "More than one woman has tried it before. And I'm still the sheriff."

"That's right!" she retorted hotly. "You wouldn't quit for any of those women and neither would you do it for me! So why are you asking me—no, demanding that I step down from the judge's bench?"

"My God, Penelope, you're going to have a baby. Did you think...were you planning to quit just long enough to give birth?"

In truth, Penelope hadn't decided how long she would take off from work once the baby had arrived. Certainly a few months. She wanted to breast-feed and give the baby plenty of time to bond to her. But Ethan seemed to have already declared her to be a negligent mother just because she cared about her job.

"You're being insulting and hateful," she said tightly.

"You're overreacting to this whole thing. If you—"

"No!" She twisted around so that she was facing him. "You don't understand, Ethan. After my parents were killed, I didn't have anything to hang on to except my dream of becoming a judge. What few relatives I had either acted as though they didn't know me or simply tolerated my presence. They were all afraid I was going to look to them for financial help."

She let out a bitter snort. "I didn't want anything from them. But I desperately wanted a law degree. The idea of becoming a judge was the only thing I cared about. And then, while I was in my third year of college, I met Hugh. He was a quiet, soft-spoken medical student. He was serious and goal oriented. Nothing like the beer-drinking, girl-chasing guys my roommates went out with. And he liked me."

Ethan could tell from the look on her face that this man had been much more than a casual boyfriend. And the realization stung him hard. He'd never thought about Penelope loving or needing another man.

"What happened?"

"We dated for several months and Hugh eventually proposed. I was so happy. I thought I had finally found someone who loved and respected me for myself. I was going to have a family of my very own. But the moment I said yes, Hugh became a totally different man. He demanded that I quit college. He didn't want me working as a lawyer or judge or anything. I was to be his wife and mother of his children. Nothing more."

"You couldn't accept that," he said quietly.

She shook her head. "I wanted to be a wife and mother. But Hugh expected me to give up my rights as a person to be those things. He thought I was crazy and selfish to want more."

"So what happened then? Did you try to change his mind?"

With a sigh, she looked down at Goldie, who had settled her muzzle comfortably across her thigh. She slowly stroked the dog between the ears.

"At first I tried. But I realized if I had to force him to see things my way, our marriage would never work. And anyway, he couldn't have loved me. Not really. When you love someone, you want them to be happy. To follow their dreams. In the end, I told him I couldn't marry him. I never saw him after that."

She might not have ever seen him again, Ethan thought, but she sure as hell hadn't forgotten. He wanted to hate the guy for hurting her. No doubt the whole incident had scarred her. Probably more than even she realized.

"Is he the reason you've avoided men all these years?"

Penelope shook her head. "Not Hugh in particular. I got over losing him. But I guess you could say the whole thing opened my eyes. I knew it would take a special man to let me be who and what I wanted to be. And down through the years, I never met him."

He stepped closer, his expression grim. "So you've lumped me with all the rest. In your eyes, I'm just like this Hugh person."

She glanced up to see he was standing over her shoulder, and as always, his nearness tugged her senses in scattered directions. "I can hardly think otherwise. You just demanded that I take a leave of absence."

With a weary sigh, he reached down and brushed a finger against her cheek. "I only meant for it to be temporary. After the baby comes, it will be up to you to...make your own choices."

Like whether she was going to remain with him or move back to town and divorce him. He didn't have to remind her of their agreement to give their marriage a one-year trial. There was rarely a moment she didn't think of it. At the time he made the suggestion, she'd thought it was a good idea. It made her feel less guilty about marrying him. But now the whole thing was like a dark cloud hanging over her, just waiting to burst.

"All right, Ethan. I'll make arrangements for a judge to fill my position. I'm not sure how long that will take, but I'll start on it tomorrow."

He sat down beside her on the rock. The more he tried

to be a husband, the more miserable and distant she became, he thought grimly. "No. Forget it. I'll get a woman
to come out and take care of things in the house. Your
work as a judge is more important. I should have realized
that to begin with."

His concession made her feel guilty and happy and tear-
ful. "I don't want a woman out here doing anything. It's
my home for now and you are my husband. I want to do
those things for you. Because I…well, because I just want
to."

Dear Lord, she'd almost said because I love you. The
words had been on her tongue as if saying them was as
natural as breathing. Had she really let her desire, her need
for him, grow into love? she asked herself. No, she
thought sadly. Her feelings for him hadn't *grown* into
love. She had loved him from the very start. She just
hadn't wanted to face the truth. She loved a man who
couldn't love her back.

The woman who'd deserted Ethan had scarred him
deeply, she thought. Too deeply for a plain, mousey
woman like Penelope to make him want to open up his
heart and try to love again.

"Are you sure, Penelope? I have plenty of money to
hire someone. You do understand I'm not a poor man?"

"Money has nothing to do with it."

He could believe that. She never asked him for anything. And though as his wife she had a legal right to
share his money and assets, from the very beginning of
their marriage she'd refused to let him list her on his bank
account or will or any of his holdings. She'd set herself
apart from him and Ethan could only believe she'd done
it to save a lot of trouble later when she divorced him.

"I'll start looking for a replacement tomorrow," she
told him, then pushed herself up from the rock. "We'd
better go eat our supper."

He stood up beside her and took hold of her upper arm. The touch dragged her soulful gaze up to his. "Penelope, I don't want you to be unhappy. Not because of me."

Her heart ached with despair. "No. You're right, Ethan. I don't want to put the baby at risk. So let's not talk of it anymore."

They went back to the house and ate the cold meal on the table. Afterward, Ethan made her leave the kitchen while he cleaned up the mess. Later, she heard the back door open and close and figured he'd gone down to the barn to check on the livestock before bedtime. He worked endlessly. As though he could never do enough on the ranch or at the sheriff's department. She didn't know whom he was trying to satisfy. Himself or others.

She was changing into her nightgown when she heard him come back into the house. His footsteps brought him directly to their bedroom. She turned as he came through the door.

"I was beginning to think I'd better go to the barn and check on you. Was anything wrong? You were down there for a long time."

Nothing was wrong at the barn, yet everything was wrong with him, Ethan thought. From the moment he'd become involved with Penelope, it seemed as if he'd become a different man. All the values, all the choices he'd made in his life before her, appeared to have fallen by the wayside. He hadn't wanted a woman. Not on a full-time basis. And he sure as hell hadn't been ready for a wife. He'd been convinced that being a sheriff was enough for him. And yet now as each day passed, he couldn't bear to think of losing Penelope. He didn't want to imagine the ranch without her. Did that mean he loved her? Dear God, he didn't know.

Tonight she'd accused him of not having a heart. Ethan had to admit he wasn't the compassionate man his father was. After Trisha had stomped on his heart and his pride, he'd been afraid to show his feelings to any woman. He'd purposely kept his emotions slumbering. But now he was deeply afraid Penelope had come along and roused them.

"Earlier this evening, I penned up two cows that are going to calve any time now. I wanted to make sure they were okay," he explained.

"Oh."

Their argument earlier had left her feeling awkward and wondering if he was still angry with her. Yet it was the notion he might be thinking like Hugh that bothered her more than anything. He hadn't come out and said she was selfish and more concerned about her career than her baby. But she'd read it in his voice and in the expression on his face. And it saddened her to think that she'd disappointed him.

His dark green eyes softened as they roamed over her pale face. "Are you all right?"

"Yes. Are you still angry with me?"

"No."

He was troubled and torn. He wanted to take her in his arms and know that she would always be there. He wanted to hear her say she loved him. More than anything. More than being a judge. More than life itself. Yet she couldn't say any of those things. Tonight he'd learned she'd already left one man for her career. She was probably going to leave him, too. Eventually. Just like Trisha.

"Are you still mad at me?" he asked.

She shook her head and wished her heart didn't ache every time she looked into his handsome face. "I don't want to make you miserable, Ethan. I really don't."

"You're not." He took a step closer, then reached out and touched the long hair lying over her breast. "It's been a while since we've been…close," he murmured. "Are you too tired?"

His hand slid beneath the firm mound of her breast and lifted its weight in his palm. The warmth of his fingers seeped through the thin cotton material of her gown and heated her needy flesh.

As her pregnancy had advanced, their lovemaking had become less and less frequent. Penelope had decided either her bulky figure turned him off or time and familiarity had cooled his desire and he was simply growing tired of her. But tonight the hunger was back in his eyes and she needed him now more than ever.

"No," she whispered, then moved close enough to slide her arms up and around his neck.

He bent his head and kissed her, then just as she thought she was going to melt, he slipped his arm beneath her thighs and scooped her off the floor.

"Ethan! I'm too heavy!" she protested.

His smile was sensual as he slowly started carrying her to the bed. "I've lifted hay bales heavier than you."

"I've gained twenty-five pounds!"

He laid her across the middle of the bed, then still dressed he planted himself over her. "And every ounce looks beautiful on you."

His face was hovering over hers and her gray eyes were full of longing as she looked up at him. "You don't have to say that, Ethan. I know I don't look desirable to you."

His lips twisted wryly at her words. "You know a whole lot in the courtroom, Judge Parker. But you still don't know very much about me." His head bent and his lips tasted the soft skin beneath her jaw, then lower on her neck until he finally reached the valley between her breasts. "Let me show you just how much I want you."

With a tiny moan in her throat, she thrust her hands in his hair and urged his mouth back up to hers. Soon she was removing his clothes and planting heated little kisses over his chest and down across his flat abdomen. And all the while, her mind was trying to block out the fact that he didn't love her. It didn't matter, she told herself. She loved him and he was her husband, and if this was all he could ever give her, she had to take it. Before everything between them ended.

As Ethan began to move inside her soft, warm body, he tried not to think of how much he wanted her or how desperate he would be without her. He didn't want to need her this much. *Love* her this much. But when the fierce ache inside him grew to be too great, he cried out her name and clutched her to his heart.

And he knew with sudden clarity he could no longer fool himself. He loved this woman. What he didn't know was how much longer he could keep his feelings hidden from her.

Chapter Thirteen

"It's nearly Thanksgiving, Sheriff, and there's almost a foot of snow on the ground, don't you think it's kinda a bad time to be serving papers on people?"

Ethan didn't bother glancing up as he scrawled his signature at the bottom of the document on his desk. "It's a bad time anytime, Lonnie. We can't let criminals go unpunished just because the holidays are coming or the weather is bad. How the hell do you think that would look? The people around here would be in an uproar."

Lonnie cleared his throat, then pushed back his hat and scratched his red head. "Well, some of 'em are anyway."

Leaning back in his chair, Ethan studied the deputy through narrowed eyes. "What does that mean? I haven't seen any complaints cross my desk."

The deputy cleared his throat again, then quickly headed for the coffeepot. "Then I guess it's not as bad as I figured."

Ethan impatiently tapped the end of his pen against a notepad on his desk as he watched Lonnie take his good easy time adding sugar and cream to his coffee cup.

"All right, I know you're just itching to tell me something. What is it? Who's been talking?"

"Oh, no one in particular. Just some of the folks down at the café."

Ethan snorted. "Lonnie, you know that place is a gossip mill."

"Well, I gotta eat someplace. And I'd have to wear earmuffs to keep from hearing some of the things they say about you and Judge Parker."

Judge Parker. Ethan inwardly winced everytime he heard the name. Although he realized it saved a lot of trouble and confusion for Penny to work under her maiden name, deep down it irked him because she hadn't changed it to Hamilton. She was *his* wife. She was carrying *his* child. She should also bear *his* name.

Ethan leaned up in his chair. "Like what?"

Lonnie grimaced, then gulped down a swig of coffee so quickly he ended up coughing a good thirty seconds.

"I'd really rather not say, Sheriff. I shouldn't have even brought it up. Forget it. Like you said, it's just gossip anyway."

More than likely it was, Ethan thought. And as far as he was concerned he didn't care what the group of loafers down at the café had to say. People would always talk. However, Ethan couldn't bear the thought of anyone saying something insulting about Penny. She'd been innocent when he'd made her with child.

"You started this, Lonnie. Now finish it."

A look of agony on his face, the deputy shook his head. "I don't want to. You're gonna get mad."

"Then maybe this will teach you to think before you open your mouth," Ethan said, then pointed his pen at

Lonnie. "What have you been hearing about me and Penelope."

Lonnie shuffled his feet, then sank into the chair in front of Ethan's desk. "Well, some people are saying you married the judge because you wanted to make sure all your arrests turned into convictions."

Ethan bit back a curse. "Do they honestly think Penelope would be biased toward my office in any way? Since we've gotten married, she's been tougher than ever on the DA. Besides, I make damn sure I have plenty of good evidence before I make arrests. You know that, Lonnie."

"Yeah. I know it. And I don't think you married her just because you got her pregnant, either."

Ethan's eyes narrowed even more on his outspoken deputy. "That's big of you."

Lonnie gulped down another swig of coffee. "I'm only repeating what I've been hearing, Sheriff, and you said to tell you."

So some of the people thought he'd married Penelope to further his career, or because she was having his child. Did any of them stop to think he might have married Penelope because he cared for her? he wondered irritably.

The self-directed question brought him up short. How could he expect the townspeople to believe he'd married Penny for love, when he'd told himself he'd married her for every reason except that one? But he'd been wrong. He did care for Penny. He might even be starting to love her. When or how his feelings had changed didn't matter. But letting her know about it, sure as hell did.

Ethan doubted he'd ever have the courage to tell her how much he wanted her to remain in his life. She'd never wanted to marry him in the first place. She was a judge. She hadn't even wanted or needed his name. How could he ever think she would need a lowly sheriff like him?

Ethan glanced at his deputy. "Is that all?" he asked tightly.

"Well, that's pretty much all. Except that some of them are surprised you took her to bed in the first place."

Ethan slapped the pen down on the desk and rose to his feet. Lonnie hunkered down in the chair as he glanced up at his boss's angry face. "What about you, Lonnie? I guess you have an opinion on that, too?"

"Do I have to say?"

"You'd better say. Unless you'd rather spend the next two weeks washing patrol cars."

Lonnie swiped a hand over his red face. "I thought you were...guarding the woman. And remember, I warned you. I was afraid she was gonna hang you! I didn't know she was going to put the noose on you in her bed!"

Ethan took several long breaths before he picked up the papers on his desk and tossed them in the direction of Lonnie's chest.

The deputy scrambled to catch them with one hand and balance the cup of hot coffee with the other. Before it was all over, he'd burned his wrist with the coffee and banged his knee on the front of Ethan's desk.

"What's...uh...what are these?" he spluttered.

"Arrest warrants."

Lonnie's brows shot up. "You mean you're not gonna wait until after Thanksgiving?"

"Hell, no! Now get out there and haul the both of them in!"

"Yes, sir!" Lonnie clambered to his feet and headed toward the door.

Just as the deputy reached for the doorknob, Ethan called his name and Lonnie carefully glanced back at him as though he was carrying a keg of dynamite.

"Is there something else, Sheriff?"

"Yeah. Just so you'll know, I didn't marry Penny to

help my career or just because she's going to have my baby. I married her because I love her. You got that?"

A wide smile spread across Lonnie's face.

"Loud and clear, Sheriff."

By Thanksgiving week there were several inches of snow on the ground. Penelope had been away from the judge's bench for nearly six weeks. She missed her work, but for the most part, her mind was consumed with Ethan and the coming baby.

Since the night she'd agreed to take a leave of absence from her office, she'd sensed a change in him. He was not unkind. He often went overboard with politeness and concern for her. But when he was near, she could feel him hiding a part of himself. Why, she had no idea. She only knew she'd much rather have the old gruff and demanding Ethan back. At least she'd known who he was and where she stood with him.

"Penny? May I come in?"

Penelope looked around to see Emily entering the spacious bedroom. The whole Murdock clan had gathered together at the Bar M for Thanksgiving dinner and all the food and merrymaking had worn her down. Chloe had graciously suggested she rest in a quieter part of the house.

"Of course," she told her sister-in-law. "I was just relaxing here by the fireplace and soaking up some of the heat."

Emily sank into an adjoining chair and gave Penelope a smile. "I hope the family hasn't worn you out. This gathering is getting bigger every year. And there'll be one more to add next year," she said happily, motioning toward Penelope's stomach.

Next year. Where would she be next year at this time? Would Ethan still want her around then or was he just biding his time, waiting until the baby came? All he'd ever really wanted was to legally give it his name. He wanted the child to eventually know he'd been born to married parents. But after that…well, he'd never mentioned remaining her husband for the long haul.

"All your family have been so good to me," Penelope assured her. "I sometimes feel like…I don't deserve their kindness."

Emily waved a hand dismissively through the air. "What is this *my* family? The Murdocks are your family, too. Or are we a little bit too rowdy for you to claim?" she asked with a laugh.

Penelope tried to smile, but the sadness in her eyes shone through to the other woman. "Oh, no," she answered, "I think you're all wonderful."

Emily studied Penelope shrewdly. "You don't look like you really mean that. Has someone hurt your feelings?"

"No! I'm just…tired. I guess I need for the baby to get here. That's all."

Emily nodded. "I can understand that. I haven't forgotten the backaches, the leg cramps, the indigestion, the insomnia. Not to mention the urge to burst into tears every five minutes. At times I wonder how Cooper survived two pregnancies. You know, I honestly think it's harder on the men. At least emotionally. They don't have hormones to prepare them for becoming daddies. The whole thing is just thrust upon them and they're expected to cope."

Penelope's gaze remained on the blaze in the small fireplace. "Ethan seems eager for the baby to come. I think…he's going to love this child very much."

Emily's smile was gentle and reassuring. "I'm certain of it. He adores kids. And deep down, I think he's wanted one for a long time. He just never could find the right woman."

Penelope glanced at Emily. Since she'd married Ethan,

his sister had become more than a sister-in-law to her. She was also a friend and Penelope loved her. "I'm...well, it's pretty obvious this pregnancy wasn't planned. Sometimes I feel very guilty about that, Emily."

Her pretty face reflecting concern, Emily left her chair and knelt beside Penelope's rocker. "Penelope, why should you feel guilty? You weren't deliberately trying to trap Ethan by getting pregnant, were you?"

The little sound that passed Penelope's lips was supposed to have been a laugh but it came out more as a sob. "No! I wasn't even sure I could have children at all. I'm very glad I was proven wrong about that. But—"

"But what?"

Penelope didn't go on. She was so afraid to speak her true feelings aloud. But the doubts and secrets had been eating at her insides for so long, she desperately needed to confide in someone. "Emily, Ethan doesn't love me. He only married me because of the baby."

Emily's mouth fell open, and then as she studied the look of misery on Penelope's face, she began to shake her head. "No. You're wrong, Penny. Ethan might have let you think that. He might even be telling himself he married you because of the baby. But I know better. My brother loves you. I was fourteen years old when he was born. I know what sort of man he's grown into. And believe me, Ethan married you because he wanted you to be his wife."

Yes, for a while, Penelope silently agreed. Long enough so that his family and the citizens of Lincoln County would believe they'd made a real attempt at staying married.

"Maybe you're right, Emily." She reached for the other woman's hand and squeezed it. "More than anything, I hope you're right."

* * *

"Sheriff, do you have your Christmas tree up yet?"

Ethan glanced over at Lonnie, who was sitting beside him in the four-wheel-drive vehicle. They were headed toward Ruidoso to talk to a family that had a missing relative. The man was an uncle, a native of Mexico, and the family feared he'd gotten mixed up with a coyote who they believed hauled more than illegal aliens into the country. They held the suspicion he was also transporting drugs across the border.

If he pulled any sort of valuable lead out of the family, Ethan could possibly break the case wide open. It was a hopeful thought. And with Christmas coming in just a few days, he should be a happy man. But he couldn't remember a time he felt so weighed down. Penelope's doctor had advised her the baby was due any day now. The long months of her pregnancy had dragged on and Ethan realized she was miserable and longed for that day to arrive.

Yet he feared that once the baby was born, it would signal the beginning of the end of their marriage. He wasn't blind. With each day that passed, he could see her becoming more quiet and withdrawn. Often he would come in at night and find her reading past trial cases or ones the present judge needed her help on. It was obvious to Ethan she missed her job terribly and was blaming him for having to give it up.

"No. I haven't had time to put up a Christmas tree," he told Lonnie.

"What about Penelope?"

"What about her? She's too pregnant to be messing with a tree."

"Yeah, but what if the baby comes?" Lonnie pointed out. "Then she'll be wishing there was a tree for the baby's first Christmas."

Ethan frowned at the deputy's sentimental notion. "The baby won't know if it's Christmas or if there's a tree within a ten-mile radius! He'll only be able to see light and dark images for a while."

"Yes. But Penelope would know," Lonnie argued.

Ethan sighed. "You know, Lonnie, sometimes I ask myself why I keep you around. And right now, I'm asking myself that very same question again."

Lonnie didn't look a bit worried that his boss was becoming annoyed with him. "Well, you said I was gettin' good at being a lawman," he reasoned. "That's probably why you keep me around."

"Yeah. But you have a nose problem."

Lonnie absently reached up and rubbed the aforementioned feature on his face. "I like Judge Parker. I want to make sure you're keeping her happy."

Ethan groaned and scrubbed a hand over his face. He couldn't make Penelope happy. Oh, he'd given her a baby. But in doing so, he'd taken away the one thing she truly loved.

"You let me take care of Penelope. You just worry about keeping me happy."

Lonnie's brows shot up. "But, Sheriff, how am I gonna do that? I ain't ever seen you happy!"

Ethan glanced at the young deputy and cursed.

When Ethan returned home later that evening, he could hear Penelope on the telephone in the kitchen.

"I know you plan to celebrate with your sons and daughters on Christmas Day, Josephina. That's why I want you to come over on Christmas Eve. We'll have eggnog and pumpkin bread. Yes. That's right. I want to light candles and say a Christmas prayer for the baby. Say you'll come. I'll have Ethan drive in to fetch you."

The old woman must have agreed because as Ethan entered the kitchen, Penelope was telling her she'd see her in a couple of days.

"Josephina's coming to the ranch?" he asked.

Penelope turned away from the telephone. "Yes, I hope you don't mind. Your family all know her. If some of them happen to drop by, I don't think they'd resent her presence."

"Of course not. She's like family to you and I'm glad you have her."

Penelope smiled faintly and he noticed her face looked drawn and there were dark circles beneath her eyes. She hadn't been sleeping at night. He'd felt every little turn and twist she made beside him.

"What have you been doing today? Are you feeling okay?"

"Just a little backache," she said. "Are you ready for supper or did you eat in town?"

"I grabbed a hamburger with Lonnie earlier. I hope you didn't go to the trouble of cooking."

She'd made beef stew and corn bread, but she'd finally given up on him and eaten the meal alone. Over the past months, she'd learned what it meant to be the wife of a sheriff. He was called out at all hours of the day and night. The times he was at home there was usually someone on the telephone wanting to complain about something or there were others who desperately needed his help. The needy cases helped her understand the importance of his job. But coping with his long hours would have been much easier to take if she knew she had his love.

"I didn't go to any trouble." She went over to the coffeemaker. "Would you like me to make a fresh pot of coffee? You look tired."

"I'm fine. Let the coffee go. I have something to show you." He took her by the hand and led her into the living room. "Stand right here and shut your eyes until I tell you to open them."

"Ethan, what are you doing?"

"Just do as I say," he said as he went out the front door.

Penelope obediently lifted her hands and covered her eyes. Moments later, she could hear him coming back through the door. An odd, swishing noise was dragging behind him.

"Okay. You can look now," he said.

She slowly dropped her hands, then blinked with shock at the tall evergreen he was balancing upright beside him. "A tree! A spruce! How beautiful, Ethan!"

"You like it?" he asked, but the wide smile on her face had already given him his answer and he wondered how he was ever going to thank that damn deputy of his.

"Oh, I love it!" she exclaimed, then rushed forward to press her nose against one of the branches. "It'll make the house smell like Christmas! But do you have any decorations for it?"

"I've never had a tree in this house before much less decorations. So I bought some. They're out in the truck. Do you feel up to helping me trim it?"

She rose on tiptoe and pressed a kiss to his cheek. "Thank you, Ethan. This is a lovely Christmas surprise."

Nearly two hours later, they were getting down to the last of the icicles when the telephone rang. A shooting incident had taken place down at Alto and Ethan wanted to make sure the investigation was handled with no screwups.

"Will you be all right?" he asked her as he jammed his Stetson on his head and shrugged into a heavy jacket.

"I'm going to finish putting the icicles on the tree and then I'll go to bed," she promised him with a gentle smile. "Just be careful. I heard earlier on the weather forecast there might be sleet tonight."

He kissed her on the cheek. "I will."

Through the little window in the door, she watched him

pull away, and then humming a little holiday tune, she went over to the tree and continued draping the threads of silver over the branches.

Within a few minutes, Penelope had completed her handiwork. She had just stepped back for a full view of the spruce when she suddenly felt a sharp stitch of pain in her side. She rubbed it until it eased, then deciding it was probably nothing more than gas, she went to the kitchen to warm a cup of milk.

She'd barely gotten the saucepan on the burner when another pain hit her. This time, it started in her back and radiated to the middle of her stomach. Once the pain had ebbed, she glanced at the clock on the wall. If another one occurred in the next few minutes, she would definitely call Ethan.

She was pouring the milk into a cup when she felt the pain begin to draw once again in her back, so she hurried to the telephone.

The dispatcher answered immediately and Penelope quickly explained the situation.

"The sheriff was on the radio a few minutes ago, Judge Parker, but I can't get a response from him now. Sometimes when the weather is bad the radio signals get lost in the mountains."

"Well, please keep trying," she told the other woman. "I really think I might be going into labor."

"Do you want me to send an ambulance out there for you, Judge Parker?"

"No. I don't think there's a need for that just yet. Just please get word to my husband."

"I'll keep trying and let you know the minute I reach him," she promised.

Penelope thanked her and hung up the phone. She drank the milk in the kitchen, her gaze glancing back at the telephone every minute or two. Finally, she decided it was never going to ring if she kept watching, so she headed to the bedroom to change into her nightgown.

She was halfway across the breezeway when amniotic fluid gushed down her legs and soaked the long wool skirt she was wearing.

"Oh my," she murmured with quiet shock.

In the bathroom, she stripped off her wet clothing and donned a heavy robe, then hurried back to the telephone.

The dispatcher quickly informed her she still hadn't been able to rouse the sheriff on the radio or by pager. "I really think the radio towers must be down tonight. I'm also having trouble reaching the deputies on duty tonight. Do you want me to send the ambulance now?"

Penelope definitely had to go to the hospital. But Roy and Justine lived fairly close by. They could be at the ranch long before an ambulance would arrive from town. And Justine was a registered nurse; she would know what to do if the baby starting coming.

"No. I'll call you back if I do," she told the other woman, then quickly hung up and dialed the Pardee ranch.

Two hours later, Ethan was nearly home when he got the call from the dispatcher telling him Penelope had been taken to the hospital.

In spite of the snowfall, he made it into town in record time. His parents were waiting with Roy and Justine in a small area off the delivery room. The moment they spotted him, Harlan stood and met him in the middle of the room.

"How is she? Has she had the baby yet?"

"Dear God, son, we thought you'd fallen off the face of the earth," Harlan exclaimed.

"I've been investigating a shooting over in Alto. It's snowing like hell in the mountains and the weather must've knocked the signaling tower out. I didn't get the message until a few minutes ago.''

Rose joined the two men. ''Well, she hasn't had the baby yet,'' she said to Ethan. ''Maybe you'd better go back there and check on her.''

Ethan left his family and hurried down the hallway to find his wife. A nurse caught him just as he was about to push through the door of the delivery room.

''You can't go in there like that, Sheriff!''

He glared at the woman. ''My wife is having a baby! I've got to go in there!''

''Not until you cover up those nasty clothes. Come with me,'' she ordered firmly as she snatched his arm.

''I beg your pardon, but my clothes aren't nasty. I may have a little horse manure on my boots, but...'' Ethan tried to peer in the small window of the door, but the determined nurse tugged him away.

''We'll take care of that, too, Sheriff.''

Minutes later, he entered the delivery room, and once he laid his eyes on Penelope's white face, the wrangle with the nurse over the hospital greens she'd forced him to wear fled his mind.

''Ethan.'' His name came out as a whisper.

He bent over her and clutched her hand. ''My God, Penelope, what happened? You were fine when I left!''

She tried to smile, but another fierce pain was ripping through her small body. Her features contorted and she gripped his hand tightly and rose half-up from the narrow bed. When the contraction finally ended, she fell back, spent and panting.

''Nothing happened, Ethan,'' she finally managed to say. ''I'm having our baby.''

''I know. But...'' He glanced desperately around at the nurse attending a nearby monitor. ''Can't you do something for her? Give her something?''

With a patient smile, the nurse shook her head. "Your wife has chosen to deliver with the least amount of pain-killer possible. It's better for the baby that way."

His attention jerked back to Penelope, who was already gripped with another contraction. He couldn't bear seeing her suffer. He knelt closer and smoothed his hand over her brow. "You don't have to be tough now, Penelope. Let them give you something."

She shook her head and tried to moisten her parched lips with her tongue. He grabbed a plastic glass of water from a small table by the head of the bed and tilted it to her lips. She took two sips, then fell weakly back against the pillow.

"It'll be all right, Ethan. Don't worry. It won't be long now."

"You shouldn't be going through this," he said in a low, tortured voice. "Not for me. I'm not worth it."

She gave him a weak smile. "You're talking silly."

Her face was white except for two flushed circles on her cheeks. Sweat misted her skin like a fine dew and dampened the edge of her hair. He stroked her brow and prayed for God to take her pain away.

"I hate myself for putting you through this."

One corner of her lips curled upward. "*You* didn't do this. We did it together, remember?"

Remember? He would never forget. And in the next half hour, he was awed by her quiet courage and strength and humbled that she was enduring it all for him. For their baby.

Just before midnight, their son was born. His small size of five pounds, six ounces bewildered Penny, who'd gained a whopping thirty-five pounds throughout her pregnancy.

As the nurse carried him away, she glanced anziously

at the doctor. "Shouldn't he be bigger, Doctor? Is something wrong with him?"

The physician's expression was thoughtful as his hand pushed and probed at Penny's enlarged stomach. "The baby appears to be in perfect health," he answered. "There's a very good reason he's small—"

Before he could get the rest out, Penny cried out in unexpected pain. "Oooh!"

Suddenly fearful, Ethan gripped her hand. "What's the matter with her, Doctor? She's not supposed to be hurting now, is she?"

The physician glanced up to give them both an amazed grin. "Your new son has a twin. How I missed a second baby, I don't know. When we did the early sonogram it must have been shadowed by the other one."

"But the heartbeat?" Penny questioned frantically, then gasped as another pain ripped through her.

"Wasn't picked up before," he said with frank concern. "We'll know in a few seconds."

The nurses hurriedly hooked up the natal monitor but by then the baby's head was already crowning. Less than two minutes later a second boy was crying lustily and the whole delivery room was sighing with relief and joy.

The second baby weighed five pounds, three ounces and was an identical match to his brother. As Ethan watched the nurses clean and swaddle the two boys in receiving blankets, he was overwhelmed with shock and joy. Penny had given him twins!

Now that the painful ordeal was over, Penelope had to fight to stay awake. "They look just like their daddy," she murmured happily.

"But they're both nearly bald," he warned her. "And their noses are flat and their faces red."

She glanced at him anxiously. "You think the babies are ugly?"

Ethan squeezed her hand and his eyes stung with moisture as he glanced down at his wife's tired face. He could never love anything or anyone as much as he did this woman and the sons she'd just given him. "Next to you, the boys are the most beautiful thing I've ever seen."

Chapter Fourteen

The surprise arrival of the twins made Christmas a special event for the whole family. They named them Jacob James and Jason Joe and everyone who looked at the boys proclaimed they were the spitting image of their father.

Penelope had always known she would love a child of her own, but until Jacob and Jason were born, she hadn't realized just how fierce or deep that love would be. When she held them and nursed them and looked down at their beautiful little faces, tears of gratitude filled her eyes. Each day she thanked God over and over for giving her not one, but two miracles.

From the start, she had planned to call the babies Jacob and Jason. But the moment Ethan held them for the first time, he immediately tagged them with the names Jake and Jase. Now two months later, everyone was using the nicknames, even Penelope.

As the car bumped over the rutted road to the ranch

house, she glanced behind the seat. The babies were safely strapped in their carriers and still sound asleep. They had both drifted off the moment she'd driven away from Josephina's that afternoon. The old woman had watched the babies while Penelope met with the mayor.

Ethan didn't yet know about the meeting. The mayor had called that morning after breakfast, and by then, Ethan had already left for work. She wasn't sure what he would think when she told him the city council wanted her to step down from her office. She supposed he would probably be relieved that her job would no longer be an issue between them. But then, she really didn't know what Ethan was thinking these days.

He certainly loved the babies. He held them and fed them, changed their clothes, crooned little tunes to them as he carried them from room to room, and rocked them to sleep. He was thrilled to be the first and only Murdock since his grandfather to have twins. Everyone could see it. Even Penelope. Yet she still didn't feel any more secure about their marriage than she'd felt before Jake and Jase were born.

Penelope could see Ethan was grateful to her for giving him two sons. But it was also obvious to her that his appreciation hadn't turned to love. She'd always prided herself in being a practical woman. Being a judge, she made herself look at everything and everyone with an open mind. She understood that some men simply couldn't say the words "I love you." They showed their love to their mates in other ways. Ethan couldn't seem to do either.

Several weeks had passed since the doctor had given her the okay to continue intimate relations and he'd also given her birth control. But so far, Ethan had not shown any interest in resuming their physical relationship. She was beginning to fear that now the babies were born, he wanted to get on with a new life, one that didn't include her. And she didn't know how she could bear to face the future without him.

When she pulled to a stop outside the ranch house a few minutes later, she noticed Ethan was already home. He met her on the porch and took both babies from her arms.

"Where have you been? I was beginning to worry."

"I'm sorry. I had to go into town and meet with the mayor. Josephina watched Jake and Jase for me."

"You met with the mayor? What did he want?"

She shut the door behind her, then went over to the couch and sank onto one end. Ethan glanced at her as he carefully eased the sleeping babies from the carrier and placed them in a portable cradle. There was a look of utter devastation on her face.

"The city council wants me to resign my office. They believe if I resume my job next month, there'll be problems."

Ethan stared at her. "Problems? What sort of problems?"

"Conflict of interest. The judge's husband is the sheriff. The sheriff's wife is the judge. If a major trial comes up, they're afraid if I'm sitting on the bench and the defendant is found guilty, it will all be for naught."

Anger spread across his face. So the gossip Lonnie had passed on to him had been true, he thought. And apparently it had boiled to a head. "That's damn crazy."

"We've talked about this before, Ethan. You know why. Because the defense will say my rulings were biased toward the sheriff's department and the accused should be granted another trial in a different court. Frankly, I can see the council's point."

He joined her on the couch. "I know we've discussed this before, but you worked for nearly three months after we were first married. No one on the city council complained then.''

"No. But if you remember, I did step aside for two trials. The other cases I sat on were not that directly related to your office. And the council didn't say anything because they knew I was going to be taking a leave of absence to have the baby.''

Ethan did vaguely remember her sitting out the two trials, but he hadn't thought much about it at the time. He'd been more concerned about keeping her and the baby well.

Penelope glanced regretfully at him. "Actually none of this surprises me. Since we first married, I've known people have been talking about us. I received a few nasty letters at my office and I even overheard the court clerk accusing you of marrying me for…well…for political reasons.''

Oh, dear Lord, he'd hurt this woman, Ethan thought ruefully. Not intentionally. But he'd hurt her just the same. He'd forced her into a marriage that had brought her ridicule and was now threatening her job. A job she valued more than anything. How could he expect her to ever love him now?

"Why didn't you tell me?''

She sighed. "Maybe I should have. But you have enough to deal with already. And besides, there isn't anything you can do about it.''

Other than give her a divorce, he thought sickly. But he couldn't bring himself to voice the suggestion out loud. He couldn't bear for her to leave him. Not now. Not ever. If he had to, he'd quit his position as sheriff to keep Penny as his wife. But would saving her job be enough to hold her?

"What did you tell the city council today?''

She shrugged. "I told them I didn't want to resign my

office. And though I'm not absolutely sure, I don't believe there is any legal way they can force me to. I haven't ever read any cases like mine. But I plan to scour my law books." She sighed and leaned her head back against the cushions of the couch. "But in the best interests of our town, I really might eventually have to step down, Ethan."

Everything inside Ethan went cold with fear. He hadn't expected anything like this to happen. He'd been counting on her work to keep her contented, to make her happy. Oh, she was happy with the twins all right. She loved the children utterly. But Ethan wasn't blind; he could see shadows of sadness come into her eyes when she thought he wasn't looking. And so far, he'd been at a loss as to what to do. He'd been hoping that once she returned to work, things would get better between them. He wished to hell he'd never suggested they marry on a trial basis.

"You can't do that. I won't let you."

She glanced at him, surprise arching her brows. "It's not a matter of whether you'll let me, Ethan. I have to think about what's best for this county and its people."

He grimaced. "What about what's best for you?"

Her head bent and she absently pushed the diamond teardrop up and down on her finger. "Sometimes we don't always get to keep what we have or what we want."

Just the way he wouldn't get to keep her, he thought sickly. With her and the twins, this ranch had finally become a real home to him. He couldn't allow her to lose her job. But how could she give up her seat on the bench just to be his wife? He wasn't enough to replace her life's dream.

Ethan had hoped that with the babies' arrival, she would begin to love him. He was the father of her children and they shared a home, even a bed, together. But she never mentioned the word "love," and since her visit to the doctor, she hadn't given him any sign that she wanted to resume their physical closeness. If anything, she was growing more and more distant. And the fear of her rejection kept him from reaching out to her.

"I'll talk to the mayor about this," he promised. "The city council doesn't always have its way."

"I wouldn't bother," she said glumly.

"Why? You know you want to keep your position as judge!"

Did she? Penelope was beginning to wonder just how badly she wanted to remain in the job. A few months ago, it was her life and soul. It was all she had. Yet with Ethan and the boys in her life now, her reasons for living, for being a judge, were changing. But how long would she be able to hold her family together? She didn't know what to do or where to turn. What she wanted most was for her husband to love her, but she could see that wasn't going to happen.

"It won't do any good, Ethan," she argued helplessly. "We are man and wife. You're the sheriff and I'm the judge. We can't consort! It would be legally unethical!"

"Unethical, hell!" he barked loudly. "Do you think I'd get anything done in my department if I ran it strictly by the book?"

Ethan's raised voice woke Jake. He began to fuss and Penelope went to pick him up from the cradle before he managed to wake his brother. Placing him against her shoulder, she gently patted his back while turning a look of warning on her husband. "I don't want to hear any more, Ethan! I don't want to talk about it!"

Ethan shot to his feet. "Then what are you going to do?"

Jake began to howl and Penelope quickly unbuttoned her blouse. "I don't know. I simply don't know!" she cried, then before he could stop her, she hurried to the bedroom and put the baby to her breast.

The next afternoon, it was cold and misty when Ethan pulled to a stop in front of the big barn on the Flying H.

As he stepped down from the vehicle, Harlan eased the bay's foot to the ground and rose from his bent position. When he saw it was Ethan, he grinned and waved. "Hello, son! You're just in time to do the back feet."

Ethan joined him and the horse by the open barn door. "What happened to your farrier?"

Harlan pushed back his cowboy hat and wiped the sweat from his brow. "Had to have a back operation."

"You will, too, if you keep this up," Ethan warned him.

Harlan chuckled and handed him a rasp. "I knew I wanted you to show up for some reason. You always could shoe a horse better than anyone in these parts."

Ethan quickly picked up the horse's hind leg and went to work. "I think your opinion might be biased."

"Hell, I'm as honest as the day is long. You know that."

Ethan grunted as he picked up an iron shoe and measured it against the horse's hoof. "Yeah. I know it. That's why I'm here, I guess. 'Cause I know you'll tell me what you really think."

"You mean your mama didn't call and tell you I was down here breaking my back? You came for another reason?"

"I need some advice, Dad."

Harlan stepped back and watched Ethan place the shoe on a nearby anvil and hammer it to the needed shape. Once the hammering quieted, the older man said, "I'm listening."

"Well, it's Penelope. I don't know what to do about her."

"What do you mean? Is she ill or something? The boys are all right, aren't they?"

"Yes. She and the twins are all fine. It's nothing like that. It's her job. Seems as though there's a problem because her husband is the sheriff. Some people think her rulings will be biased toward my department."

Harlan smiled faintly. "Well, personally, I'd be pretty damn mad if they weren't. But I know Penelope. She's strictly business straight down the line. She would never make an unfair ruling."

"I know that. But—"

"But what? What does your wife say about all this? Is she anxious to keep her job?"

"Dad, being a judge has been Penelope's whole life. She'd be devastated…miserable if she had to give it up. And she'd resent the hell out of me for being the reason."

"Ethan, you don't know that. Penelope loves you and she's not a foolish woman. She wouldn't blame you."

Penelope loves you. Dear God, if that were only true, Ethan thought. Then this whole thing might not matter so much. "I can't be the reason she loses her job, Dad. Our marriage couldn't stand the strain. I'm not so sure Penelope wants to continue being my wife as it is."

He reached for the horseshoe nails and jammed a few between his lips, except for the one he held between his fingers.

"What are you talking about, son? Penelope isn't going to leave you!"

Ethan carefully matched the shoe to the horse's hoof and drove the first nail in the center of the toe. "She doesn't love me, Dad. She never has. She only married me because I forced her into it."

Harlan chuckled. Ethan shot him a resentful glare.

"Sorry, son. But I really think you must be as blind as a bat. Maybe I better take that shoeing job back. I don't want you to quicken my mare's feet."

"I can handle this job," Ethan said gruffly around the nails between his lips. "It's Penelope that's giving me the trouble."

Harlan groaned with disbelief. "The woman worships you. Whatever happens with this thing about her job isn't going to change that. You mark my words."

Ethan thought about his father's words as he finished nailing the shoe tight, then he straightened and looked at Harlan. "I can't take that chance. I've decided I'm going to turn in my resignation. That way, Penelope can keep on being judge without any problem."

"The hell you are! Have you forgotten how long and hard you've worked to become sheriff? Have you forgotten that you've wanted to be the sheriff of Lincoln County ever since you were a little boy?"

Stone-faced, Ethan propped the horse's hoof on his knee and began to file away the protruding ends of the nails. "I haven't forgotten any of it."

"Then how could you do such a thing?" Harlan demanded.

"Because I love Penelope. I don't want to take anything away from her. You'd do that much for Mother, wouldn't you?"

Harlan let out a long, resigned breath. "I'd do anything for your mother."

"Then I guess I have my answer."

No more words passed between the two men while Ethan finished shoeing the mare. He and his father were putting away the equipment when his pager went off.

"You want to use the telephone here in the barn?" Harlan offered.

"I'd better. It's Tate Jones and he doesn't call me unless it's for a good reason."

Harlan stood nearby while Ethan talked to the deputy. By the time he hung up the phone, his expression was grim.

"What's happened?" his father asked.

"I've got to go," he answered, and started striding toward his Blazer. Harlan followed alongside him while Ethan explained, "Tate says the Border Patrol was in some sort of high-speed chase with three men. Shots were exchanged and both vehicles were wrecked over on 70."

"The desert or the mountains?" Harlan asked.

"Mountains. And the three suspects have fled on foot." Ethan opened the door of the Blazer and reached for his revolver. He glanced at his father as he strapped the Colt around his hips. "Thanks, Dad, for listening."

Harlan softly slapped his son's shoulder. "It's times like these I almost wish you weren't a lawman, son. But I'm proud of you. And I realize you wouldn't be happy any other way. Just don't do anything foolish out there. Penelope and the twins need you. And so do your mother and I."

"I'll be careful," Ethan promised, then slid behind the wheel and started the engine.

Harlan lifted his hand in farewell, then stood in the misty ranch yard and watched his son drive out of sight.

It was growing dark when Penelope heard the sound of a vehicle pulling to a stop in front of the house. She glanced at the sleeping twins and walked out on the porch to see if it was Ethan. To her surprise, Harlan was sprinting to the steps to avoid being soaked by the rain.

"Hurry and come in out of the cold," she invited.

After he quickly followed her inside, she took his wet hat and jacket and put them on a chair near the fireplace.

"I know this is a nasty time to be barging in on you like this," Harlan began, "but I wanted to talk to you and I didn't want to do it over the phone." He glanced around the room, then back toward the entrance to the breezeway. "Ethan isn't here?"

"No. I haven't heard from him since early this morning. Frankly, I thought he'd be home by now."

"You haven't talked to anyone at the department?"

Penelope shook her head, then alarm raced through her as she looked at her father-in-law. His normal jovial mood was more serious than she'd ever seen it. "Why? Is something wrong?" she asked sharply.

"I'm not sure. He was at the ranch earlier this afternoon and got a call while he was there. Something about the Border Patrol being in a high-speed chase. Both cars were apparently wrecked and three armed suspects have fled into the mountains. I haven't been able to find out anything else since."

Penelope's knees went weak and she slowly sank onto the edge of the couch. "I didn't know," she said with a shake of her head. "Why hasn't anyone told me? Why didn't Ethan call me?"

"He probably didn't have time. Or he didn't want to worry you." Harlan walked over and took a seat in the armchair facing her. "But none of that is why I'm here."

She stared at him with wide eyes. "You mean there's more?"

He nodded. "Normally, I don't meddle in my children's personal lives. Rose and I have always wanted to stand back and let Emily and Ethan choose their own way. If they need us, we're there. Otherwise, they're grown adults and what they do is their own business. But in this case, I can't stand by and watch Ethan make a big mistake. I feel like I would be a negligent father if I didn't at least try to do something to stop him."

The alarm that raced through Penelope earlier now turned to icy fear. Her face paper-white, she stared at her father-in-law. "Stop him? From what? He wants to divorce me, doesn't he? He wanted you to be the one to tell me!"

Harlan vigorously shook his head. "Dear Lord, you must be as blind as he is. No. It's nothing about a divorce. He's planning to resign his position as sheriff."

Penelope shot to her feet. "Resign? No! I don't believe it! Ethan *is* the sheriff. No one could ever take his place!"

Harlan sighed. "So you knew nothing about his intentions?"

Still stunned, she could hardly find the words to speak. "He—he hasn't implied any such thing. Why would he do it? Being sheriff is who Ethan is. It's what he is. He would be totally lost without that badge on his chest and all that it means."

"Ethan came by the ranch today to talk to me about this problem you're having with the city council. He thinks the only way you can keep your job is for him to resign."

"Oh my. Oh my!" Slowly, her hand covered her mouth as a strange mix of emotions swirled through her. In her wildest imaginings, she could not have pictured Ethan giving up so much for her. It didn't seem possible. Yet she could see that Harlan was deadly serious, so Ethan must have been, too. "Harlan, I would never let him do that. It wouldn't be…" She stared at him with tortured eyes. "Why? Why would he do such a thing for me?"

A wry smile touched the man's face. "Don't you know how very much he loves you?"

Suddenly, all the doubts and fears and longings she'd harbored for the past months boiled up inside her and culminated in a burst of tears.

Harlan rose to his feet and gathered her against his

chest. She sobbed quietly into his shirt until she could compose herself enough to lift her head and look up at him. This man was her father-in-law. He loved her just for being plain Penelope. All the Murdocks loved her and she was a part of the family. No matter what.

"Thank you for coming, Harlan. For telling me this."

He patted her wet cheek. "Thank you for loving my son."

Hours later, Penelope was walking from room to room, watching and listening for any kind of sign that Ethan was driving up the long dirt lane to the ranch house. So far, the only news she'd heard from the department in town was that Ethan and several other law enforcement people were still out in the mountains.

In the past hour, the rain had turned to snow. It already covered the ground and was growing deeper by the minute. Ethan had left the house this morning wearing a lined jean jacket. He had to be freezing in this weather. But that would be the least of his worries if those men were armed and dangerous. And obviously they were. She's been told they had shot the windshield out of the Border Patrol pickup.

For years now, Penelope had worked in conjunction with law officials. She was very aware of the enormous risk they took and she had married Ethan knowing he would, more often than not, be exposing himself to all sorts of dangers. Yet that didn't make her worrying any less great.

The sound of Jase's crying pulled her away from the living-room window and she hurried back to the bedroom. The baby was wet so she changed his clothes, then sat down with him in a nearby rocker and offered him her breast. He latched on hungrily, and as the baby nursed, she silently prayed that Ethan was safe.

She was still in the rocker when she heard the sound of a vehicle. Moments later, footsteps echoed on the tiled floor and then he was standing in the door of the bedroom gazing at her and the baby feeding at her breast. His hat and clothes were wet with snow while blood was smeared along one cheekbone, but she'd never felt so relieved in her life.

"Ethan! What happened?"

The sound of her voice snapped him back into motion. He entered the room and quickly pulled off his hat and jacket and shirt and tossed them in a heap on the floor. His holster and Colt came next, and as he carefully placed the weapon away in a drawer, he said, "It's a long story. But right now I think I still have prickly-pear spines stuck in my cheek."

"Lie down on the bed and I'll get the first-aid kit," she told him.

She quickly rose from the rocker to put Jase back in his cradle, but Ethan motioned to her from the bed. "Bring him over here and put him beside me."

Ethan stretched out on his back and Penelope placed the sleeping boy in the crook of his arm, then hurried to the bathroom to fetch the medical supplies.

When she returned to the bedroom, she sat down close beside him on the edge of the bed. He looked so cold and tired she wanted to weep. "Did you catch the men?"

"Yes. They're probably being booked as we speak."

She breathed a sigh of relief, then bent closer to examine his face. The wound was red and puffy and still oozing blood. "How'd you do this?"

He grimaced. "When you're running down a wash in the dark, it's hard to see what's in front of you."

"You weren't wrestling with one of the suspects?"

One corner of his mouth lifted sheepishly. "Not exactly."

Sighing, she shook her head. "Ethan, a general sits behind the lines and sends his soldiers out to do battle. When are you going to learn that's supposed to be the case with a sheriff and his deputies?"

He muttered a curse. "I would never do less than what I ask my deputies to do. You know that."

"Yes. I know it." And a lot of other things, she wanted to say. But she didn't. She wanted to get him clean and comfortable before she said all the things she had to say.

There were four small spines still stuck in his cheek. She pulled them out, then cleaned and disinfected the wound. And all the while she worked, she was acutely aware of his warm skin, his earthy smell and the ever tempting nearness of his lips. Touching him for the next fifty years would still not be enough.

"Do you feel better?" she asked as she began to put the medical supplies back in their box.

"Much better. Thanks."

She set the box aside, then turned back to him. "Good," she told him, "because I need to talk to you."

"About what?" he asked, his wary gaze traveling over her face.

She reached over and pulled Jase from his arm. "Let me put the baby back in his bed first."

His eyes followed her movements as she rounded the end of the bed. "Why? He was sleeping just fine where he was."

"When you hear what I have to say, you might get loud and I don't want you waking him or his brother."

This brought him straight up off the pillow and he swung his legs over the side of the bed. "All right, Penny! You might as well come clean with all of it. At least that would be better than having you going around in miserable silence. You want to end our marriage, don't you?"

With both boys snug in their cradle, Penelope returned

to the bed and sat down beside him. Her gray eyes solemnly searched his. "Do you want to be free to find another woman, Ethan?"

His lips parted with shock. "No! Why would you ask such a question?"

"Because it seems clear you're not very happy with me. If you want to be free to find someone you can really love, then I'll let you go."

The frown on his face said that her every word had stabbed him. "I don't want another woman!"

She drew in a deep breath, then slowly released it. "Do you love me?"

Like the curtain lifting on a stage, she could see the hard expression on his face change to soft, vulnerable hunger. The sight caused Penelope's heart to soar on wings of sheer joy.

Ethan groaned. "Yes. I do love you, Penelope. I—"

He couldn't say more. She wouldn't give him the chance. She leaned into him and placed a long, searching kiss on his mouth.

When she finally eased her head back, he stared at her with shocked wonder. "I thought you didn't want me. I thought you wanted to leave. Ever since the twins—"

"I've been waiting, hoping you would give me some sign that you loved me. I'd given up expecting that you could ever care—until today."

With another groan, he reached up and touched her cheek. "For a long time now, I realized I love you, Penelope. But we'd agreed to try this marriage for a year and see what happened. And you never mentioned loving me. So I figured you'd want to leave sooner or later." Regret twisted his features as he tangled his fingers in her long hair. "I guess...well, each time I thought about telling you how I felt, I would get sick with fear. Fear that you wouldn't believe me. Or that you simply wouldn't care how I felt. Another woman left me because I wasn't good enough for her. I never thought I'd be good enough for you, either.''

The anguish and doubt in his voice tore at her heart. "Ethan," she said softly, "I've loved you for a long time. Even before we made love at the cabin, I worshiped you from afar. But I knew there wasn't any chance you would ever look at me as a woman. And then when we married, I knew you had done it all because I was pregnant.''

Regret twisted his features. "I didn't marry you just because you were pregnant. But even if I did, I'm asking you to stay for *me*. Not because we have children together. I'll fix this thing with your job, Penelope. I won't let you lose it.''

She pushed him back against the pillows and pinned him with a stare that was both tender and accusing. "You're going to fix it all right. How? By resigning?''

"How—''

"Harlan came by this afternoon,'' she interrupted. "And I thank God he did. Otherwise, I would never have forgiven you if you'd pulled such a stupid stunt as resigning your office!''

"Dad had no right to tell you my intentions!''

"He had every right. He's your father. He wants you to be happy. Just as I do.''

"Well, I'm your husband and I want *you* to be happy!''

She smiled because no matter what happened in the future, now she knew they would be together. They loved each other so much that they'd both been willing to sacrifice their careers.

"Ethan, you don't understand. I don't *have* to be a judge to be happy.''

His eyes were full of disbelief as he met her gaze. "Why are you trying to make me believe such a thing? Because you know I feel guilty about your job and you don't want me to?'' He shook his head, then reached for her hand. ''Penny, you and I both know that working in the courtroom has been your whole life. You've already told me you wouldn't give it up to marry that other guy.''

She reached out and smoothed her fingertips over the tired lines on his face. ''I didn't love that other guy. I didn't know what love was until you came into my life. Ethan, after your father left this afternoon, I didn't have to do a lot of thinking to know what was in my heart. You and the twins have brought love into my life. Before you three, my only aim was to seek restitution for my parents' deaths. I was bitter and lost, and deep down I wanted to make every felon pay for my misery.''

''You were never unjust in the courtroom, Penelope.''

She sighed softly. ''No. I believe I was always fair in my rulings. But I'm different now, Ethan. I guess love changes the way a person looks at the world. I still want people to pay for their crimes, but it's no longer the sole driving force inside me. You and our children mean more to me than anything. We're a family now. You and the boys are my family. If I never sit on the judge's bench again, my life will still be full and happy because I have your love.''

His solemn gaze continued to search her face as though he found her words incredible. ''You worked hard to get your law degree. You're proud of your position and I'm proud of you. You know you don't want to give it up.''

One of her slender shoulders lifted and fell. ''No. I don't necessarily want to give it up. And I'm not going to. I've been studying a few cases today and it's clear to me that the council can't force me to give up my office. I'm an elected official and I'm going to keep on doing my job. If I see there's going to be a conflict of interest, I'll step down and call in another judge for that particular case. Otherwise, I'm going to do my job just as I always have."

Hope began to spread across his face. "I know there's been talk about you and me. But I believe the people of this county will stand behind you. You've earned their trust and respect."

"I like to think so. But if they ever do start to doubt me, I'll quit and become a defense attorney."

His jaw dropped. "A defense attorney! Hell, I can't have you as the opposition! Besides, you know I never arrest anyone who isn't guilty."

She laughed softly and took his face between her hands. "I might just prove you wrong on that count, Sheriff Hamilton."

His chuckles joined hers and then his arms were around her, pulling her down to him. "You've already proved me wrong, my beautiful wife. I didn't believe I could ever love a woman like this. I had decided there wasn't any woman who could love me just for what I am. And then you came along and I was afraid to trust you with my heart. But you—" He broke off as the words choked in his throat and his fingers touched her cheek. "Well, now I can see you're willing to give up all that you cherish just to make me happy. You really are proud of me being sheriff."

Her eyes filled with tender understanding. "I couldn't be more proud."

His arms tightened their hold on her. "You mean more to me than anything, Penny. And you know what? I thank God every day for our having the chance of making you pregnant. Jake and Jase are little miracles."

She rose far enough to untie her robe and slide it off her shoulders. Ethan's eyes glittered with longing as she slipped back into the circle of his arms and snuggled her naked body next to his. "Maybe we can have another little miracle, a sister for the boys, by the time they get to be two or three," she murmured against his ear.

He leaned his head back far enough to look into her eyes. "You would go through that much pain again for me?"

Her lips curved up into a smile as she pressed her cheek against his. "I would do anything for you, darling. Anything."

With a groan, Ethan found her lips, and as he kissed his wife, he finally understood that this was how his father had felt about his mother for all these years. This was a bond nothing could break.

"I'd do anything for you, too," he whispered against her lips.

They tilted into another smile. "Good. I'm glad we got that out of the way. Now don't you think it's about time we did something for each other?"

The laugh beneath his breath was full of joy and love and promise. "High time, my darling."

* * * * *

COMING NEXT MONTH

#1261 I NOW PRONOUNCE YOU MOM & DAD—Diana Whitney
That's My Baby!/For the Children
Lydia Farnsworth conveniently wed her former flame, Powell Greer, so they could adopt their cherished godchildren. Although the once-smitten newlyweds didn't know the slightest thing about being parents—or reconciling the past—they embarked on a mission of love....

#1262 THE MOST ELIGIBLE M.D.—Joan Elliott Pickart
The Bachelor Bet
Her past had been erased, while her life seemed to begin the moment Dr. Ben Rizzoli rescued her. Though there was an irresistible attraction between them, the dashing M.D. tried hard to hold his emotions in check. As though he was keeping some secret. As though he was desperately afraid of falling in love....

#1263 BETH AND THE BACHELOR—Susan Mallery
Beth Davis was aghast when Texas bachelor Todd Graham set his sights on *her.* Didn't the suave, sophisticated tycoon have more sense than to woo a widowed suburban mom? And could she trust that her Prince Charming was ready to be a husband and father of two?

#1264 SECRET AGENT GROOM—Andrea Edwards
The Bridal Circle
Life was about to change for shy Heather Mahoney when she found herself powerfully drawn to her elusive new neighbor. Ultrasecretive Alex Waterstone was a man to be avoided—that much she knew. Why then did he inspire dreams of wedding bells and shimmering white satin?

#1265 FOREVER MINE—Jennifer Mikels
When Jack McShane gazed into Abby Dennison's beautiful brown eyes again, he realized she still had a hold on his heart. *Then* he realized this woman he'd foolishly left behind had secretly borne him a son. So the wanderin' rodeo champ vowed to hang up his hat and become a bona fide family man....

#1266 A FAMILY SECRET—Jean Brashear
Maddie Collins knew Boone Gallagher wasn't any more pleased than she was when his father's will stipulated they must cohabit before she could sell him his old ranch house. But the city sophisticate hadn't counted on unearthing a shocking secret—or the allure of this gruff, gorgeous cowboy!

Looking For More Romance?

Visit Romance.net

Check in daily for these and other exciting features:

Hot off the press

View all current titles, and purchase them on-line.

What do the stars have in store for you?

Horoscope

Hot deals

Exclusive offers available only at Romance.net

Plus, don't miss our interactive quizzes, contests and bonus gifts.

PWEB

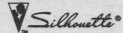

Silhouette ® SPECIAL EDITION ®

presents **THE BRIDAL CIRCLE,** a brand-new
miniseries honoring friendship, family and love...

THE BRIDAL CIRCLE

by

Andrea Edwards

They dreamed of marrying and leaving their
small town behind—but soon discovered there's
no place like home for true love!

IF I ONLY HAD A...HUSBAND (May '99)
Penny Donnelly had tried desperately to forget charming
millionaire Brad Corrigan. But her heart had a memory—and a
will—of its own. And Penny's heart was set on Brad becoming
her husband....

SECRET AGENT GROOM (August '99)
When shy-but-sexy Heather Mahoney bumbles onto secret agent
Alex Waterstone's undercover mission, the only way to protect the
innocent beauty is to claim her as his lady love. Will Heather
carry out her own secret agenda and claim Alex as her groom?

PREGNANT & PRACTICALLY MARRIED
(November '99)
Pregnant Karin Spencer had suddenly lost her memory and
gained a pretend fiancé. Though their match was make-believe,
Jed McCarron was her dream man. Could this bronco-bustin'
cowboy give up his rodeo days for family ways?

Available at your favorite retail outlet.